JACKIE
LOVES
JOHNSER
OK?

JACKIE
LOVES
JOHNSER
OK?

NEVILLE THOMPSON

JACKIE LOVES JOHNSER OK?

NEVILLE THOMPSON

POOLBEG

Published 1997
by Poolbeg Press Ltd
123 Baldoyle Industrial Estate
Dublin 13, Ireland

© Neville Thompson 1997

The moral right of the author has been asserted.

The Publishers gratefully acknowledge the support of The Arts Council.

A catalogue record for this book is available from the British Library.

ISBN 1 85371 880 7

Cover illustration by Eoin Stephens
Cover design by Poolbeg Group Services Ltd
Set by Poolbeg Group Services Ltd in Times 11/14
Printed by The Guernsey Press Ltd,
Vale, Guernsey, Channel Islands.

ABOUT THE AUTHOR

Neville Thompson was brought up in Ballyfermot in Dublin. Having spent some time in Corfu, he now lives in County Westmeath with his wife, Jean. *Jackie Loves Johnser OK?* is his first novel. He is currently working on his second.

ACKNOWLEDGEMENT

Many thanks to Poolbeg for their support, professionalism and their policy of publishing new Irish talent. Every member of staff deserves credit for the finished article you are about to read. In particular, I thank Kate Cruise O'Brien for her editing and enthusiasm throughout.

Many years ago two teachers influenced me greatly, Dymphna McCarthy and Angela Russell. I'm pleased to let them know that their efforts were not in vain.

Thanks to my mum and dad for all they did throughout the years. Sadly, my dad died before I was published. He was the greatest role model a son could have. I miss him.

I thank Harry for never cutting a long story short, Bri and Linda for their enthuasism and Mick, Lucy and the gang for their home thoughts from abroad.

To Joanna, whose arrival into this world coincided with my signing for Poolbeg. May you always be my lucky charm.

Last but not least I thank Jean, for her support and encouragement when all I was receiving were polite rejection slips. Her advice changed my style and I will always be indebted to her for that. This book is as much her achievement as it is mine.

Dedicated to Jean,
a beautiful woman,
fabulous wife but, above all,
my best friend.

In the night you hide from the madman you're longing to be.
But it all comes out on the inside eventually.

Western World by Steeleye Dan.

CHAPTER ONE

I couldn't fucking believe it.

10.30 on a Saturday night and he was home.

"What's wrong?" I asked as he walked into the kitchen.

He didn't bother answering, just walked straight to the brown formica press and took out the bread and a jar of strawberry jam.

"Johnser!" He'd the jar open and was looking around for a knife as he answered.

"What?"

"I said what's wrong?"

"Nothin'."

He ripped open the wrapper on the bread, buttered one slice and, using the same knife, slapped on a large dollop of jam. Folding it in half, he stuffed as much of it as possible into his mouth.

"Why does somethin always have teh be fucking wrong?"

He stuck the knife back into the butter, leaving it streaked with jam.

"Ah, for fuck's sake, Johnser! Don't do that."

He looked down at the tub and laughed, bits of well chewed bread falling from his mouth as he spoke.

"Looks like a used jam-rag, eh?"

1

I threw the tea cloth at him.

"Go way, yeh dirty bastard."

He laughed loudly, ducked and ran down the hallway.

I stooped to pick up the tea cloth and watched him stumble as he went. Maybe he was half pissed, or it could just be that his mate hadn't turned up, or maybe he had and his missus was with him, Johnser hated that. Whatever, it was only 10.30 on a Saturday night and he was home. The kids were in bed, the dishes were done and the only jam-rag in sight was on the table.

This was looking like a good night.

CHAPTER TWO

I stumbled down the hall.

Mouth full of bread and jam, belly full of beer. Jackie had fucked the tea cloth at me so I knew I was in the good books.

Pat Kenny was talking to some dry-arsed fucker about his one-man voyage around the world. Well, if he was so fucking alone, who was holding the fucking camera? A load of bollocks. I changed channels, *Match of the Day*, Jasus, I couldn't remember the last time I'd seen that. No Jimmy Hill, wonders will never cease and Gary fucking Lineker. I thought he was all washed up in China or Japan or somewhere like that. I'd hated him ever since he scored that goal against us in the World Cup in 1990, but I had to admit he knew his football. For an Englishman, anyway.

I went for a James Dean jump on to the sofa, you know the type, supercool over the back like a high jumper. Me body was over but me legs got caught and catapulted me to a sudden and ungainly stop. I hit me head on the wooden arm and landed hard on me arse on the floor. Fuck it, I bet James Dean had two or three takes before he perfected that jump. I'd just struggled back on to the sofa when Jackie came in with a six-pack of Harp and a large packet of popcorn. She slipped in under me arm and I knew I was on for a ride. I gulped down a bottle, opened another and grabbed a handful of popcorn. I decided to watch the goal of the month before making me move.

The front door opened and Jackie jumped to her feet.

"Ah, fuck," I snapped, I knew I should have got me leg over when I had the chance.

"Oh Jasus, that'll be Ann looking for a lend of the Hoover."

She stood in front of me straightening her skirt and I cursed the fact that Ann hadn't got her own fucking Hoover. I slipped me hand up her leg and touched her knickers.

"Fuck off," she whispered, trying to sound annoyed but failing.

I looked at her face, she was like a teenage girl whose parents were about to walk in. I wouldn't tell her because she'd tell me to fuck off again, but she was beautiful.

The door opened and her smile faded, her mouth opened but nothing came out. Then she croaked –

"Oh, God!"

I looked up and saw the barrel of a sawn-off shotgun looking back at me. It was like an old film, I swear to God, you know the ones where the hero is just about to get blown away and his whole life flashes in front of him. In those few seconds, it was as if Cecil B DeMille had taken over and I saw my life as clear as if I was sitting in the front row of the Adelphi.

CHAPTER THREE

I was born on a large estate, with long rolling gardens and horses rambling through the sprawling meadows. Uniformed footmen stood by your doors day and night. That's how the film would have gone. Reality was something totally different.

I was born in Ballyfermot, Ballyer to those who lived there. It was the Corporation's crowning moment. A concrete jungle that finally proved, without a shadow of a doubt, that they didn't give a shit about the poor unfortunates who were herded in in droves to live there. Horses roamed OK, every fucking bin day, dragging the arses out of bin-bags. Every Monday we woke to the sound of the aul fella screaming at the little piebald fuckers.

And the uniformed footmen, the Garda Síochana, were always at our door. If it wasn't for the aul fella being drunk, it was cause one of us twelve kids had been caught robbing. I can't remember a week when they didn't call.

I was the youngest. Ma dropped babies like they were going out of fashion, she had eighteen in all, six died. Eighteen pregnancies between the age of seventeen and forty-three. We're talking *Guinness Book of Records* here. Da used to say she shouldn't bother getting out of bed, cause it was a waste of time. She used to laugh at that. We'd all laugh, even though we hadn't a clue what was so funny. Once, when a young doctor had tried to advise her about contraception, she'd looked at him as if he had two heads and told him it was God's wish.

"God's wish!"

God's wish that none of us ever had a pair of trousers with an arse in them.

God's wish that Santy always brought broken toys. Some wish.

I swore that God was like everyone else, and had never been to Ballyer. I suppose in truth I couldn't blame him.

Things were really hard.

I was christened John Kimble Kiely. Kimble, cause me mother thought the actor was a ride and John, after an older brother who had died at birth. The funny thing was, it wasn't John who had died, it was Jimmy. So we ended up with two Johns and I became Johnser. Well, I was fucked if I was going to be called Kimble.

Ma had weird names for all of us. Famous singers, film stars, even names from the Bible, it didn't seem to matter where they came from. They say some women eat strange things when they're pregnant, Tommy Gormley's sister ate coal when she was preggers. My ma thought up names.

I suppose life must have been pretty boring for her, after all she was pregnant for years at a time. She had to do something to spice up her day, so she thought up strange names. Or maybe it was her way of getting revenge for the labour pains we put her through. I'm not sure, all I know is that we had the weirdest names in Ballyer.

We had a Marilyn after Monroe, an Ava after Gardner and

an Elvis after Presley. There was Luke from the Bible and Heston after the actor in *Ben Hur*. We had a couple who were lucky, Bette after Davis and Bobby after Kennedy. But Jasus, what was she thinking of with Bela (Lugosi) and Rudolph, who was some great lover, though for years we thought it was after the fucking red-nosed reindeer. So I guess meself and John were lucky in a way.

Maybe it was God's wish that Boris, Greta, Toby, Fanta, and Dev died, rather than have to carry those stupid names around for life. The only one with a decent name was Rita and that was only cause me ma reckoned she was the spit of Rita out of *Coronation Street*. So there you have it, twelve kids, four girls and eight boys. Aged between newborn and twenty, an aul fella who drank every penny that came in (and God knows it wasn't a lot) and me ma. All this under one roof, a slimy little three-bedroomed house in a god-forsaken concrete jungle.

Like I say, times were hard.

CHAPTER FOUR

I stood straightening meself, pushing Johnser's hand down off me knickers and trying to sound disgusted when all I really wanted was for his hand never to move. Jasus, I had to admit it, I loved this man more than life itself. Although it was easy to forget love when he came in pissed out of his head, having spent half the night in the pub. But, even so, life without him would be nothing.

Christ, it had taken me so long to get him and now all I could do was stand staring at some bastard who was about to blow his fucking head off. I was powerless, rigid with fear, I couldn't even scream. Me, Jackie Clarke, who couldn't keep her mouth shut or her nose out of an argument. The screamer from Kimmage Road, bigmouth Clarke, old bellow-lungs Jackie, standing silent like a fucking gobshite. The one time Johnser wouldn't have minded the neighbours hearing me and I was struck dumb. The man I'd waited for for fifteen years, the man I'd schemed and plotted to get for meself, was lying on a sofa in my sitting-room with the barrel of a sawn-off shotgun pointing at his head and all I could do was watch.

Me mind drifted from Johnser to the bastard standing over him and all I could think was that I'd seen him before.

Like it mattered, like if I turned to him and asked had I met him in such and such a pub, or didn't I have a dance with him on Children's Allowance day up in the *Embankment,* he was going to put the gun down, grab a beer and forget all about covering the wallpaper with Johnser's brains.

I looked at Johnser. He was still the same, he still had that look of control on his face, like he'd planned the whole thing.

For once I wished he'd forget how tough he was. For once I wished he'd panic, shit himself, beg this fucker to spare him.

But I knew in me heart of hearts he wouldn't, he would go out with a smile, that same smile that drove me mad all those years ago.

CHAPTER FIVE

Ignorance is bliss.

If we'd known any different we'd have revolted. We'd have grouped together, all forty thousand of us. Grabbed every spade, hammer, every knife and fork, anything that could be used as a weapon and we'd have stormed the Government Buildings and took over. We'd have hung the bastards from the scrawny little trees that surrounded our miserable glass-splattered playground. The fuckers.

Da said that the only time a politician came near Ballyer was when he was looking for a vote and he was right. They'd come to the gate, you could see them hesitate before they came in. Only for it would have been too obvious, they'd have worn gloves so they wouldn't have to touch us. You could see their faces cringe as they shook hands. Once Ma invited two of them in and, out of politeness, they accepted. One was a snobby young girl, the other a real posh aul fella, in a fancy three-piece suit and a cashmere coat. He tried to sound like one of us, a common Dub, but he sounded more like Kermit the fucking frog.

Ma did it on purpose, to show them how we lived, to show them what they were really dealing with. She never admitted it but I think her and Da had it all planned. Before the duo could refuse, she handed them both a cup of tea, the cups dragged from the pile of dirty dishes that sat continually in the sink. You could see the colour drain from their faces. Ma shoved me on to the girl's lap, saying I was the baby. I was five and I stank to high heaven, it was bath night and I was last in line. Even after the bath I never smelt that great, the water was never changed, just another kettleful thrown in after every second person. Most of the time, I was dirtier getting out than I had been getting in.

The man asked if Da was at home and Ma screamed his name at the top of her voice, then turned politely towards the politician explaining that Da was having a bath. The bath was a big steel tub set in the middle of the kitchen. Da came out as he always did, without a stitch on. There he stood, bollock-naked, and his flute hanging down dead level with the prudey girl's face. I doubt if she had ever seen a flute before cause, hard as she tried to look away, she kept getting drawn back to it. Even when they were leaving, Da stood naked at the front door waving them off. We never seen either of them again.

Da never voted anyway, he said it was a waste of time. It didn't matter who was in power, in Ballyer things never changed.

They said that one in every five Dublin families was unemployed; well, there must have been one part of Dublin where everyone was working, cause none of us or our neighbours, or our road for that matter, ever had a job.

CHAPTER SIX

I was a great robber.

The older kids used to hate bringing me to the shops. It was embarrassing being seen with the old crock of a pram that had known better days before coming to our house. Now, seven fat kids later, this three-wheeled danger to society made at least four daily trips to the Elephant supermarket. Like it or not, someone had to go and they had to bring me, cause if they didn't, I'd scream like a child possessed and me ma would fucking kill them when they came home. I thought it was great, they were so embarrassed they used to boot down the road at breakneck speed, turning corners as if their kacks were on fire. For me in the pram, it was like a rollercoaster ride, it frightened the shite out of me, but it was great. They weren't allowed to take the pram around the shop, cause the security man said that they would be robbing. So I was parked close to the checkout, out of breath in me lopsided pram. The Elephant was huge, a big warehouse-type building with endless shelves, packed with glorious colourful goodies. It was pointless really, cause we always got the cheap dreary products. I used to sit there right beside the sweets and, as the security man walked every inch of the store after me brothers or sisters, I helped meself to whatever I fancied. Once the others found out what I was capable of, they all wanted to take me shopping. I was five and already I knew what I was going to be when I grew up. A robber.

CHAPTER SEVEN

I cried.

The first day I went to school, I cried. I'd been looking forward to it all summer. God bless Marilyn, cause she patched up her old schoolbag for me and glued on a load of Batman pictures to make it look better. The pictures hid all the holes and I felt the gear. Ma brought me down by the hand. The night before I'd been put into the bath first and Bela had let me have some of his Brut aftershave, so I smelt great. Me hair was gelled neatly to one side. I looked like one of Hitler's Youth.

Da had swapped a radio with Lar Harris for his clothes voucher, so I had a great pair of second-hand trousers and a brand-new jumper with just one tiny rip in it. I was the bee's knees, the cat's pyjamas, delighted with me new clothes and me new bag that held two copies and a pencil with a rubber on the top. Walking as tall and straight as I could, proud of me gorgeous hair with all its gel, the smell of Brut and Ma. Yeah, proud of me ma and she of me. There she stood in a normal dress, no maternity wear, make-up done and a look on her face that told me we were as good as anyone else. I walked into the class and looked around at all the other kids with their mothers. Some of them looked at us the way the security man in the Elephant

13

did, but most of them looked at us like we were all the same.

Ma pushed me into a seat beside a fat kid who had his head buried in his folded arms. He was bawling his eyes out and his ma was trying to tell him that everything was going to be OK.

I looked around at the other kids and they were all bawling. Ma kissed me then, wiping the lipstick from me cheek, told me that Rita would be picking me up after school.

"Rita!"

Rita never came near me, even after I'd had a bath, she wouldn't touch me. Something was up. I looked at the other kids again, they were still crying. They knew something that I didn't. I began to cry.

The door opened and in walked the tallest woman I had ever seen. Tall, gangly and specky, she looked like she would break in two in a strong breeze, but in fairness she was OK.

Boring as fuck, but OK.

Looking back, she was the best teacher I ever had. The problem with all the other ones I had was that they knew me brothers, cause they'd all been in trouble, so they immediatley assumed that I'd be the same. I didn't like to disappoint them.

CHAPTER EIGHT

I remember the first time I saw Johnser.

We'd told our mas that we were going to a dance in the school hall, but we cut across the waste ground at the back of the church, down through Bluebell and ran the last hundred yards to Inchicore and *Sgt Pepper's* disco. They had real bouncers, not someone's older brother or over-protective da, but real bouncers, with dicky bows and scars on their faces and cauliflower ears. They looked you up and down, asked you your age and then, after what seemed like an eternity, they let you in. The place was packed, we had to push our way through the crowds and on to the dance floor. We all squealed as our favourite Mud song came on, "Tiger Feet". We knew all the steps, rehearsed in our bedrooms, perfected at the school dance, and now we were ready to show the real world what cool chicks we really were.

The fellas were so much older and wiser. At least eighteen, some maybe even twenty, and they were like flies around shite within minutes. We all paired off and, once outside, their hands homed in like hungry babies on to our tits. I remember panicking, things were moving too quickly. I didn't like being this old, but I'd already said I was eighteen and we all knew that eighteen-year-olds let fellas feel their

15

tits, at least through their jumpers. I could feel something hard being pushed against me pelvis, oh Mammy, then just as I thought I was going to be pregnant, someone let a roar – "Millee."

And all the lads were gone.

Girls appeared from every darkened corner, fixing blouses back into skirts and hair back into ponytails. Tara Coyle was pulling up her tights but we all knew she was a slut.

A huge crowd had gathered and they were all shouting –

"Kill the fucker."

"Kick the shit outta him."

"Knife the bastard."

Above the noise I could hear the thud of bare fists smashing skulls, the sickening sound of a boot being driven into a stomach. Despite my revulsion I couldn't turn away, I found myself being pushed to the front of the crowd and there he was.

Standing over the three bodies lying helpless on the ground, he looked wild, furious, out of control. He was Johnser.

And I knew from that moment that I loved him.

CHAPTER NINE

Take no prisoners.

Some big film star once said those words and they had stuck with me. Every time we were out for a fight we'd chant – "Take no prisoners."

It was stupid, but we said it all the same.

Fighting was what it was all about, if we didn't have a fight the night seemed boring. You had your mates, you had your mot, but if you didn't have a fight, you had nothing.

School was a washout, they knew we were never going to do anything with our lives. We were in the gutter and had no intentions of getting out of it. They were wasting their time trying to convince us that if we studied really hard we would get jobs, we knew it was a fucking lie. All we wanted to do was have a laugh, no matter where we were. It didn't matter a shite to us whether it was in the school, at the church or out in a field, we were always acting the clown. It wasn't us I felt sorry for, nor was it the teachers, they were getting paid for looking after us. I felt sorry for the kids who believed all the shite about how a good education would open doors for them.

Sure it would open doors, but as soon as they realised you were from Ballyer, they would be slammed hard in your face.

Michael Butler got a job with a big ice cream company, a good job, the first rep in Ballyer, and fair dues to him. Then gear started going missing and suddenly all eyes were on Michael. In no time at all he was out the door and on the dole with the rest of us.

I learned how to read and write. I liked reading, I read loads of war books and I would have been good at writing if me spelling hadn't been so bad. I knew how to count, how to multiply and divide. I'd never get diddled in a bookie's and I knew every finish in darts without even thinking about it.

I wasn't going to be a banker, (although I did some bank jobs of a different nature) but, so what, it always looked like a boring fucking job.

I left school the year of the Group Cert, I didn't even bother sitting it, didn't see the point. The school inspector never came looking for me and everyone silently agreed that it was the right thing to do.

Ma asked me if I was going in one day and, when I said no, she never asked again.

I wasn't alone, there was always a gang of us. We played football on the street all day, one eye on the ball and one eye on the world. You never knew when Lady Luck would come your way. Like the day a rookie driver came into the roundabout too quick and overturned his lorry. We didn't give a fuck if he was dead, we were into the lorry like vultures, scavenging every crate of orange and lemonade that we could. We gorged ourselves until we were sick drinking the stuff. In the end we gave half of it away. There was always a chance, someone leaving a window open or a car door unlocked. In those days we never thought of doing a job unless there was no one in sight.

Night-time was when we came into our own. Suddenly

we were alive and no one fucked with us. At night we hung around menancingly, bullying anyone who let us. I say "let" because it wasn't as though we hung out in a different place every night. We could always be seen at the corner of the shops. There was an alley at the back of the shops with three lanes going off in different directions, a web of getaways for us and a stranglehold for anyone who dared enter our domain. Every night we were there, waiting, watching and if you wanted to avoid us you could. Anyone who dared to venture by we considered fair game.

I wasn't really into kicking the shite out of some poncey git.

I liked a good millee. Like the time that Crumlin gang came up to the Gala or, even better still, a major snarl-up in town. God knows who'd show up, it was fucking great.

A good fight was everything, it gave you power, respect, but, above all, it gave you contacts. Contacts outside your own patch, in parts of the city you knew little or nothing about. Suddenly people would know your name, respect your name and want to do business. I was eighteen and starting to move in the right circles. I was going to be playing with the big boys.

CHAPTER TEN

Two weeks later I was Johnser's mot.

I couldn't believe he'd asked me to go with him. I had entered a whole new world. When I was on his arm, I was it. Girls who had turned their noses up at you suddenly wanted to go to the toilets with you. When we got there, they wanted to know all about Johnser. I used to say that Johnser didn't like me telling our secrets, that drove them mad. Because I never told them anything, they made it up. I heard that Johnser had a ten-inch dick, that he fucked all night, how he had a thousand pounds from a bank robbery hid under his mattress. How he always slept with a gun by his bed. How he beat the crap out of four, then five, then ten coppers, all in the one night, all at the same time. Bruce Lee, eat your heart out. It was fun, fun listening to the folklore, fun being the envy of them all. Fun being Johnser's mot.

The strange thing is that looking back, being a cynic with age, it had all been a big fuss about nothing. It's like with the Beatles, all that screaming, all that stuff about the "Fab Four", all that "there'll never be another Beatles". Thanks be to Jasus. Some of their stuff was shite, pure rubbish. I hated them.

Went out tiger hunting with my elephant and gun,

For added protection I always took my mum . . .

If anyone else had released that they'd have been laughed out of the recording studio, but it was the Beatles so it had to be good.

And so it was with Johnser. In truth where we went was never that exciting. If anyone else had said, "Com'on, I'm takin yeh on a date," and I ended up standing at the side of their local shops, with their gang, all shouting, "Get up yeh ride," at every little tart that passed, I'd have told him where to get off. But this wasn't anyone else, it was Johnser and, because it was Johnser, it was the best date I was ever on. It was like being whisked off on the Concorde to Paris and having a four-course meal in that restaurant that spins around at the top of the Eiffel Tower. It was the gear, life didn't get any better.

The fact that I got the arse frozen off me didn't seem to matter.

When Johnser was on his own he was different. He was quieter, more down-to-earth, more natural. Trouble was getting him alone long enough for him to stop acting so tough. There was always someone hanging around, always some mates in the background or someone he had to see, and once there was something going on the real Johnser was hid. While his mates were around he was the boss, the main man. He liked his position, he'd fought hard to get where he was and there was always some smartarsed kid who thought he'd like to have a go, some fella from another part of town, sick of hearing about crazy Johnser Kiely, sick of seeing *Johnser Rules OK* on every wall in Ballyer. Every second night Johnser fought, if it wasn't his fight he made it his. If there wasn't a fight he caused one.

"What are yeh lookin at?"

"Yeh talkin teh me?"

"What did yeh say 'bout me mot?"

They didn't have to be looking, they didn't have to talk to him, they didn't have to say anything about me, or his sister or his granny, the poor fuckers were just in the wrong place at the wrong time. There was no point in grovelling, he hated that. At least if you fought he'd have some respect for you. Grovel, and he'd show you no mercy. To be honest, I loved it. At first, anyway. I was going on sixteen, acting eighteen and, if I was going to be eighteen, this was all part and parcel of the game.

It was great having me very own bodyguard. Before Johnser, I was one of those girls who got called a little ride as I walked by the shops. As soon as I was Johnser's mot I got me name back.

It was always, "Howya, Jackie?"

All the others were still rides, but I was Jackie, I was special.

Things changed. In school I was suddenly in demand, the girls we were all afraid of now wanted me to be part of their gang and I was only too willing to join. I stopped hanging out with the squares, stopped rehearsing those stupid Mud songs, those stupid dances. Quo were everything. Rossi was a ride. I stopped wearing me uniform, started smoking in full view of the teacher's staffroom, cut, *Jackie loves Johnser forever OK*, into every desk I sat at. For the first time in me life I saw the inside of the principal's office.

I chewed gum day and night. Me answers were always short and said with that, "I-couldn't-give-a-fuck-who-the-hell-yeh-are" attitude.

"So?"

"I don't care."

22

"So what?"

"I didn't ask teh be born."

Da was worried. Thought I was fucking possessed. *The fucking Exorcist*. Ma said it was a phase I was going through.

Me schoolwork suffered. I was never an A student but now I was barely a D, and that was only when I looked over Brigid "brainy arse" Brennan's shoulder. God, to think she used to be a friend of mine.

Ma and Da were called to the school. To discuss me reports.

"What reports?"

All eyes turned to me.

"What?"

I know now that I broke me Da's heart. He had such great expectations, I was going to be the first in the family to go to university. A doctor, well at least a nurse. At the time, I didn't give a fuck. When he talked, all that went through me mind were the words of a *Sweet* song –

"Recognise your age, it's a teenage rampage."

Brian Connelly is a ride.

I ended up barely scraping a Group Cert and getting a job on the factory floor of Caffrey's. Where all the rest of Da's family had started.

Friday was great. We got our wages, ran home or, if the weather was really good, cycled. Once I got the bus but, more times than not, it was a waste of time waiting, because the bus had to go through the industrial estate and would be packed by the time it got to me. I had to give me ma twenty pounds a week. Fucking daylight robbery. And for what? Shite grub, two veg and potatoes. I hate veg. And me clothes washed . . . big deal.

On Friday we got fish and chips, not a veg in sight . . . bliss.

Then it was straight to the bath . . . hair dried . . . and out the fucking door before they had a chance to start.

"Where are you going?"

"What time will you be home?"

"Have you got your key?"

"Don't be late."

"AH, FUCK OFF!"

CHAPTER ELEVEN

I'd get off the eighteen and he'd be there. Never looking, back turned to the bus stop. I used to try and act real cool. I'd walk to the traffic lights and wait for the little green man, even if there was nothing coming I'd still wait. Then I'd saunter across, skirt up to me arse, happy in the knowledge that no one would be brave enough to comment. They'd save their dirty remarks for some other poor bitch who just happened to get off the same bus. As she passed they'd say things like, "Get up, yeh ride. Are those tits hand-reared?"

Then they'd break their shite laughing, you'd think they'd just heard the joke of the century. Fucking eejits.

Johnser always greeted me with, "Howya?" No kiss.

Fuck off, kiss me in front of his mates and him stone cold sober, are yeh mad? I'd stand beside him smoking me brains out, freezing me arse off and answer in me usual supercool way.

"Shurrup, you."

"Fuck off!"

"Yeah, yeh would alrigh."

And when I got fed up answering or some smartarse had got the better of me, I'd say, "Did yeh hear what he called me, Johnser?"

. That soon shut them up. Depending on his humour it would either end with Johnser saying, "Give it a rest," or else he'd give them a good old-fashioned kick in the balls.

He was brilliant at it, everyone agreed. No matter how ready they were, he landed that kick every time. Crunch. And they'd end up on the ground in agony. We never said anything, just laughed as the poor fucker got to his feet rubbing himself.

You could set your watch by us. Half seven and we'd be outside the Quinnsworth off-licence, it was really the Elephant with a new name. Johnser collected all our money and went in, they never refused Johnser. He'd come out laden down with bags. Mainly cider but always a few cheap beers, one hundred cigarettes and, on the odd occasion, if the dosh stretched far enough, a bottle of vodka.

We drank down by the railway tracks or at the canal. The Naller, as we called it, was the best. The police never hassled us down there. The railway was different, they were afraid we'd do damage or play chicken with the late trains as they passed. The lads loved to play chicken. Jasus, looking back it was madness, they could have been killed.

I remember one night Fat Larry, pissed drunk, fell on to the track. Face down, straight between the lines and the train bombing along. He was flaked out. I started screaming and two other girls who were there that night started bawling their eyes out.

Johnser was like lightning. One minute he had his hand up me top, next he had Fat Larry up on his shoulders and was throwing him over the other side of the track. The train's signal screeched into the night and we could see the driver's face as it passed, he looked like death. As the train passed, we lost sight of Johnser and Fat Larry. Us girls kept on screaming as the lads shouted Johnser's name. Then the train was gone and there he was, screaming at Fat Larry as he kicked the living daylights out of him.

The cops came down that night and Johnser was taken to the station.

Johnser saved Fat Larry, saved a train-load of culchies, drank twenty pints and kicked the shite outta the cops. He wrecked the cell, he wrecked the station.

"Did Johnser really do all that?"

"Can't say, Johnser doesn't like me teh talk about it."

No one hassled you down at the Naller. Every gang had their own patch, a bridge or a lock and a little patch of grass. We had a bridge. In the summer, the bottles were hung on a rope and left in the water to stay cool. The lads would go for a dip and, when they were getting dressed again, they'd wrap towels around themselves and try to step out of their swimming shorts, while at the same time trying to get into their clothes. They were forever pulling the towels from each other and us girls would laugh and point at their mickies. Later, when we were alone, we'd swap notes about whose we'd seen and what size it was.

No one ever saw Johnser's, no one was ever brave enough to pull his towel off. We all agreed that Slash had the biggest one, we nicknamed him Donkey. Whenever he walked by we'd all chorus, "Heehaw, heehaw." And go into fits of giggles.

Slash would curse us from a height but he never knew what we were laughing at.

The little finger was raised whenever Fat Larry walked by and once again we'd be reduced to fits of laughter. It was all good fun. I loved those nights, we were all happy then.

There were always more fellas than girls. I was with Johnser; Slash had started going with a girl from Palmerstown, Sally was her name, so she became one of the gang. Fat Larry and Froggy never had a girlfriend. And Tommy Brady, Scall, Baldy and Tiny were forever switching between Mandy, Linda and Donna. We were like one big family, we had our ups and downs, our fights, but at the end of the day, we all looked out for each other. When darkness fell, we all paired off.

Johnser was so predictable, he'd start to sing. He always sang the same song, "Two outta three ain't bad."

He wasn't the greatest singer in the world, but because he was Johnser, it sounded good.

"Now don't be sad, cause two outta three ain't bad."

As soon as the word "Bad" hit the air, his arm would slip around me shoulder and, with the final note still ringing in our ears, we walked away from the others and made for our well-worn patch of grass, then we kissed.

He kissed with experience, tongue straight in, licking the top of me mouth, tickling, then touching me tongue. They banged against each other as if fighting, his always winning. The first time we kissed me mouth felt like it would cramp, it was numb for a day after. Every time I went to move me tongue it hurt, and I thought of Johnser.

Tongue fight over, he buried his head into me neck and his hands undid me blouse. He loved me tits, played with them for ages, squeezed them, tweaked them, sucked them, sometimes even bit them then, as the bulge in his jeans stood to attention, he dropped the hand.

I always said "no" and he always got annoyed.

"For Jasus sake, Jackie."

"No!"

"But I'm mad about yeh."

"Me da'll kill me."

"Fuck yer da."

"Suppose I got . . . yeh know?"

"Yeh won't."

"How can yeh be so sure?"

"I'll take it out before I come."

"No, Johnser, I can't."

"Well, let me feel it."

So I did. Every Friday, Saturday and Sunday night. I let him pull me knickers down, never off, and he ran his fingers through the mat of curly black hair, while I rubbed his mickey through his jeans. I always had one eye on the others, just in case Fat Larry had any ideas about becoming a peeping Tom. He said that he used to spy on his sisters while they were having a bath.

Well, he could fuck off, he wasn't going to see mine.

The winter was the worst, we spent the whole time getting pissed on. Tiny was sent ahead to light a fire under the bridge and we all sat huddled around it. Our parents couldn't understand why we wanted to go out on nights like that, when we had our lovely warm homes, but it wasn't that simple. Under the bridge we were special, we were adults. Winter changed things, the couples stayed under the bridge while all the singles drifted back to the shops.

It was me sixteenth birthday. Ma and Da gave me twenty pound in a card. Ma snuck me a bottle of *Tweed eau de toilette.*

"Now don't let your father see that, he still thinks you're six, not sixteen."

It was great, at least me ma knew I was a grown-up. Not like Aunty Carmel, she'd given me a three-pack of knickers with little rabbits on them. I could imagine Johnser's face if he saw them, no thanks.

Johnser bought me a necklace, gold-plated, with a real fancy design set around the number eighteen. I'd have to take it off before I went home. I could just imagine the questions I'd be asked about wearing a necklace with eighteen on it, never mind who I'd got it from. They didn't know about Johnser. I knew they'd want to meet him and Johnser wasn't into that kind of thing, so to save all the hassle I never mentioned him. He gave me the necklace by the fire and we kissed. Within minutes, the usual questions were being asked and I was giving the usual answers. Me knickers were at half-mast and his fingers probed, like never before. At first only one finger slipped inside, ever so quick, just parting me, just enough to wet, not enough to protest. Then again, lower, deeper, moving along and touching me. God, it was . . . I don't know . . . different.

The clit, that's what we called it, he rubbed it, and it was great. I looked over at the other couples under the bridge, no one was watching. I opened me legs further and a second finger entered and, as I got wetter, a feeling I had never felt before, or as good since, happened and I came. I had to bury me head in his shirt so as not to scream out. I wanted to jump up and shout, "Oh yeah, Johnser, take me."

But I just bit down hard on me lip. He rolled on top of me, his jeans rubbing against me, and I felt his thing, harder than ever, begging to be let free. He was moving as though he was riding me, but he was still wearing his jeans. I lay under him and we gyrated, like the real thing, like in the films and he held me so tight I knew he was coming. He rolled off me and I could see a large damp stain on the front of his jeans and I felt good. I felt like a woman, a woman in love.

CHAPTER TWELVE

I still hung around the shops, but I was moving on.

They were still me mates, but I was ambitious. I wanted a profession, a career. Not the everyday profession like a fireman or a doctor. I wanted to be a robber, a full-time criminal, a twenty-four-hour-a-day menace to society, and Slash, Tiny and Fat Larry just weren't in that league. So it was like any group of lads, we hung out together, played together, fought together, but our jobs were different.

Townies are a law upon themselves. Less trusting, clannish. I was lucky that some of me uncles still lived there. I worked for the Brush. The Brush ruled everything, and I mean everything.

"Looking for a bike for the kids at Christmas?" Go to the Brush.

"Need a loan?" The Brush was your man.

"A crate of whiskey? A camera? A fridge?" The Brush, the Brush, the Brush.

In order to keep ahead of demand, the Brush needed jobs done.

The Brush had the brains, he needed the brawn. He needed foot-soldiers, trusted men, he needed me. So I worked for the Brush, I worked hard. I drove, I carried, I did whatever it took, and soon I gained his trust and I was put in charge of jobs and my jobs were always done right.

One day I got to meet the Brush in person, a rare treat.

It was straight out of the movies. A car came to the house. I was dead embarrassed, no one ever called to the house, I was too ashamed of it. Here was me, dressed to the nines, throwing money around left, right and centre, yet living in a kip. The driver was known as Blue, he was Brush's right-hand man. Cocky fuck, I knew he was smirking at where I lived.

"Nice decor," he said. "Woodchip always looks so well, doesn't it?"

Anyone else and I'd have fucking killed them. Then again, anyone else wouldn't have said it. Because he knew he could, he did. That to me was taking liberties, not showing respect. His day would come . . . no fear.

We drove without talking. He turned up the radio full volume and sang along to the songs.

"Yellow river, yellow river, it's in my mind . . . "

"An' up your hole," I thought.

It was the longest journey I'd ever had in a car. We stopped a few times and Blue would get out without a word. Disappear into a doorway for a few minutes, then back into the car, radio on and it was sing-along-a-Blueboy all over again.

"Winding your way down to Baker Street . . . "

I began to see the same places twice, three times. Harold's Cross from the right, Harold's Cross from the left. Down Camden Street, up Camden Street, across Camden Street. Fuck this, I've had enough.

"What the fuck's up?"

"What do yeh mean?"

"This is the fucking fourth time I've seen Christ Church. If I wanted teh see the sights, I'd take a fucking tour bus."

It did the trick. He got out, made a call and within minutes we were down an alleyway and entering a snooker hall by the back door.

There was only one game being played when we went in. An old man and what I took to be his grandson. I pushed by, fed up with all the delays.

"Watch it," the old man said.

I turned, said nothing. Just stared at him. I thought of me own granda. I wouldn't like some smartarse talking down to him, telling him to fuck off. No matter what, no matter if he was out of order or not.

"Sorry."

Apology given, I turned to Blue.

"Where's Brush?"

He smiled. Jasus, I'd like to kick his fucking teeth in. If he wasn't one of Brush's men I'd . . .

The old man walked, cue in hand, towards me.

"Hello, John, I'm hearing good things about you."

Me face must have told the story. He continued, "Not what you expected, eh?"

From every darkened corner of the hall, laughter echoed.

"Let's go to my office, you and me need to talk." He gestured towards a small door to the right of the table. Blue and the young snooker player made to follow us.

The Brush waved his hand. "Blue," handing him the cue, "you take over from me."

I smiled.

Yeah, Blue, stay with the boys, us men have some business to discuss. I'd have loved to have said it, but I just smiled.

I could feel his eyes piercing into the back of me head, little daggers being thrown, aimed at me skull, wanting to blow me fucking brains out. I could feel them and it felt great.

The office was small but, in contrast to the darkened hallway, it was bright and colourful. The walls were painted light blue, like the skies back in the summer of me childhood . . . Jasus, listen to me, talking like a fucking aul fella. But back then the summers *were* so much brighter. We'd get up in the morning and pull on our shorts and T-shirts. You never gave it a second thought, you knew that the sun would be out there, waiting. A big orange ball sitting amid a light blue sky. And we'd run and run all day. Not giving a fuck about rain or hose bans or drought.

I liked this room.

I'd have loved this colour for our house, but I knew that within a week, two at most, it would look like every other colour that had been painted on to the woodchip wallpaper . . . chip-pan yellow.

It was unbelievable, paint the walls magnolia, paint them mint green, salmon pink, paint them scarlet fucking red and within a week they'd be chip-pan yellow again.

The Brush moved to the other side of a small oak table and sat in one of those plastic chairs that adorn every bingo hall. He waved his hand (the Brush seemed to like waving his hands) in the direction of another plastic chair.

"Sit down, John, we don't hold with airs and graces here." I don't know what the fuck airs and graces had to do with a plastic chair, but I sat down anyway.

The Brush wore a waistcoat, like the snooker players, and from one of the pockets he pulled a ten-pack of Player's. He searched his pocket again. I knew he was looking for a light so I threw a box of matches on to the table. He picked them up and lit his cigarette. Took one long hard pull and, sitting back, allowed smoke rings to bellow out of his mouth.

"One of the last great pleasures left to a man my age."

I pulled out me own cigarettes and reached for the matches.

"John, I'm sorry, where are my manners?"

He reached into his pocket.

"No, honestly, I only smoke tipped. Those things kill me."

"Kill us all, John, kill us all. The doctors are blue in the face trying to get me to stop, and Mary, the missus, won't let me smoke in the house."

* * *

I remember the first cigarette I ever had. It was one of me da's non-tipped and it nearly fucking killed me. I was nine and all the rest of the family smoked. Puffing their brains out and at the same time telling me not to. Bobby kicked the shite out of me one time when I asked him for a butt. So I learned me lesson. If I was going to find out what the big attraction to cigarettes was, I was gonna have to get me own, and fuck the lot of them. I decided to nick the aul fella's. He'd come in pissed and, after having a smoke, go for a shite and straight to bed. It was his ritual. The cigs were always left on the mantelpiece and the poor drunken fucker never had a clue how many were left.

I'd only rob two, maybe three, depending on who I was meeting the next day. So there I was, two cigs, four matches and me gang behind the school shed. We'd put Tommo Ellis on *Ello* and the poor fucker would be shitting himself in case the head caught us. It was almost tribal, a sacrifice, some mystic ritual. All we were short of was offering up a prayer to the god of smoke.

I lit it on the second match, the breeze having blown out the first. I took a huge pull, letting me lips wet the end of it. The smoke went all the way down to me toes and, as I exhaled, it turned to fire and ran the length of me body, burning me guts on the way. I could feel me eyes watering, stinging me to death. I passed it to Slash. They all asked at the same time, "What's it like?"

I could hardly talk, me insides were on fire and me stomach retched. I thought I was going to throw up the currant bun we had every Wednesday. I didn't. I gulped and it returned to me stomach. It would have been a terrible waste. I loved school on Wednesdays cause we got buns. And I loved Friday cause we got bread and jam. If it had been Tuesday I wouldn't have minded, cause I hated corned beef.

They asked again, "Johnser, what's it like?"

I gave a hoarse whisper, "fucking cool."

I was a hero.

"Hurry up, Slash."

"Yeah, Slash, hurry fucking up an' get it outta yer gob."

"Slash thinks it's his aul one's tit. Don't yeh, Slash?"

"Fuck off, yous," Slash retorted.

"Hurry up, what's wrong? Yeh chicken?"

"No, now fuck off."

"Then smoke the fucking thing."

Slash inhaled and I watched his face change colour. As he exhaled, out came the smoke and his bun. He let the ciggie fall into it and followed that with a helping of cornflakes.

"Ah, for fuck's sake, Slash."

37

Slash looked around, puke dribbling from his lips. Too weak to say anything.

"Sketch!" shouted Tommo Ellis. "Here's Lurch."

We scattered in all directions.

Lurch caught Slash and held him up like a rag doll in his huge hands. We'd named him Lurch after the character in the *Addams Family*. He must have been six foot six, brainy Bannon said he was nearer seven foot. Whatever, he frightened the shite out of us.

Poor Slash had to clean up the vomit and got fifty lines.

"I must not smoke in school."

That afternoon the head gave us a lecture on smoking, but on the way home we all shared the second cigarette even though it nearly killed us.

* * *

"I've been hearing good things about you, John."

I didn't know what to say, so I said nothing.

"How do you feel about doing a job with me?"

Brush was legend, if there was a bigger criminal in Ireland I hadn't heard of him. Just working for this man gave you street cred. Working with him put you on a different level.

"Great."

I felt like a right wanker the minute I'd said it. "Great!" "Great," was what you said when someone asked you to play a game of football or gave you a can of beer.

The Brush stubbed his cigarette out in the ash-tray.

"Listen, John, not a word about this to anyone. If I hear one word . . . and believe me, I'll hear."

For the first time in me life I was genuinely scared. Here

was a man smaller than me, thinner than me, older than me and yet he scared the shite out of me. He must have sensed me fear.

"But . . . like I say . . . I'm hearing good things about you. I think you and I are going to work well together. I've a few details to sort out, I'll be in touch."

He sat back and waved his hand towards the door. I knew our meeting was over.

CHAPTER THIRTEEN

Two days later the job was on.

I got the bus into town and Blue pulled up in a battered old van. As soon as I got in, he told me to change into workman's overalls. I looked at the state of the van, it was held together with rust.

"Jasus, I hope teh fuck we don't have teh make a quick getaway."

"Don't let the framework fool yeh, son, this engine has some poke."

Five minutes later we picked up the Brush. He was standing on the corner waiting for his lift like any man going to work, his canvas hold-all on the ground beside him. We picked up two others along the way. Nobody spoke. We sat quietly on a makeshift bench along the side of the van.

It wasn't even eight o clock and already Blue was singing his fucking brains out as we travelled through the early morning traffic. We arrived outside the bank's gates and the security man, more interested in the girl passing, let us in without any fuss.

Inside we worked . . . fucking worked. For four and a half hours we sanded doors and stripped off old paint. I looked at the Brush like he had two heads. We were in the basement carpark when the security van arrived. Blue moved to our van and started the engine. The security van pulled up beside us without anyone taking any notice. As the van backed towards the lift door, Brush opened his hold-all and handed us guns. The security men got out, we waited. The shutter at the back of the van opened and the security men grabbed two bags each. Before they knew what was happening we were on top of them.

The Brush had a sawn-off shotgun, his voice was distorted with anger.

"Give me the fucking bags."

The security men froze. The Brush grabbed the bags from the first man without protest, but the second man held on. Out of the corner of me eye I could see the bank's security man looking over. Still the man struggled with the Brush.

I ran towards the bank man, me gun pointing.

"Down, get fucking down."

He dropped, as if I'd shot him. Arms spread, face down. I stood over him and looked back towards the Brush. The security man continued to struggle. Brush stood back, aimed his sawn-off at the man's knee and let off a single shot. In the confined space it sounded like thunder, the whole place lit up. The man screamed in agony. Brush picked up the bags and ran towards Blue and the van. Moxy, one of the other men, got to the van first, pulled open the back doors and jumped in. As Brush and Domo approached they threw the money bags in. Moxy caught them and the lads jumped on board. Blue shouted, "Com'on Johnser, hurry!"

Fuck you, Blue, I thought, why don't yeh give them me name an' address while yer at it.

I bent down, pointing the gun at the bank man's face.

He closed his eyes.

"Don't, please don't . . . I'm married."

"Don't fucking move, right."

I ran and jumped into the van. As we sped away I looked back: the bank man remained riveted to the spot. Ah, the power of the gun. The Brush was high, high as a kite. But still in control.

"Take it easy, Blue. Slow down, we want to get away in one piece."

Round the bend, sharp left and a sudden stop.

"OK, Moxy, Domo, take the bike." The Brush threw them the keys.

"John, you come with me and Blue."

We ran down an alleyway to a waiting Jag, bags in hand. We got changed, suits for all of us, and four minutes later we were at a wedding.

* * *

The Brush was hauled in by the police.

We had so many names for them. Pigs, coppers, bobbies, guards, we even picked up "the fuzz" from *Starsky and Hutch*. It made no difference, call them what you like, we hated them. All this shite about how much they were needed, how they protected the ordinary Joe Soap. As far as we were concerned, they were nosy fuckers who deserved no respect and got none. If you were hauled in, you said nothing. Never cooperated, even if they had you by the balls. You kept stum, said nothing and did your time. If you needed a lesson in how to do it, just video the Brush at work.

He picked a spot on the wall and stared at it. It freaked

them out. They wanted to beat the crap outta him, put him up against a wall and pull the trigger, but they couldn't. The only thing those thick culchie fuckers knew was, no matter what, you didn't fuck with the Brush. If you did, you and yours suffered the consequences. A guard in Phibsboro did it once. Within the week his house was burned out, his wife had a beautiful double blade scar across her left cheek and his three-year-old daughter went missing for a few hours. The charges were dropped and the guard left the force.

For six hours they questioned him. They slagged his wife, he sat and stared. They slagged off his daughter, he sat in silence.

They asked where he had been all day, still he said nothing. In those six hours everyone attending the wedding was asked for a statement and everyone gave the same answers, even the priest. Brush, like the rest of us, had been there for the whole day. Sixty statements all saying the same thing. By the time the Brush was released, a whole row of cars near the police station had had their tyres slashed. Two sergeants at the station had the windows in their houses put in.

The wedding reception was paid for by the Brush. The priest's church got a much-needed new roof. It paid to be on the right side of the Brush.

The Brush was happy with me, the way I'd handled meself. The way I'd taken care of the security man. I got four grand and was told not to be stupid with it. It was me first real lesson in crime. Here I was, money to burn, but I couldn't touch it.

I still signed on the dole, hit the social for new shoes and butter vouchers. You name it, whether I was entitled to it or not, I made sure I got everything that was going.

I was never even a suspect. I was inner circle now and yet to me mates, to the pigs, to everyone, I was still only Johnser. No one knew how much that job had changed me.

The following day Ma died and I knew there was no turning back.

CHAPTER FOURTEEN

Johnser was always very secretive about how he spent his days.

I knew he robbed but he never went into detail. It was unusual, cause back then fellas boasted about everything. If they pissed in a straight line, God forgive me, they told you about it. If they got a hand on a tit, the whole world heard about it.

Nothing was sacred, except Johnser's job. I often asked him about it. I'd ask when all the lads were around, thinking he'd want to brag about it in front of them. But he'd give me daggers looks and tell me to fuck off.

I even tried asking him when we were alone. One time he had me tits out, normally I could get him to promise me the sun, moon and stars when he was at them. So there he was kissing them one at a time and I was running me hands through his hair the way he liked. I whispered, "Johnser."

As one nipple left his lips and the other was on its way, he answered, his mind on the matters in hand.

"Yeah?"

"How deh yeh earn a livin?"

He stopped, pulled his head up and lit a cigarette.

I had to pull me own top down.

"For God's sake, Johnser, what's yer problem? We've been going together over a year and I still don't know what yeh do."

He wouldn't answer. Ten minutes later I was on the bus home.

Things were changing. Johnser started getting real moody. He wanted to go all the way, I didn't. It's not that I didn't want to do it, but I wanted it to be special. I didn't want it to happen down at the Naller, in the middle of winter, with me arse frozen off and me mates only yards away. For fuck's sake, Fat Larry would probably be peeping. I wanted us to go somewhere special, just me and Johnser. We planned to take a caravan in Brittas the next summer and I thought that maybe I'd lose me virginity then. If Johnser wanted to do it before then, I'd do it in a hotel or a bed and breakfast, but I wasn't doing it on the Naller.

Then his mother died. He never talked about her. And just like he had never been to my house, I had never been to his. In fact, I'd never even seen his ma. I'd seen some of his brothers, and one time one of his sisters had come down to the shops with a message for him. He got really annoyed and left, cursing her from a height. I wouldn't have known about his ma's death only for one of the girls in Caffery's who lived on his road told me. I checked it in the paper and went to the church.

Johnser was wearing a suit and had his hair combed to one side.

He looked great. If it wasn't such a sad occasion, I'd have told him he was a ride. I wished that he'd turn up to meet me wearing that suit, maybe a different tie, though if push came to shove I'd settle for the black one. Still, he'd look a right gobshite dressed in a suit standing at the corner of the shops or down by the Naller.

Johnser looked like he'd been crying. He was the image of his brothers, he looked nothing like his sisters, they must have taken after the ma. I went over and handed him a card.

46

"Johnser, I'm so . . . "

He interrupted.

"Jackie, what are yeh doin here?"

"Jasus, Johnser, I just wanted teh say I'm sorry."

"Right, I'll see yeh later." He took out a twenty-pound note.

"Do us a favour, get Slash teh get the drink in, an I'll see yeh later down the Naller."

"Yeh can't go there tonight!"

"Why?" he asked, genuinely puzzled.

"What about yer family?"

"What about them? I don't wanna spend time with them."

"But, Johnser . . . "

"Jackie, yeh don't know what yer on about."

He walked away and I knew that Johnser would do his own thing.

That night he came down, dressed the same as normal, and after singing, "Two outta three ain't bad," we walked away from the others and I wanked him for the first time. I can't remember why, I just felt that I couldn't say no. He had drank more than he usually did and his eyes looked like he'd been crying again. As he kissed me, it felt different and as he sucked me nipples it felt as though he was a child, breast-feeding. He still had a horn, still had me knickers at half-mast and he still fingered me, but he didn't try to force me like he usually did. I wanted to do something special for him, something I had never done before. I un-zipped his jeans and took it out. It was hard and warm to touch. I wanted to look at it but he was suckin me tits and I couldn't see. I'd never wanked a fella before, but whenever the lads were calling someone a wanker, they always cupped their hand and shook it up and down. So I cupped his thing in me hand, holding it loosely and

47

moved me hand up and down. Johnser held me hand and squeezed. I knew that meant I wasn't holding it tight enough. I squeezed hard and started pushing and pulling again. He lay back, and pulled his jeans down to his knees. At last I saw it. I wanted to laugh, thinking about the lads when their towels were pulled away from them. It was weird, the weirdest thing I'd ever seen, never mind held. The sac that held his balls was the same as Slash's or Fat Larry but his mickey was huge. It stood straight like a candle, veiny and ugly. Its top (me knob, as Johnser called it) was like a hat, a purple hat with a slit in the top, and as I wanked him, all the loose wrinkly skin went over the top, covering it completely. Every time I pulled it back, he moaned in the same way that I moaned when he played with me. I began to move me hand faster, trying to ignore the ugly veins, everything was purple. Purple hat, purple veins. His moans became closer and faster, suddenly his whole body stiffened and his mickey jerked in me hand. Through the veins I could feel a warm flow of liquid and through the slit in the little purple hat a large splurt of creamy white stuff shot out. I stopped pulling.

"Keep goin."

I grabbed it again and kept wanking. His body tilted and he kept coming. I kept going even when his mickey didn't feel hard. He reached down and moved me hand away. His shirt was full of the stuff but he was smiling. He kissed me.

"That was fucking great."

I spent the next three weeks wanking. Every time we slipped away from our mates, it was out and in me hand. Some nights I did it as many as three times. Then, suddenly, wanking wasn't enough.

Tara Coyle joined our gang and I knew she spelled trouble.

Johnser couldn't understand why I didn't like her and I couldn't really tell him. I mean, what was I supposed to say – "She's a ride,"?

That would be like showing a red flag to a bull. None of us had gone all the way; if we had they would all have wanted to go with us, but we knew that as soon as they got their hole they'd be gone. But it wasn't only that, she was good-looking and she knew it. Her dresses were always much shorter than ours and, when someone told her they could see her knickers, she wouldn't cross her legs and tell them to fuck off like the rest of us. No, not Tara, she'd just sit there smiling. Everyone seen her knickers, even Fat Larry.

Johnser was getting more and more frustrated, then one night he didn't show up and neither did Tara.

The next night we headed to the Naller. Tara was looking at me and Johnser all night. When Johnser finished singing we went to our little patch. Soon he was pulling me knickers down. He tried to pull them off.

"Johnser!"

He ignored me. He began opening his fly. I knew what was happening but, before I could stop him, he was on top of me.

"Johnser, fuck off!" His hand moved to me fanny, finger in, he tried to make me wet.

"Johnser!"

He tried to part me legs with his . . . succeeding . . . spreading me.

"No, Johnser!" His other hand pulled roughly at me top . . . tits out . . . head down . . .

Biting.

"Johnser, fuck off."

I fought. Fought Johnser, what a laugh.

His hand moved to his thing, pulling it close to me fanny, trying to enter me.

I screamed.

He bit me tit hard, the hat trying to enter, missing.

Hand down again, fingers in, hat missed again.

Me mind raced with thoughts of me da, he was looking at me and I was pregnant with no boyfriend.

"Johnser, I mean it, fuck off."

He was hurting me. Hurting me tits, hurting me fanny, hurting me dreams. Johnser, my Johnser was gone, as dead as his ma.

Still he missed, it hurt like hell but he missed. I struggled me knee free, connected hard with his balls and he crumbled. He rolled off me in agony, curled up like a baby. I grabbed me knickers and ran. He didn't follow.

* * *

I stayed away from Ballyer for a week. But, finally, I convinced meself that Johnser was feeling guilty, that he was sorry, that he was too proud to ring me. After all, I was the one who had run off home. I could see the gang as the bus rounded the corner.

They were all there, Fat Larry, Slash, Johnser and Tara. Tara Coyle, skirt up to her arse in the middle of winter, hanging on to Johnser's arm, kissing him.

Tara in his mouth, Johnser in her knickers.

I didn't get off the bus.

Word spread like wildfire. We were finished. Tara Coyle was his mot now, Tara Coyle was preggers. They were engaged to be married.

Life ended for me.

I walked to me local shops and, as I passed a gang on the corner, they shouted, "Get up, yeh ride!"

CHAPTER FIFTEEN

I didn't go out very much, in fact I didn't go out at all.

Oh yeah, I went to work all right and home again.

Ma and Da started to worry about me, even more so than before.

Me attitude changed. I changed back to the old me, I became nicer. Not nice nice, but nice in the way of someone who is broken-hearted, because their partner has died. Someone who is in mourning, yeah, mourning, that's probably the best way of describing how I felt. Nothing seemed to matter any more, life had no purpose. I got up in the morning, and had me usual shower, came downstairs, had me usual breakfast, walked the few steps to me usual bus stop and went to me usual dreary job. It seemed even drearier now that I hadn't got Johnser to think about, knowing that I would never see him again.

What was I talking about? Who was I trying to fool? I did nothing but think about Johnser. About the days when I had enjoyed the walk to the bus stop because I knew I was going to see him that night. I thought about him as I packed the little marshmallows that came down my side of the conveyer belt, as I packed each one, I thought about him. I thought about him as I ate my lunch, I thought about him as I walked down the road and the fellas on the corner shouted, "Get up, yeh ride!"

Johnser, Johnser, Johnser, he was all I could think about.

Ma and Da tried their best, they knew something was wrong but were too afraid to ask what it was. Ma really went out of her way to try and please me, you know the kind of thing –

"Scrambled eggs for breakfast, love? Will I do your toast on both sides? Is that tea too strong?"

And Da, Da actually came from behind his newspaper for the first time I can remember and tried to make conversation about stupid things on the television like *Coronation Street,* a programme I never fucking watched. He knew I never fucking watched it, he knew it was the one thing on television I detested. I was the only person I know who hated Mavis, I hated Rita and I hated Bet, I hated the whole fucking lot of them. I wanted to become a terrorist for a day, just one day and I'd blow the whole fucking cast of *Coronation Street* out of it. And here was me Da asking me, "What do you think of Mavis? What do you think she'll do about Derek's birthday party?"

I don't give a fuck what she does, I'd say, in me head of course. Outwardly I'd just sit staring at the screen nodding and grunting when necessary, he didn't seem to notice my indifference. In fact, if the truth be known, Da was probably happy now because I was home all the time, I was back, I was Daddy's girl again.

If only he knew, if only he could see inside me head for one second, if only he could see that inside I was crying. And it wasn't only inside. Every single night I cried aloud. I didn't sleep any more, I would close me eyes and the tears would start.

I couldn't help it, I just couldn't stop, I just cried and cried and cried.

I thought about Johnser and Tara, Tara doing the things I

52

used to do with Johnser, but of course, she was doing the other thing too. I cursed meself, I honest-to-God cursed meself for not having opened me legs, I hadn't given it to Johnser, and fuck it, here it was and no one was getting it and I didn't want anyone to get it, I wanted Johnser. I wanted Johnser to take me cherry, I wanted Johnser to take first go, I wanted Johnser to break me hymen, call it what you like, I wanted Johnser to be me first ride and I knew now that he was never going to be. He was Tara's, but fuck it, Tara had had them all, every one of them, she didn't need Johnser, she probably didn't even want Johnser.

I used to have stupid dreams about how I would go up to Tara and explain to her, the way Dolly Parton had done in the song *Joleen*, when she had told the other woman, "You can have your choice of men but I will never love again."

I even thought that was the way I'd say it, can you imagine? "Now listen, Tara, this is the way it is, right, you can have your choice of men but me, well, I can never love again."

And of course, she was going to give him back, we'd do a little bartering. I'd give her two of me miniskirts and a jumper that I knew she liked, and she'd give me back Johnser.

As I lay awake crying in the middle of the night, not having had a proper night's sleep in weeks, this all seemed perfectly logical. I actually convinced meself that she'd do it, that Tara Coyle would give me Johnser Kiely for two miniskirts and a jumper. But in the cold light of morning I knew this was never going to happen. I knew that Tara would never give him up, especially if she knew that I wanted him back.

She'd gloat on that, she'd jump for joy, she'd sing a hallelujah chorus on the altar, she'd tell the whole bloody congregation, all twenty of them attending early Mass, how much I wanted him, and if it had meant getting him back, you know, I don't think I would have minded.

I thought about going up to see him, thought about saying to him, "Look, Johnser, remember what we had together? well, I'm willin teh give it all now. I'm willin teh lie on me back, in the wet grass down by the canal, and let yeh have yer way with me."

But something inside always stopped me.

Oh yeah, I thought about him every single minute of the day and I cried every single minute of the night, I wanted him more than life itself. But, deep down, I knew that if I gave in, if I submitted, he'd be like all the other fellas I'd heard about. The minute you gave in they didn't want you any more. I tried to convince meself that Johnser respected me, respected me because I wasn't easy, respected me because I hadn't gone running back, respected me for giving him a kick in the balls when he'd tried to have his wicked way. But at the end of the day, what good had it done me? I had no Johnser, that fucking slut Tara Coyle had Johnser.

Tara-I'm-everybody's, Tara-open-like-a-tollbridge, Tara-fuckin-margarine-legs-Coyle had Johnser.

She had my Johnser and there was nothing I could do about it.

CHAPTER SIXTEEN

The Brush was like a contractor, he got so many jobs he always had one in his pocket. We were never out of work for very long.

I mean to say, after the bank job I thought well, that will be that for a while, but the very next Wednesday we were back on another job. Not as big, of course, just a little post office down the country. In we went, pointed the gun over the counter and left with a few grand in our back pockets. He didn't even bother his arse showing up for the job, but we still had to split the money with him, and of course he took the biggest percentage. No one seemed to mind, cause, after all, the Brush was the brains behind the whole operation. Every Friday I had to call to some of the shops around Pearse Street, to collect the protection money they had to pay Brush. It was funny, really, funny to see these men who, on another day, in another life, when I was a kid hanging around the Elephant supermarket, would have fucked me out of their shops. Now they just nodded to me, nodded in that fearful way knowing that at any minute I might decide to knock their fucking blocks off, they gave me the money and, if I picked up a Mars Bar, they gave me that as well. In fact they'd have given me a box of Mars Bars had I wanted them.

But I never did, I never wanted them to see any sign of weakness. I never wanted them to think this was anything more or less than business. I didn't speak to them, I never said anything other than what had to be said, "Howya, the Brush sent me."

They always kept the money in a little envelope stuck in behind the cigarettes, they'd hand it to me and I'd be gone. I never opened the envelopes. Can you believe that I didn't even know how much he charged them? Why should I want to know? I was on a nice little earner every week, that's all I cared about.

I was driving a car now. And I think I was the only person in Ballyer who was happy in the knowledge that it would never be stolen. It wasn't much of a car, an old Ford, but still, it was a car. The gas thing about it all was that the police were now beginning to respect me, they started calling to the house to ask me about the big crimes, no more of this, "Did yeh rob a car? Did yeh rob a Mars bar, a Snickers bar?"

You know, things like that. Oh no, there was no more calling to our house because the aul fella was drunk. They only called now when they knew there was business going on, a big meeting, the board meetings I used to call them. They'd bring me down to the station and start asking me all sorts of questions, questions about what jobs the Brush had on. I'd just sit there staring at that space on the wall, the way the Brush had told me to, and I'd say fuck all, and it felt like paradise. I could see their big red thick culchie necks getting redder by the minute. They'd start scratching their heads, scratching and thinking, how can we get this bastard to talk? I remember one time, looking at me little spot on the wall and thinking to meself that they could easily be two farmers looking up the arse of a cow waiting for a calf to be born. All they were missing were the wellies. Jasus, they were thick. I felt like telling them what I was thinking.

In the old days I would have said something regardless of the thick ear I would have got, but not now, now I just sat concentrating on me little spot. Eventually, after two or three hours, they would get tired of their little game and let me go.

I was fast losing contact with me old mates, I didn't see them as friends anymore, they were just people I'd grown up with, they were like Batman, something I had liked once but had grown out of. I was no longer into Batman, and I was no longer into me mates down by the canal. I wasn't into drinking cans sitting on the wet grass. I wanted something more, much more, and I was getting it. I was eighteen years old and everything was starting to fall into place. I was going to be the top man. I would look at the Brush, look straight at him and think, man, you better make the most of the next few years because I'm going to be taking over. After all, I had the intelligence. I was going to treat the next few years like an apprenticeship, I was going to learn everything there was to learn. How to rob, who to rob, where to rob, when to rob, why to rob, and by the end of it all I'd be the best fuckin robber Dublin had ever known. I was already one of the best fighters in Dublin, and I knew that once I put my mind to something I could become the best.

I still seen the lads from time to time, but things were different now, they didn't seem to be going anywhere. I had outgrown them. I knew that at 7.30 pm on any given night if I drove past Quinnsworth they'd be outside with their takeouts, still shouting abuse at any girl who passed by. Anyway, I had a full-time girlfriend now, I had Tara, and Tara rode. After the first ride I decided that I wasn't going to do it in the grass again, I didn't want Fat Larry sneaking up on us to see what we were doing. This was my woman and what we done was private. I didn't want anyone else knowing about it. So, me and Tara got together, I never planned it, it just happened. I suppose I was flattered that she fancied me, after all she was a fine-looking thing. She had a great pair of tits on her. All the lads agreed that she had the best pair of tits we'd ever seen on a sixteen, seventeen, eighteen, even a twenty-year-old for that matter. She looked really great and we all knew that she rode, well at least we hoped she did.

Jackie was a nice girl but I was getting sick of her. I mean to say, here I was doing bank jobs, putting me life at risk, holding guns to people's heads and I still couldn't get a ride, Jackie was still off-limits. No way, I wasn't having that, nothing is off-limits to JK any more. So why not, Tara offered and I took. She let it be known that she wouldn't refuse me. Any time I wanted her she'd be there, and there was nothing she wouldn't do. She didn't mind the cold, she didn't mind the wet grass, she didn't mind anything. She loved me for what I was and I convinced meself that she was the one I wanted. After all, Jackie had kicked me in the balls and no one had ever done that before. Respect is respect and Jackie hadn't shown any. Like, fuck it, I appreciate that she didn't want to be known as a ride but we'd been going together for over a year and we'd done everything else . . . me mother had died, for fuck's sake, and where was the emotional support? She could easily have opened her legs for me but she wouldn't. Tara had, so I took Tara. End of story.

I'd be lying if I said that I didn't think about her, Jackie that is. Sometimes I thought about the good times we'd had together, times away from the rest of the gang, times when I had sang, "Two outta three ain't bad."

She understood me, I didn't have to be tough when I was with her. She didn't want me to be tough and, even though that annoyed me at times, cause girls are like that, there were times when I was happy not to be tough. I was happy to show a side of me that didn't have to be smashing people's heads in. Jackie was that side. Tara didn't want to know anything about tenderness, all she wanted to know about was me being a hard man. And, in order to keep her happy, I started bragging about the jobs I was doing. Sure, I kept quiet at the beginning, but now that me name was being bandied about, why not tell her what she wanted to hear? She always asked at the right time, buttons opened, dick hanging out, then she'd say –

"Johnser, tell us about . . . this job, that job, the other job." I wondered how she knew so much about the different jobs. In truth, I think I was flattered by her interest. I was flattered by the fact that this girl with the great body, who let me shag the arse off her, was so much in awe of me.

Things seemed to move really quick with her, in fact, looking back, maybe things moved too quick. She let it be known she wanted to be mine and I was happy enough with that. After all, a ride's a ride.

Then suddenly she dropped the bombshell, "Johnser, I'm pregnant!"

I couldn't believe what I was hearing, she was pregnant.

The only thing I could think of was me ma, eighteen in a row, bang-bang-bang. Women are like that, all you have to do is look at them when they're fertile and they end up preggers.

So we got engaged, for the simple reason that I was

59

Johnser Kiely. Sounds stupid I know, but that's the way I was.

I was always tough, always a fucking nut, a headcase, but I was always respected. Me biggest fear in life was that people would think, "Ah Johnser, he's gone and got his mot up the stick and now he's done a runner. Typical." I wasn't going to let anyone say a bad word about me. I was getting engaged and that was that, it had nothing to do with love. I had no intention of ever marrying her, but six months later I found meself walking down the aisle with Tara on me arm. That girl moved so fucking quick, before I knew what hit me she was Mrs Kiely.

CHAPTER SEVENTEEN

Nothing seemed to change.

I was crying and crying and crying. It wasn't even days, it was weeks, it was heading towards months. At one stage I thought to meself, for God's sake, girl, pull yourself together, you can't go on like this, you can't spend the rest of your life crying. OK, Johnser is gone, Tara has him, they're engaged, there's a baby on the way, they're going to live happily ever after, but your life has to go on. I thought about suicide but I knew I wasn't brave enough. It was one of those thoughts that showed how immature I was. After all, imagine me with a knife, slitting me wrists, is that what I was going to do? Or was I going to take tablets? Knowing me, I'd take the wrong ones. I'd take Brutlax and end up shitting for three weeks. I couldn't kill meself, for fuck's sake, I couldn't kill anything. I hated spiders but I couldn't kill one. I'd watch as it climbed the wall and I'd crouch further and further into a corner, terrified, as if it was going to kick me to death with its legs. And the poor spider was probably only trying to get back home to her web to feed her little babies. I couldn't even kill a fly. Remember *Psycho*, when they said she wouldn't even harm a fly? Well, that was me. I just couldn't, I couldn't kill anything. So why was I sitting here thinking I was going to kill meself, commit suicide. "Suicide is painless." That's all me arse.

Eventually, like it or not, I decided that life had to go on. No matter how I felt about it, I would have to get meself back out and about. The girls in Caffrey's were great. Some of them knew what was going on, some of them knew that Tara Coyle was going out with him. For a while it was a bit awkward, they didn't know what to be saying to me, so they avoided me. But that was all right now, they were all back to normal, talking about the usual things, their nights out, and what they had bought for the weekend. About the Television Club, about all the fine-looking fellas who went there, about how they were all rides. About how much they loved the place. I thought to meself, well, why not, it's about time you started having some kind of life again. Teresa Cummins was getting engaged or married or something like that. Something big was happening in her life that I wasn't particularly interested in, but I might as well go along and if it didn't work out I could always go home early. So I went with them, I got all dressed up and went drinking with them. And it was funny, it was a funny sensation sitting drinking in a pub with a cushioned seat under me arse instead of wet grass. It was comfortable, but I didn't enjoy it. The music was blaring, it was bouncing off the walls, I thought me eardrums were going to burst.

I said it to one of the girls and she just laughed, saying, "Jasus, deya hear yer one? It's like havin me fucking granny with me." And continued to knock back her pints. I was on vodka, vodka and orange of course, and I just sat there sipping at me drink and listening to the ear-splitting music. The music wasn't even that good, I didn't like the songs they were playing, I wasn't into Wham! or any of that other disco crap. I wanted to hear "Two outta three ain't bad". But I didn't want fat Meatloaf singing it, I didn't want to know that Jim Steinman had written the lyrics, clever fucker that he is. I wanted to hear Johnser singing it, I wanted Johnser sitting here singing it to me, but he wasn't. So I had another vodka, and another and another.

Eventually the music didn't seem that bad, and the noise didn't bother me so much any more. Me head was starting to feel a bit woozy and me legs felt a bit funny as I walked to the toilet. On me way back, Teresa Cummins pulled me on to the dance floor.

Here I was trapped in the middle of all these flailing arms and legs, like branches on a tree waving about in a breeze. Caught in the middle of three hundred gobshites acting like fucking trees, and I was going to become one of them. I stayed for what seemed an eternity and, when Teresa wasn't looking, I made me escape back to me vodka and orange. We became best friends. No, not Teresa, not fucking her, me and the vodka and orange. We met every day, same time, same place, usually me bedroom. I took it out from underneath me knickers, that's where I kept it, in me knicker drawer. Me ma never went near that drawer, every other drawer in the house, yes, but not that one. She was always rootin around, but never there. I knew by the way the knickers were left on me bed that she didn't go near the drawer.

Maybe in her bedroom that was her private little place, I don't know, but for some reason she always left me knicker drawer alone.

So I kept a naggin of vodka there. A little drop into me cup and down the stairs. I suppose I could have drank it anywhere in the house. Ma and Da never noticed. I don't know how, cause when I came in of an evening I never had a word to say to them but by 10.30 pm you couldn't shut me up. They'd want to go to bed, Da would be standing with his two milk bottles, ready to put them out, and I'd start yakkin about anything and everything. I'd even start on about *Coronation Street*.

I'd start saying things like, "Isn't Rita lovely, Da? Do yeh think Mavis is funny?"

And he'd look at me like I'd two heads cause he'd tried to have this conversation with me earlier and I hadn't even bothered to answer him.

He'd say, "I think it's time to go to bed, love."

"Ah Da, ah Da but . . ."

I'd go on and on and on. I knew he liked James Bond so I'd start on about Bond films and, like it or not, he'd always have to get in on that conversation. Then I'd hightail it to bed. Poor Ma would have to listen to him going on about how *Octopussy* was the greatest film of all time. If it wasn't so pathetic, it would have been funny.

CHAPTER EIGHTEEN

We were after doing loads of jobs, but the Brush was growing more and more impatient, because he couldn't be in on them. The police had him hounded. Every time he walked out the front door they had him. Down to the station, into the interview room, three hours later he was back out, back home. A knock on the door and he was back in the station again. They wouldn't leave him alone. The only thing he was getting to do was plan jobs. He wanted to take some paintings. Fucking paintins, maybe that was why they called him the Brush, maybe it had nothing to do with him having worked for the Corporation. It suited him better, after all, in his own way he was an artist. We'd go to his house and sit for hours planning jobs. When we were leaving we'd wave to the coppers sitting outside in their car. Although they tried to ignore us, we could see their big thick red necks getting fucking redder with frustration.

There were some paintings down Wicklow way, big gaff, posh place, I drove by it one night with Blue. Blue was still the same as ever and I hated him, fucking hated him. I used to cringe any time I had to go anywhere with him and I think he knew it. He enjoyed this, it was the effect he wanted, he liked to have on people. He was the most ignorant fucker you could ever meet. Music blaring, singing aloud out of key, fuck you, fuck you, Blue, some day, some day I'll have you. I think what gave him the most pleasure was that he honestly thought I would never be big enough to do him any real harm. What he wasn't aware of was that I was watching the Brush. Brush wasn't getting any younger and I was getting that little bit more involved. Some day this was all going to be mine. I was going to run the whole show, just like the Brush did, I was going to have everybody in the palm of me hand, just like Brush had. People would respect me even more then, because they'd know where I'd come from. They'd remember the old gang wars, cause they'd all be the same age as me, and they'd remember how good of a goer I was. I'd be able to ask for whatever I liked and I'd get it.

But for now I had to sit in a car with Blue and suss out this big old house. We used to watch the old Bentley coming down the drive. It was a fucking enormous driveway, as big as the Phoenix Park. We'd sit at the side of the road and watch. They were two old dears, the man must have been about a hundred and the aul one wasn't much younger. The Bentley crawled along at a snail's pace, I'm not exaggerating, we could have jogged alongside it. But they weren't our target, it was their paintings. We had a look around one day, after they'd gone out, and I noticed that all the windows were alarmed.

I went back and told the Brush, told him all about the place. What time the old dears left at and what time they came back. I suggested we hit one of the windows and set the alarm off. Blue started laughing, like I had just told the joke of the year.

"What the fuck are yeh laughin at?"

"Hit the window, what good is that gonna do us?"

He looked baffled, totally baffled. I couldn't believe the fucking gobshite didn't know why I wanted to set the alarm off. Surely to Jasus even he knew that one, sure it's the oldest trick in the book. Set the alarm off a few times, get the cops out, cops get fed up, tell the owner they have a fault, alarm is switched off, bye bye security . . . hello paintings.

I looked at the Brush and knew that even he was embarrassed by Blue's lack of cop-on. Ignoring him, he turned his attention to me, "Excellent idea, John. Do you think you can organise the job?"

Blue reacted without thinking.

"What the fuck, Brush? What are yeh thinkin of, lettin that little bollocks take control?"

Big mistake. No one ever cursed at Brush.

The Brush glared at him, a real I'm-gonna-kick-your-fuckin-head-in-despite-me-age look.

Blue retracted immediately, "Sor . . . sor . . . sorry, Boss," he stuttered.

Brush lit a cigarette, took a long drag and blew the smoke around the room.

"Can you arrange it?" he asked again.

I couldn't believe it, this was one of the biggest jobs we were ever likely to do and, not only did the Brush want me in on it, he wanted me to organise the whole thing.

I was now the Brush's number one, ahead of Blue. I looked across at Blue, and knew by the expression on his face that he knew it too. I think that if we had been on our own he would have begged me to let bygones be bygones. He would have turned to me and said, "I'm sorry about all

NEVILLE THOMPSON

the differences we've had in the past. For slaggin the
wallpaper in yer ma's house. But please don't do this to
me."

This is what I'd been waiting for. Fuck Blue. I turned to
Brush.

"Yeah, I can arrange it."

The Brush stubbed his cigarette out.

"Good. I'll give you the exact details on what paintings I
want in a week or so."

68

CHAPTER NINETEEN

A week later I was back with the Brush. This time I was alone.

As usual, Brush spoke first, "Do you have the men for the job or do you want my lads?"

I knew I had to take the bull by the horns.

"No disrespect, Brush, but I think I prefer me own men. The less ties you have with this job, the better."

He smiled. "You're like a son to me."

And I guess I was. I felt like I was his son, what's more he was more of a father to me than me da ever was. OK, so Da had gone off the drink since Ma died, but things were never going to be the same again. He was going with some aul tart, some aul one he had met when he was drinking. They were both trying to clean up their act. I knew it would never work. For a couple of weeks he'd be fine, everything would be hunky-dory, but eventually he'd have a row, he'd have to, it was part and parcel of the man. And when he did row, that's when it would all blow up in their faces and he'd hit the drink again. I'd seen and heard it all before. Da had never been what you could call a father, he had never been someone you could lean on or depend on for support. I mean to say, he was always too busy wondering where he was going to get the next tenner for drink. We never had anything, we'd fuck all in Ballyer in them days. It wasn't as though money was scarce, yet the rent was always behind, and the food, fucking yellow packs or whatever the hell the cheapest was at the time. As for clothes, all hand-me-downs, and Ma, Ma never got anything. Apart from the day I started school I never seen her in anything new, it was always the same old summer frock she called a dress, and then in the winter she wore a big skirt, a tweed skirt and a woolly jumper that she'd knit herself. She looked crap, she really and truly looked crap. Sure was it any wonder? When me da drank every single penny that came into the gaff. He didn't care, he didn't give a shite what was happening. He didn't give a fuck if there was another baby on the way.

New books for school, are you fucking joking? Even if we'd had someone in the house with brains, they'd never have had a chance. Da never gave us the opportunity of getting on in life. He never gave us the chance that other kids got, the chance of going on and bettering ourselves. So there we were stuck in a fucking hell-hole of a concrete jungle, and Da out every night of the week drinking every penny.

Every once in a while Ma would lose it, she'd just crack. "That's it, I've had enough."

She'd go beserk, fuck him out and his clothes after him. His three-piece pin-stripe suit out the fucking window, his only suit fucked into the dirty aul street. And he'd go, he always went and for three days we wouldn't see him. We'd know where he was all right, the next-door neighbour took pleasure in telling me ma.

"I seen Mr Kiely . . . I seen him here, I seen him there . . . "

And it was always a pub. Eventually he'd come back. He'd sit in the kitchen and he'd cry, bawl his eyes out. He'd beg me ma to take him back and, like a fucking eejit, she would.

I remember I used to sit there and I used to say to meself, in me head, cause I'd never say anything out loud, "Ma, please don't take him back, fuck him out, leave him an' his three-piece suit out on the street. He's useless, he's a piece of shite."

You see, without him, me ma went to the social . . . after all, she was a deserted wife. And for those few days we got decent grub. I remember one time he left for a whole week and I even got a pair of shoes out of them. A brand new pair of shoes, the first fucking new pair of shoes I'd ever had. They cut the fucking toes off me but I felt great. That's all you want when you're a kid, that's all you need. When you walk into your classroom, you don't give a fuck if Daddy's played happy families with you all weekend, as long as you have the gear, as long as you're dressed the same as your mates, you don't give a fuck. When your mates are starting to wear Wranglers and you're still in shorts, that's when you feel like a fucking gobshite.

That's how I felt. That's how all the Kielys felt.

That's why we were so tough.

There were other kids just like us, just as poor, who had nothing, who walked into school in their shorts and got the bollocks slagged out of them. Not us. We learned to defend ourselves. Like in that song by Johnny Cash, "A Boy Named Sue", Walking into Ballyer in your little shorts was like being a boy called Sue. You had to fight to earn respect, cause as sure as Jasus, you didn't look like someone people should respect.

A little pair of shorts, I always remember them. I was eleven years of age and I was going into school wearing the skimpiest fucking shorts you ever seen. They were like hot pants on me.

Stripy fucking hot pants, with me arse bet into them.

Da let this happen. He let me ma get all them letters from the ESB. It was his fault the electricity was cut off, it was his fault that me ma's hands cracked open from having to handwash the clothes. As far as he was concerned, a washing-machine was a luxury she could do without. There was no fear of him doing without the luxury of his fucking pints. It was his fault we were the only family on our road without a colour telly. And, after all, what was Ma supposed to do? She could hardly go out and get a job, she was too busy having kids for that. So I didn't have a da. I didn't have anybody who I could refer to as a father-figure. I used to resent Fat Larry. Fat Larry was always going on about his da, he liked him. I used to give him an awful time about his da, his aul fella. I used to say he was bender. I'd tell everybody that Fat Larry's da was a child molester, but deep down all I really wanted was to have a da like his. Someone who liked me, someone I could be proud of. I knew that someone would never be me aul fella.

In all honesty, although I felt that Brush was the nearest thing to a father I was ever likely to have, and he had already told me I was like a son, it was all too late.

It was only business now. I was too hard, all those times when I needed support, I'd been alone. I was old enough to look after meself now, I didn't need anybody. And, although I appreciated all the Brush was doing for me, and although I liked the relationship we had, deep down inside I knew the day would come when I would take over and, when this happened, I would be as ruthless about it as I had been about everything else in me life.

So we worked the plan through. The Brush showed me photographs of the paintins. I thought they were crap, serious shite. There was one that made a little bit of sense to me, but Brush laughed and said I was holding it upside down. I thought to meself, where in the name of Jasus do people get their taste from? Brush seemed to know what he was talking about, he started going on about different strokes and different eras and the greatness of this man, that man and the other man. All I could see was a big ugly-looking bunch of fucking flowers. A vase full of flowers on a table that looked full of woodworm. I wondered what all the fuss was about. I swear to Jasus, Jimmy McEnteer who had been in me class was a better painter than this so-called artist, whoever he was. I looked down at the name but I couldn't make it out, he couldn't fucking write, never mind paint.

But anyway, that didn't concern me. We were going to do the job and I was in charge, that was all I wanted to know about. The problem now was to find guys I could trust.

73

CHAPTER TWENTY

Everyone said that Jeffrey was lovely, nice. Sweet was how they described him. Me ma used to say he was sweet, me da thought he was nice, and all me friends used to say, "Ah, he's lovely." But he wasn't what I wanted. Jeffrey Adams, it sounded very English, or very posh or poncy, it just didn't sound right. But anyway, I started dating him. He was very nice, he really was and he was sweet. If Jeffrey said he'd call for me at eight, he'd arrive at ten to eight. He always brought chocolates or flowers, even though I told him I didn't particularly like flowers. And he always had time for a chat with me da, they'd talk about *Coronation Street* or *Octopussy*. And Da was won over straight away. And he'd talk to me ma. How nice the day had been, wasn't it great to see such good weather, how he'd noticed the flowers in the garden looking beautiful. He was a nice fella, he had a good job, a car and he was presentable.

He was no great shakes in the looks department, he was no Brian Connelly or Rossi, but he'd do. It was very hard to describe Jeffrey. His only outstanding feature was his height.

Now, don't get me wrong, there was nothing wrong with the fella, I mean, it's not as though you'd say, "Ah Jasus, not him, for fuck's sake what are yeh doin goin out with that eejit?"

74

It was just that he was nondescript. And another thing was that everyone called him Jeffrey. No one ever called him Jeff, and he didn't have a nickname, so it was always Jeffrey.

Jasus, it sounded so fucking formal.

He worked in the office in Cadbury's. Assistant trainee manager or something, I don't know. He had some job that some day was going to be big and important, but at the minute it wasn't. He wore a shirt and tie and, like I say, he had a company car. We used to go for drives and it was nice in the winter, sitting in the heat of the car as we drove to different places.

We'd go to restaurants, fancy restaurants. Italian one week, Indian the next, Greek, Chinese. Not for a takeaway, but a sit-down meal, with about one hundred and twenty courses being served at the one time. It was OK, but I always felt there was something missing.

Jeffrey declared his love for me on the first night, and the second, and the third. The minute he stopped the car outside me house he'd whisper those three little words, "I love you."

And I hated it. I didn't want him, I'd never wanted to go out with him, I didn't want to be with him and I definitely didn't want to kiss him. But I went along with it. Because at least he was somebody, at least he was there.

I was always late for our dates. He would arrive ten minutes early and I would arrive an hour late. He'd sit with Mammy and Daddy discussing the ups and downs and the ins and outs of life.

And when I eventually made me entrance he wouldn't get angry.

He'd never say, "For fuck's sake, will yeh ever hurry up, we're after missin the start of the bleedin film."

He'd just say, "You look great, you look lovely, beautiful."

Whatever. And life went on like that.

I wouldn't let him kiss me, not even one kiss. Not at first, anyway. I remember the first time I went out with him, he arrived at the house at ten to eight, we left at nine and I was back home and in me bed by a quarter to twelve. I'd given him a quick peck on the cheek and ran.

I ran in, up the stairs, back to me best friend. Back to me little bottle of vodka. I didn't even bother with orange juice because I'd forgotten to get some earlier on. Straight down it went, I took two gulps and that was it. Once again I cried meself to sleep.

He must have been a glutton for punishment because he asked me out again.

Suddenly we were an item, we'd been going out for seven weeks. Seven whole weeks and I finally let him kiss me. Well, I didn't really let him, it just sort of happened.

It was one of those nights when I was particularly fed up and he stopped the car on the way home. I'd had a lot to drink, there was plenty of vodka and orange inside me, and I was really missing Johnser. If we'd still been together it would be our anniversary. So, when he leaned over, I pretended he was Johnser, and as he stuck his fucking rigid tongue into me mouth, I responded. Not too much, just enough to tickle the tip of his tongue with mine. His hands were all over me, mauling, touching, feeling me tits. I pulled away.

He spent the rest of the journey telling me how sorry he was, how I must think him a proper monster, telling me how bad he felt. I felt like screaming at him, "Will yeh shut fucking up. There's nothin wrong with yeh, it's me."

Why did he have to blame himself? Why did everyone pussyfoot around me? Why didn't someone tell me off? How come nobody ever said, "Now listen here, you, it's about time yeh got your act together, what the fuck is wrong with yeh? Why are yeh being such a bitch? Why don't yeh just get on with yer life, Johnser's gone an' he's not comin back."

Jeffrey was just like Ma and Da, ignoring the situation, blaming himself, pretending I was doing nothing wrong, acting as though me behaviour was normal.

But I knew, I knew I was wrong. I was the one who was drinking too much, I was the one being the bitch, but there was nothing I could do about it, I just couldn't stop.

I took full advantage of their niceness.

I took every single thing Jeffrey gave me. Every apology, every "I love you", every box of chocolates, every bunch of flowers, every free meal. I just fucking took and took and took.

I hated meself. I truly hated meself. I hated meself for not being brave enough to go up and see Johnser, I hated meself for not having rode Johnser when I'd had the chance. I hated meself for treating Jeffrey so badly, I hated meself for watching fucking *Coronation Street*. I even hated me best friend at time; there it would sit, tucked away under me knickers and I'd go over, take it out, and we'd make up. Together, we'd go to sleep.

News about Johnser always came through on the grapevine. Some of the girls in Caffrey's lived in his area, and others lived beside Tara Coyle. So I always heard what was happening with them. They were engaged, that hurt. The thought of her wearing his ring. I wondered what it was like, I wondered if Johnser had actually walked around jewellery shops looking at rings, or was it one he'd robbed.

I heard later that it was a three-stone twist, I also heard

that it had cost a fortune. I couldn't imagine Johnser walking into Weir's of Grafton Street and paying a fortune for a ring. But it still hurt. It hurt me to think that he was engaged to her, it hurt me to think about her showing off his ring – real schoolgirl stuff, I know, but it still hurt.

I knew that the wedding was planned. I knew it was only three months away, three months, what the fuck was happening? How the fuck was she getting him to marry her so quick? All because she lay on her back, it couldn't be that simple. Don't anyone try to tell me that if I'd opened me legs and got pregnant I'd be marrying Johnser now. That I would have been the happy little mother-to-be and she would have been the one crying herself to sleep. It couldn't have been that easy.

CHAPTER TWENTY-ONE

I had all the information I needed for the job. All I needed now was to get a gang together. I had to think carefully about it, I had to make sure I got men who knew how to keep their mouths shut. Fellas who'd be up for the job, fellas who'd be tough enough to handle themselves. I'd met a lot of new people, all inner-city guys, guys I knew I could trust. These men were me friends now; some of them were relatives, distant I know, but relatives nonetheless. They were good blokes, they knew how to keep shut and I could trust them.

I needed someone who could drive a car really well, a good fast clean driver. Someone who could rob a car, maybe two, even three cars. Set them up all over the place and give us plenty of escape routes. There was one guy I knew who could do the job, that was the Pocket. The Pocket was a tiny little fella, he'd fit in your pocket, hence the name. But, by Jasus, could he drive. I've never seen anyone like him, fucking hell. Don't talk to me about Evil Knievel or any of them stunt men. This guy was it, he was the main man, he could turn a car on a penny.

He was brilliant. And I knew he'd love the job, I knew he'd love the opportunity to work with me, because anyone with a bit of sense knew that I was going to be Mr Big. They knew that if they wanted to get well in with me, now was the time to do it.

So I met the Pocket and asked him was he interested in doing a job with me. He nearly died, I think he nearly creamed himself. He said yes, of course, so I told him what I wanted. Two fast cars and a Land-Rover to get us over the fields without getting bogged down. He told me that would be no problem, it would take him about three weeks to get everything organised and he'd keep them in a lock-up until I needed them.

I also needed muscle. So Stan the Man would be me next recruit.

He was the biggest fucking ugliest-looking bastard I've ever seen. He was like a sack of potatoes with eyes. He was ugly, damn fucking ugly, his face was ruined from all the fights he'd been in. But he didn't give a fuck. If anyone needed to be sorted out, if things got a bit physical, Stan would be the man.

Five hundred pounds, that's what he cost me. But, judging from what Brush was saying, this was going to be well worth me while. Money well spent.

I needed one more man, someone small. Not the Pocket, he was the driver. Someone about his size would be ideal but with bigger hands. Johnny Fingers. Fingers was a bit mad but he was small, he was nimble, he was quick. We'd only need to break the smallest little window and he'd be in. He'd open the doors and we'd do the rest ourselves.

Four men on the biggest heist ever, this was something that was going to be talked about for years to come.

I had another problem, though. The wedding, it was getting closer and closer. Tara kept going on about me meeting her father. I didn't want to. I didn't even want to meet her half the fucking time. I kept on putting it off, but I knew that sooner or later I was going to have to meet him. I hated the thought of going up to her gaff. All that smiling and saying the right thing, fuck it, I wasn't into all that crap.

I was giving her money hand over fist. Buy the dress, buy the cake, buy this, buy that. But she kept saying, "No, me da's doin it, me da's doin it."

I felt like saying, "Well why don't yeh marry yer fucking da, then? If he's so bleedin great."

The only enjoyable moments were when I felt the little movements in her belly. All the little kicks that I could feel coming from me baby. Johnser Kiely's little son. I never thought about a girl, it was always a boy. I wanted to do the things with him that me aul fella hadn't done with me. I wanted to give him the new shoes, I wanted to send him to school, I wanted to give him a clip round the ear if he didn't go. I wanted him to have the best of gear, the best clothes. I wanted to show him how to be tough if he had to be, but also how to be gentle. I wanted to go for walks with him, go to football matches, things like that. And every time I felt that little kick, that's when I thought, "Yeah, I will marry yeh, I don't particularly fucking like yeh, but I'll marry yeh anyway."

She kept on telling me that her da wanted a big wedding, a society wedding, she was calling it. She lived three miles up the road from Ballyer and she wanted a society wedding.

I'd give her a fucking society wedding, a fucking kick in the society, that's what I'd give her.

I really couldn't be bothered, you know what I mean. At the end of the day it was her aul fella's money, so let them do what the fuck they liked with it. One night I got really fucking annoyed and I said to her, "Who the fuck's yer aul fella? What's he own? How come he's able teh throw all this fucking money around?"

All she said was, "Yeh must know him, he knows you."

That didn't surprise me, in fact I laughed. Maybe he was someone I was collecting money from every week for the Brush. Yeah, maybe he was one of those pricks who paid for protection.

I used to meet her nearly every night. I'd bring her to the pictures the odd time, but most nights we'd just drive around in the car then I'd drop her home. I didn't even leave her to the house because, when we'd started going out together, she wouldn't let me near the place, and now that she wanted me to go to the house, I wouldn't. I'd tell her, "No, get out here, this is where yeh always got out before."

I was sitting with her one day in the car and I got the biggest surprise of me life. Like I say, she wasn't a bad-looking girl, I didn't mind being seen with her. Anyway, who pulls up in his car beside us but the Blue. We were just sitting there. I was having a smoke, she was staring into oblivion, rattling on and on about the invitations she was getting made up, and who was coming and would I ever tell her, would I please ever tell her how many were coming from my side. And I said, "I don't fucking know, I'll tell yeh when I find out."

I didn't want to get involved in stuff like that, it wasn't me scene. I'd put the girl up the pole, I was marrying her, end of story. I was going to get a little house and that would be that. County Council house, Corporation House, who cared as long as it was a house. And here he was, the man I hated most in the world, pulled up beside us. He got out of the car, a big smile on his face. And I thought to meself, one word, Blue, just one word, and that would be it. But, for the first time ever, he was actually nice to me. He came over, we nodded to each other, and he started chatting. I couldn't believe me ears when Tara said, "Howya, Da."

I spun around and looked at her.

"What, your da?"

She smiled.

"I knew yeh knew him, I told yeh yeh did."

I looked back at Blue, he was smiling too.

"Can't yeh see the family resemblance? No?"

I could have fucking throttled her at that moment. If I'd known that she was Blue's daughter I wouldn't have gone near her, not in a million fucking years. How could you, how could you touch anything that came from the Blue's dick?

"I hear we're gonna be a family, Johnser. How 'bout that? Who'd have thought it?"

Not fucking me, anyway, I thought, no fucking way. I knew then that I was snared, that he had me by the bollocks, that's why he'd been so smug lately. There was no way out now, I had to marry her. I couldn't lose face to this bastard.

Ah Jasus, I cursed me prick, I cursed the fact that I went for a ride that night. One lousy fucking ride. I couldn't keep me mickie to meself, no, I had to have a ride. I couldn't stay with the girl I was happy with, no, I couldn't stay with Jackie, I had to be the man. I had to have me own way, I had to have a ride. Well, fuck you, Johnser Kiely, How big and smart are you now? You're stuck with this fucker for life.

Any time I met the Blue after that, he done nothing but talk about wedding arrangements. I couldn't believe it, me stomach churned at the mention of the "Big Day".

I hated getting up in the mornings knowing that I was one day nearer to becoming his son-in-law. I wondered whether she got pregnant on his orders, whether he'd told his own poxy daughter to, "Go in there, luv, an' let that fella lie beside yeh."

I wouldn't put it past him, I'd put nothing past that wanker.

And in the middle of all the arrangements, the cake, the photos, the cars and the, "We'll have teh invite the Brush, an' we'll have teh invite this man an' that man," he threw it in – "So what's the story with me an' you on the paintins?"

I knew he had me. I knew I couldn't refuse him now, there was too much to lose, there was too much at stake. There was going to be five of us now, now that the Blue was getting involved.

We organised the job for the day of the wedding. It seems ludicrous, but it would give us the perfect alibi. I mean, how could I be involved in a robbery when I was getting married? I had to attend me own wedding.

Everything had to be perfectly arranged, the timing had to be spot on. There was going to be a gap of about four hours allowed cause we were going to have the wedding first thing in the morning.

The old couple always left the house around twelve and got back at six. We were going to have to get in during that time. It was all organised, the Brush had everything laid out and Blue was only too happy to arrange the wedding around us.

Blue arranged a stag night and everyone was going to be there, me own da included. The Blue knew this would embarrass the shite out of me, that's why the bastard done it.

CHAPTER TWENTY-TWO

Jeffrey was really beginning to get on me nerves. I was walking all over him. I might as well have put on me high heels and trampled up and down his back and he'd still come back for more.

So I started to abuse him, I wouldn't give him an inch. I started leaving him downstairs with me ma for two hours, sometimes three. At other times I wouldn't bother coming down at all or maybe, after a few vodkas, I might come down and say I wasn't feeling well and could we leave it for another night. And he'd sit there for the night with Ma and Da talking about the weather and films and who was the best Bond. Both of them agreed it was Connery.

Johnser's wedding was getting closer. I would wake up in the morning with a terrible feeling of apprehension hanging over me, as if I was the one getting married. As if I was the one having to make all the arrangements. I'd think to meself, they'll be ordering the cake today. They'd be looking at photographers tomorrow. And I wondered how many cars they'd have and how many bridesmaids, and on and on and on. I thought about everything, I felt like I was cracking up.

Jeffrey had to go away on a course and it was like all me birthdays had come at once. I decided, this is it, I'm going out with the girls tonight. I couldn't give a shite about Jeffrey.

We headed out on the town. I knew there was only one week to go to Johnser's wedding and I couldn't bear it. I needed to go through this week in a state of oblivion. We got to the pub and I started knocking back the vodka. None of the others could keep up with me, I was ordering two at a time. The girls were getting to the stage where they were wondering should they take me home, and I kept telling them to fuck off an' leave me alone.

Then suddenly, there he was, standing in front of me. I thought the drink was causing me to hallucinate, making me see things that weren't there. But he was, he was real. I reached out and touched his hand and he said, "Howya?"

He sat down beside me and suddenly I felt sober.

"Howya," he said. "How's it goin?"

I couldn't speak, I was like some tongue-tied teenager who had just met her idol, having planned for years what she would say and do if she ever got the chance to meet this person. And when she finally got the opportunity, all she could do was sit staring with her mouth open.

I felt stupid, I couldn't think of anything to say except, "Fine." One fucking syllable. "Fine." That's all I could manage.

What I really wanted to say was, "Johnser, I fucking luv yeh. I want yeh back."

I felt as if I'd been struck dumb, like me brain had ceased to function.

"Everythin OK?" he asked.

"Yeah, fine." There it was again, that fucking word.

There was silence for a few seconds, then I said, "I hear yer gettin married."

86

He looked at me. He had a look in his eyes that I had never seen before. It wasn't hatred or sadness or anything like that, it was more a look of frustration, bewilderment. A look that said for the first time in his life Johnser Kiely didn't know what to do.

"Yeah, I'm gettin married."

He started talking. Talking about Tara, talking about us, talking about the old days, Fat Larry and the rest of the gang. The times we'd spent down at the canal, how they'd been good days. We were like two old fogies remembering. Talking about the only good memory they had, after spending a lifetime on earth.

"Good times, weren't they?" Johnser asked.

I agreed. We talked about the time Fat Larry had lain on the train track. About the time the truck took the roundabout too fast and all the crates of orange fell off. I told him why we'd given Donkey his nickname, and he laughed. The laugh I loved so much, a boyish laugh, an ordinary laugh but, coming from Johnser, it sounded like the nicest laugh in the world. I laughed too, for the first time in what seemed like years, I actually laughed. Our hands touched, and held, our eyes met, and we kissed.

He pulled away.

"Jackie, I'm sorry, really sorry."

"Sorry for what?"

"Yeh know . . . "

Suddenly I had this violent urge to slap him across the face.

I'd never before felt such anger.

"No, Johnser, I don't know. All I know is that I wouldn't let yeh ride me, that's all I know. I was actin the same way as I always had an' yeh fucking dumped me."

87

"I know."

"No, yeh don't know, that's the thing, Johnser, yeh don't fucking know. Yeh never bothered yer arse teh know."

I couldn't believe I was talking to Johnser like this. What's more, I couldn't believe he was taking it. What was wrong with him, was he patronising me, or did he really not know?

"Why, Johnser, why did yeh do it teh me?"

He looked down at the floor, like he had some great interest in the carpet. He apologised again.

"I was a fool, Jackie. I shouldn't have done what I done. I know that now. Fuck, but I know it. But what can I do? It's too late for us, she's pregnant."

We kissed again. This time he didn't pull away. It was like we were back down by the canal on those cold winter nights. Those nights when I thought I would freeze to death until Johnser kissed me. Then I would forget about the cold and everything else, everything except him and the fact that I was his girl.

I responded, I responded with all the passion and excitement I'd felt when I was his girl. He asked if he could take me home and I said yes.

We got into the car and I smiled.

"You've come up in the world, Johnser."

He just laughed.

We drove in silence. It wasn't an awkward silence, it was the compatible silence of two people who are at ease in each other's company. When we stopped at the traffic lights he reached over and took me hand. He squeezed and I squeezed back. The lights changed and he moved his hand back to the gear-stick. He drove towards the Phoenix Park but I didn't protest. I knew what was going to happen.

We found a nice quiet spot, stopped the car and, without saying a word, we kissed again. This time he reached inside me blouse and I let him. It was lovely, it felt so good to have him back. He was mumbling something about missing me, I don't know whether he was talking to me or me tits but I didn't care, I didn't care about anything. I ran me hands through his hair as his head went lower and lower, kissing me belly. He lifetd me skirt and started kissing me tights. I cringed, what in the name of God had possessed me to wear tights. Fucking tights, I hated them, I wouldn't even let me ma see me in tights and here was Johnser kissing them. Jasus, I was scarlet.

He was pulling them down, I couldn't wait for him to get them off, not for any sexual reason, but purely so as I could get rid of the fucking things before I died of embarrassment. Why hadn't I worn me fish-net stockings and suspender belt, or me holdups, or fucking ankle socks, anything, anything other than big ugly tights with their reinforced gusset. When he eventually got them off, I thanked the Lord that I had at least worn a nice new pair of knickers. Imagine if I'd been wearing one of those old offwhite pair you keep for when you're having your period, I would have been rightly fucked, or on second thoughts maybe I wouldn't.

I was naked. Naked from the waist down and his head was between me legs. He was kissing me, licking me, making me come, it was brilliant. I couldn't believe it. Here I was in a car, in the middle of the Phoenix Park having an orgasm. Where were me morals now, me big ideas of how I would lose me virginity in a hotel room we had booked for a weekend? Fuck it, who cared.

I wanted him, and I wanted him now. He reclined me seat and climbed on top of me. He was fumbling at his jeans, like a kid desperate to go to the toilet. Suddenly he was in. It hurt but I didn't say a word, I wasn't going to stop him this time. He was in and he was riding me, I was having the first ride of me life and it was with Johnser, the man I loved more than life itself.

I can't say I enjoyed it, I felt no sensation other than that of Johnser on top of me. It was no different to what he had always done, except this time there was a little bit of pain, so I knew that we were making love. He was touching me everywhere, and he was whispering in me ear, "I luv yeh, Jackie, I've always loved yeh."

And I was saying, "I luv yeh too, Johnser."

I could see his face and I knew that at that moment he meant it.

I held him tight against me and suddenly his body stiffened, he jerked backwards and I knew he'd come. I could feel his stuff shooting up through me body. I grabbed his arse and pushed against him as hard as I could, until finally he was finished.

We got dressed and he handed me a cigarette.

"Jackie, I'm sorry, I didn't mean teh . . . "

I stopped him in mid-sentence.

"There's no need to apologise, it's what I've always wanted, it's what I've waited for for years."

He leaned across and kissed me.

"I luv yeh, Jackie," he said again.

This was the first time he'd ever said he loved me. And I knew then, without a shadow of a doubt, that he meant it.

We sat there holding each other. We kissed, talked, kissed again. We talked about the old days, talked about what had gone wrong between us, talked about everything under the sun. The only thing we didn't talk about was Tara Coyle.

I just couldn't. I couldn't even bring meself to ask how she was, how the wedding plans were going, no, I just couldn't.

I didn't want to know. All I wanted was Johnser, all I wanted to know about was Johnser. I wanted this night to last forever. And I suppose, in a way, it did. We sat in the park all night, just holding each other, drifting off to sleep for a couple of minutes, waking up, talking, drifting off again. Eventually, the birds started their dawn chorus and the sun began its journey to the centre of the sky.

His head was resting on me shoulder as he whispered. "I think I'd better take yeh home."

I sighed as I ran me hand through his hair. I loved his hair, the soft silky feel of it, the smell, the colour, he had lovely hair.

"OK, John, whatever."

I had called him John. I couldn't believe it. He was no longer Johnser the boy, he was John the man.

He drove up to me house, right to the front door.

We talked for a few minutes and then he kissed me, "Goodbye, Jackie, take care."

I liked him for that. For not starting any bullshit about, "If only things were different."

We both knew that he was getting married, so what would be the point. We'd had our one night. I'd had my Johnser and that was all that mattered. Now I would have me memories for the rest of me life.

I opened the front door and went in.

Ma and Da were sitting waiting for me. Da was furious.

"And what time do you call this, madam?" he greeted me.

I didn't answer. I walked into the kitchen and put on some

91

toast. Ma was sitting there smoking, she hadn't smoked in years.

"Your father's talking to you, Jackie Clarke."

I spun round.

"What? What the hell's wrong, now?"

"I said what time do you call this?"

I looked at me watch.

"Yeh know what time it is, Da, yeh know fucking well what time it is. Yeh also know that I've been cryin meself teh sleep for months. Yeh know that I've been drinkin like a fish, an' yeh also know that I couldn't give two fucks about you, me ma, Jeffrey, James Bond or anyone else for that matter, so just fuck off. I'm in love with someone who's just about teh get married an' there's not a damn thing I can do about it, not that I'd expect yeh teh understand. So don't be annoyin me about the fucking time."

I couldn't believe what I'd just said. Jasus, I'd be fucking killed. But I wasn't.

They just sat there looking at me, speechless. The toast popped but I was no longer hungry.

"I'm goin teh bed."

I got into bed and within minutes I was asleep, with Johnser.

I woke up later that day and I could feel the dampness of Johnser's spunk still in me knickers. The house was silent so I went and had a shower. When I eventually came downstairs, Ma and Da acted the way they always did, pretending there was nothing wrong. They made me sick.

Jeffrey rang and asked if I'd like to go for a meal. I told him to fuck off. It felt great. I couldn't believe that, after just one night with Johnser, I could feel so good about meself.

92

I hadn't felt so happy in years, in fact, I don't think I'd
ever been this happy.

Later that night Jeffrey called to the house.

"How are you? Is everything OK? Are you OK?"

"I'm fine, Jeffrey. I'm honest to goodness fine."

I knew he'd like that, all that goodness stuff, Jeffrey
didn't like cursing, he liked people to be refined. I knew he
wanted me to be refined.

"Are you getting ready? Are we going out?"

And I thought to meself, why not? So out we went to
another fancy restaurant, ate another fancy meal, and life
went on.

CHAPTER TWENTY-THREE

I hated meself for the way I'd treated Jackie, the way I'd just dropped her home and driven away. Why wasn't I big enough, man enough, to call off the wedding? To tell Tara that I didn't love her, that I loved someone else, that I wanted to marry someone else. I'll tell you why, said a little voice in me head. Because you're afraid of the price you'd have to pay. Afraid of losing face to the Brush. Afraid of not being Mr Important, of not being respected. That's why, Johnser, that's why.

I tried to convince meself that maybe I didn't love Jackie as much as I thought I did. After all, it was only a ride.

But I couldn't. It was more than that, it was making love. It was the first time I'd ever made love and that made it different. It wasn't any better, sexually, I mean; if anything, I had to admit that Tara was a much better ride but, it was different, it was nicer, it was clean. Despite the fact that it had taken place in a car in the Phoenix Park, it was clean.

I wanted to tell her how I felt, tell her how much I loved her, how she was the only woman I had ever really loved, but I couldn't. I hadn't wanted the night to end, and I don't think she did either. But eventually morning had come and I'd had to leave her home. I knew there was no point in asking

Jackie to meet me again, I didn't want it to be like that. I didn't want her as a bit on the side, I wanted her to be permanent. I knew that could never be because I also wanted me life. How could I give all that up? Who was going to employ me? What straight person was going to say, "Oh great, Johnser, you've turned over a new leaf, please let me give you a job."

I'd no education, none worth talking about, anyway. I could read and write but that was about it, full stop. I never planned on having an education, never planned on learning any skills at all. I couldn't even put a fucking nail into a wall. I couldn't imagine meself going into an interview, couldn't imagine putting on a shirt and tie and asking some greasy little fucker for a job. Trying to explain to him why he should choose me ahead of the other two thousand people sitting in the waiting-room, just so as he could pay me one hundred and twenty pounds a week before tax. I could never see meself doing that, and I knew that, if I did, I would only end up hating Jackie and blaming her for everything.

A life of crime was a good life. I made a good living, I was doing well. I wanted for nothing other than the love of that woman, and if that was the sacrifice I had to make, so be it.

It was like being a priest although not as bad, it wasn't as though I had to stay celibate, I just had to do without Jackie.

I don't know, maybe I'm being bigheaded, but I think Jackie would have accepted the role of mistress; still, I couldn't do that to her.

Jackie deserved better than that. Jackie deserved someone nice, with a good job, who could give her a decent standard of living, a nice house and a couple of little kids. She couldn't be expected to accept what I had to offer.

The wedding day was fast approaching, like it was

travelling on a rollercoaster and there was nothing I could do about it. Although I have to say me mind was elsewhere, it was on the job. This was going to be it, the big one, the one I'd been waiting for. And me father-in-law-to-be, the Blue, was going to be involved whether I liked it or not. I was going to have to try and get on better with him; after all, me and Tara were going to have a kid and he was going to be the granda. And, in fairness, he seemed to be making an effort to get on with me. He had got what he wanted, he was in on the job.

I remember talking to him one night, and he said something that really shocked me. He said he didn't think we needed the Brush any more, that as far as he was concerned me and him were well capable of taking over everything. That we'd both been in charge of big jobs, so we knew the story. And why should the Brush always get the biggest slice of the cake and not have to take the same chances as us?

I knew he meant it, it wasn't a test, he wasn't checking me out or anything. He honestly thought that we were good enough to take over.

He could see I was interested, he knew that being number one was a dream I had always cherished.

"Think about it, think about it, son."

Son, he was still calling me son, and I fucking hated it. I cringed, I wasn't his fucking son. Just because I was marrying his daughter, that still didn't make me his son, son-in-law maybe, but not his son. It wasn't as though it was a figure of speech cause I never heard him saying it to anyone else. And he emphasised it, everywhere we went he referred to me as son. Even in front of the Brush. I think he wanted everyone to know that I'd put his daughter up the spout, and now I was part of his family. I tried to ignore him but it really bugged the fuck out of me.

"Think 'bout it. Like I say, why should the Brush get any of this? Is he goin teh be on the job? No. He knows where teh get a few fucking paintin's, big deal. We're the ones takin the risks, we're the ones settin the job up."

We. Where was he getting this "we" from? It was *me* who was setting the job up, it was all me own work. The Brush had given me the job, I'd arranged the men, I'd arranged the cars. I knew the times, I knew what we were going in for.

I tried to be rational, tried not to cause any conflict with only a week to go to the wedding . . . and the job.

"Look, Blue, I agree with yeh, some day we'll be tops. But we've no contacts who'll get rid of paintins. Nobody knows us, nobody's gonna deal with us."

He shook his head.

"Listen, son, the way it is, if yeh have pictures like them you'll find a market. I know some of the people the Brush deals with, I'll deal with them, there's no problem."

"I don't know, Blue, I'd rather let Brush deal with this one. We've plenty of time teh do other jobs on our own."

He looked at me. "You, maybe, not me. I want it now. The Brush's had his day, let's take him out. The time's right."

CHAPTER TWENTY-FOUR

It was Saturday the 6th. I would never forget that date, it was the day Johnser was getting married. I couldn't stop thinking about it. I was thinking about her going to the hairdresser, about him getting up, about the cars arriving, about what colour the bridesmaids would be wearing. I wondered if Fat Larry had been invited, if any of the old gang were going. Somehow I doubted it, Johnser had moved on, hadn't he?

That evening Jeffrey came over. Lovable lanky Jeffrey. And we sat in the sitting-room and talked. Ma and Da had gone out, there was a new Bond film on in town and Jeffrey had got them tickets. Jeffrey was being his usual lickarse self, telling me how beautiful I was even though I hadn't bothered to wash me hair. I was sitting there wearing an old track suit that used to be pink, that was until Ma put it in with a dark wash and it was now a shitty purply-blue colour, and he was telling me I was beautiful. I felt like telling him to fuck off, I was more interested in what was going on in me mind than I was in listening to his shite. I wanted to think about the wedding, what songs were being sung, what speeches were being made. I wondered if Johnser was singing "Two outta three ain't bad" and, if so, was he thinking about me.

As the words of the song went through me head, "I want you, I need you, but there ain't no way I'm ever gonna love you," I wondered if that was how Johnser felt about me. But no, Johnser had told me he loved me, he just couldn't marry me. But it sure as hell was how I felt about Jeffrey. I did want him but, not in a sexual way and on lonely nights when me friends were out on the town I did need him (I hated being alone). But there was no way I was ever going to love him. There was no way I was ever going to love anybody but Johnser. Johnser was the bee's knees, the cat's pyjamas and I loved him. Nobody was ever going to take his place. Certainty not this eejit.

"Jackie," he said. "There's something I have to ask you."

I was watching the telly. It was only 9.30 pm and there wasn't really anything on, but I was watching it anyway. I was pretending to be interested in whatever it was I was watching, but I can't for the life of me remember what it was. The programme may as well have been about fleas on a camel's arse, because at that moment in time I would have been more interested in them than I was in Jeffrey.

"Jackie?"

"Yeah, yeah. What? I'm listenin. Ask, ask me what?"

He got up, walked across the room and turned off the telly.

I shouted at him, "Turn that back on, I'm watchin it."

"In a minute," he snapped.

Jasus, what was happening? Jeffrey actually sounded annoyed.

That was a turn-up for the books. Jeffrey, the mouse, sounding aggressive. I couldn't believe what happened next. He knelt in front of me, "Jackie, I love you."

"Would yeh fuck off, an' turn on the telly."

I was scarlet for him. Who did he think he was, fucking Romeo. Oh Jasus, what was he fucking like?

"Give me a minute, please. I've asked your father . . . "

"You've what?"

"I've asked your father for your hand in marriage, and he's said yes."

"You've done what?" I jumped up. "You've done what?" I walked over to the window.

"I can't fucking believe it. Yeh asked me father before yeh asked me."

He followed me to the window, pulling at me arm. I pushed him away.

"Get the fuck away from me, I can't believe you've done this teh me."

"Jackie, please . . . "

"Jackie please, me fucking arse. If yeh want teh marry me, yeh ask me. Not me father, not me mother, yeh ask *me*. What deyeh think I am? Some kind of fucking Indian woman?"

"Jackie, please, please," he begged.

But I was on a roll. I couldn't believe it, I couldn't believe that I was going to be part of an arranged marriage.

"No, Jeffrey, I won't listen teh yeh. I'm not some little Indian who's given by her father teh the highest bidder. I'm an Irish woman an' if yeh want teh marry me, yeh ask me. An' if I say yes, well, then, yeh go an' talk teh me father."

"I'm sorry, Jackie, I'm so sorry . . . "

"I know yer sorry, a fucking sorry sight. What deyeh take me for? Some kind of gobshite who can't make up me own mind?"

"I thought it was the right thing to do."

I just couldn't believe him. There was a book on the chair

100

and I picked it up and threw it at him. He ducked and it hit the telly.

"Jackie, please . . . "

"Jackie, please, nothin. Yeh thought it was the right thing teh do. Why deyeh always have teh do the right thing? What is it with you? I thought we were livin in the twentieth century, but obviously I was wrong because you seem teh be still livin in the dark ages. Jeffrey, just go . . . get fucking out."

He went.

I started crying. It wasn't him. OK so he had annoyed me, I'll admit that. Asking me father before asking me, but that wasn't the real reason for me explosion. The real reason was because I knew that Johnser was gone and the best I could hope for now was Jeffrey. I was going to have to accept second-best because Tara Coyle had got the best.

I was crying for something that was never going to be, me and Johnser. Me tears were interrupted by a ring on the doorbell. I was tempted to ignore it but I didn't. It was Jeffrey.

I turned and walked back into the room leaving the door open, he followed. He apologised.

"Jeffrey, please, stop it. It's not you, it's me. I'm annoyed with yeh for askin me da before yeh asked me, but you've already said yer sorry so just leave it, OK?"

"OK. I'm sorry."

"Jeffrey." I shouted, "Stop it. Just do me one favour, stop sayin yer sorry."

We sat in silence and I picked up me mug of vodka and started drinking again.

"Well, will you?" he asked, kneeling in front of me. "Will you marry me?"

I looked away. I looked at the clock on the mantelpiece and seen the time. Ten to eleven. I wondered if Johnser and Tara were still dancing the night away or had they slipped away up to their room. Were they making love? Was he holding her close to him? Was Johnser Kiely holding his new wife, his lawful wedded wife, Mrs Tara Kiely.

I turned towards Jeffrey.

"Yeah, Jeffrey, I will."

His face broke into a smile.

"You mean yes . . . you will marry me?"

He hugged me, I didn't hug him back, I just let me hands lie limply on his shoulders.

I stared at the clock thinking about the other vows. Till death us do part.

Jeffrey kissed me. I looked at the clock again. Well, fuck you, Johnser, I thought. If you were going to have that slut Tara, then Jeffrey was going to have me. I took his hands and placed them on me tits.

He looked shocked.

"Jackie, what about your parents? They could be home soon."

I didn't say a word, fuck them, I couldn't care less any more.

I opened me top, placed his hands inside and kissed him.

Jeffrey tried to protest.

"Jackie, please, we can't . . . "

But I could, I had to.

Jeffrey fucked me. He'd call it making love, I'd call it a fuck.

I didn't move. I just lay there staring up at me ma's chandelier, the light blinding me, while he humped away. Two, three, four, it was over. He zipped up his trousers and lay beside me.

"I love you, Jackie, I love you."

That's all I ever heard, after "sorry" that was the most annoying thing he ever said. He started giggling to himself.

"What are yeh fucking laughin at? What's the big joke?"

I couldn't find anything to laugh about. A life with Jeffrey was not my idea of fun. He continued to giggle, and I could feel meself getting annoyed again. I slapped his face.

"What's wrong? what's so fucking funny?"

He reached into his pocket. "I forgot to give you this," he said, pulling out a box.

That annoyed me too. It annoyed me that he had chosen the ring. He hadn't even given me the satisfaction of picking it meself.

He'd chosen a real expensive-looking solitaire, but I didn't want a solitaire, I wanted three diamonds just like the one Tara had, the one Johnser had given her.

Ma and Da came home shortly after that. Jeffrey ran to the kitchen and grabbed a bottle of champagne from the fridge.

They had it all organised, they all knew what was going on, all except me. Ma was behaving like a teenager. Giggling and laughing at nothing.

"Isn't it great," she cooed. "You thought we'd just gone to the pictures, but we knew, we've known all along about Jeffrey's plans."

It is in its fuck, I thought.

If you're all so fucking happy, so wonderfully happy, why don't you all live together? Why don't you all just fuck off and leave me alone. This had nothing to do with me, it was all about Mammy and Daddy and Jeffrey.

But I didn't really want to be alone, that's what the

trouble was. So, once again, I found meself going along with the plans.

Ma assumed that every cat, dog and devil would be coming to the wedding, but I said no, I didn't want a big fancy do, I only wanted immediate family. I told them I wanted the wedding to be as soon as possible. Jeffrey took this as a huge compliment, he thought that I couldn't wait to spend the rest of me life with him. How sad.

If only he knew. I was never going to meet another Johnser, I was never going to be swept off me feet again. I was never going to love again, so it didn't really matter who I married.

CHAPTER TWENTY-FIVE

In the end, Blue agreed that we would stay with Brush. Only because he didn't know where to sell the paintings, but he was still anxious to break away as soon as possible. I agreed. I agreed because I thought I would be able to stall him until I was ready to take over.

The morning of the wedding arrived and everything was going according to plan. Pocket had the three cars in the lock-up and it was arranged that him, Fingers and Stan the Man would drive them to the locations. They would be well hidden a couple of miles apart. I went and got married. It was as simple as that.

Tara walked up the aisle and I have to admit that, even though she was a couple of months pregnant, she looked nice. She looked fucking great, she looked stunningly beautiful despite her ugly father's presence at her side.

There were friends of mine there, who were more business aquaintances than friends. Me family was there, me da and his aul slut of a girlfriend. And surprise, surprise, he was still sober. I could see Fat Larry at the back of the church. He hadn't been invited, but I was glad he was there, I was glad he had taken the time to come and see me off. Then I seen the rest of the gang and it made me smile. They waved, and Fat Larry looked like he was going to shout but then, realising where he was, changed his mind. I nodded to them.

The Brush sat in the second row looking as proud as punch, anyone would think he was the father of the groom. He'd asked me what I wanted as a wedding present, I couldn't think of anything so in the end, he bought me a new car. I couldn't believe it, the day before the wedding he'd handed me the keys. A Ford Escort, brand spanking new, registered in me own name. It was the best thing anyone had ever done for me, but I wished he hadn't. I don't mean, "Oh God, yeh shouldn't of," while at the same time ripping the keys from his hand. But I felt guilty about it cause I knew that, one day, I was going to move in on his territory and take over, kill him if that's what it took, and here he was repaying me for my loyalty, what loyalty?

But I had to admit it was a beauty. Bright red, with a lovely walnut finish on the dash. It was the nicest car I'd ever seen and I was going to be driving it.

Blue gave us a holiday. Two weeks' honeymoon he called it, but it was only a holiday to me. Still, I shouldn't be so ungrateful, it meant I'd be away while the heat was on.

So we got married. The ceremony seemed to last for hours, thanks to Tara and her fucking family.

* * *

Eventually we got to the reception. We were going to have a breakfast first, then some music, then an evening meal.

The police were everywhere, they were watching us like hawks but there was nothing they could do. The breakfast was taking place behind closed doors so, once we got to the dining-room, we made our escape.

The speeches had begun, everybody made one. There was no need for them, they were an excuse to linger in the dining-room, while we got outside. Everyone attending the wedding had an idea that there was something going down. And I have to admit I was very excited about the job I was about to do.

While all the fuss had being going on in the church, me mind drifted to thoughts of Jackie. It wasn't that I was comparing Tara to her, it was just that I felt I would have been a lot happier if it had being her receiving me ring. But it wasn't Jackie, it was Tara, and now I was married to her. And there was no point in thinking about what might have been, I had to concentrate on the job in hand. After all, I was a professional.

CHAPTER TWENTY-SIX

All the lads got changed and we slipped out. Pocket was waiting to drive us as far as the Land-Rover. When we got there, we drove across fields to the house. The old couple were out. I hit the window and set the alarm off. We hid and waited for the police to arrive. They arrived within the hour and done a quick search of the garden area, noticed that there was a small window broken, blamed it on kids, and drove off again. As soon as they left, we broke in. We knew what pictures to take so it shouldn't take long. The alarm was ringing like mad in the background but we knew that the police weren't going to come back. Anyway, the Pocket was on look-out and he could see across the fields for miles. We got all the pictures the Brush had marked in the catalogue and the Blue chose one or two that he wanted. They were probably fucking worthless, but he wanted them anyway. We had twenty-eight pictures in all, they were fucking huge. Brush had told us to remove the frames, this would make them handier for storing. I shouted to Pocket to come in and give us a hand. We had only three to go when the door opened and in walked the old man.

Fuck it. The one time I take a chance and I fucking blow it. Before I had time to react, before I could even speak, Stan was on him. He hit the old man full force and sent him reeling across the room. As he fell, he hit his head on the corner of a table.

The old woman came in and started screaming. She knelt over her husband. Stan kicked her so hard I could hear the crunch as his boot connected with her stomach. The man started moaning, Stan jumped on him. I heard the crack of his neck breaking.

"For fuck's sake, Stan."

But it was too late, Stan had lost it. He ran at the woman, angry because of the interruption. He gritted his teeth and lashed out with another kick.

"Yeh stupid fucking cunt."

He kicked her again and again and again.

"Cunt, cunt, cunt."

That's all he was saying. I grabbed him.

"For fuck's sake, Stan, give it a rest."

He turned. I could see the evil in his eyes but I knew, if push came to shove, I'd be well able for him. I pushed him across the room.

"Giv'it fucking up."

I shouted to the Pocket, "Get this fucking gear outta here, now!"

We ran. As we got to the Land-Rover I could see the police cars in the distance. Fuck them, why did they want to check the house again, had they nothing fucking better to be doing? Jasus, the fucking alarm had been set off every day for the last week, it was bleeding obvious there was a fault.

The Pocket took off like a bat out of hell across the fields.

The police speeded up and headed towards the house. I could see one of them on the radio obviously calling for back-up.

The Pocket drove like a madman, avoiding trees by the

skin of his teeth. I don't know what the police done. I don't know had they checked the house, had they found the bodies, whatever. I didn't give a fuck, all I knew was that we were out of there, we were running, we were on a high. The adrenaline was flowing, that feeling of fear mixed with excitement. Stan was laughing, talking about what he had done.

"Didyeh see her? Didyeh see the aul one? Didyeh see the way I shut her up?"

Blue was laughing, too. I wasn't. I turned on them.

"Just wait till Brush hears about this, just fucking wait."

Stan shut up. But Blue didn't, he turned to me.

"The Brush doesn't need teh hear."

"He can't fucking help but hear. This isn't somethin that can be written off. It's not as if someone in Pearse Street didn't pay their protection money, an' we beat the crap outta them. They're fucking dead back there, deyeh realise that?"

"How deyeh know? How can yeh be so sure?" he asked.

"Just read the fucking papers temorra an' you'll know."

We changed cars twice and were back at the reception three hours after we'd left.

The wedding was in full swing, but I couldn't enjoy it.

I had to talk to Brush, had to tell him what had happened.

Once he'd established that the paintings were safe, he wanted to know how the Blue had handled the situation. I told him everything, and as I spoke he stared across the room at Blue.

The Blue tried to outstare him, but couldn't. He turned away, laughing nervously. Brush never flinched.

"Johnser, I'm only going to say this once, so listen carefully. Blue is getting out of hand, he's a liability. I know you've just become part of his family but you're going to have to choose between him and me. Now, don't answer immediately, think it over while you're on your honeymoon. I'll expect an answer when you return." He smiled.

I appreciated his honesty. He didn't pull punches, he knew what was happening. I also appreciated his giving me the time to make me mind up. There was no point telling him that it wasn't Blue's fault. Once the Brush got something into his head, actual facts didn't matter. He wouldn't want to hear about Stan the Man, and besides, if I did put him straight I'd be up to me neck in shit. After all, I'd picked the fucking gang. No, fuck Blue, he was old enough to look after himself.

The wedding went on into the early hours. We all danced and sang and laughed. We done all the usual things you do at weddings. I tried to forget about Jackie but I couldn't.

This whole fucking thing was a joke. Tara was a joke, Blue was a joke, the fucking wedding was a joke. But there was nothing I could do about it now, it was too late.

The Pocket and Stan had gone to the Dublin mountains to hide the paintings. They were to store them there until Brush got in contact with his buyer. They knew where to hide them. We'd dry lined a ten-foot hole in the middle of a forest, you could have lived in the fucking thing. But it had to be just right, otherwise the paintings would get ruined, so said the Brush. When they arrived at the wedding later on that night, they assured us that everything had gone according to plan.

The meal looked great but I couldn't eat a bite. Tara more than made up for me. I'd heard about eating for two but this was ridiculous, she must have eaten enough to feed a football team. The band started with "When you're in love with a beautiful woman". I hated dancing but I knew I had no choice, so I shuffled to and fro and was happy when the song ended. I made a hasty retreat to the bar and watched as her aunties and uncles demolished every song that was ever written.

Uncle Albert started off with "That old devil called lurve." I don't know who he thought he was, skipping across the stage like a teenager and scrunching his lip up like a demented Elvis every time he said *Lurve*. As he dipped his head to take his applause, his wig slipped. It was like something out of Monty Python, no, it was worse, cause it was real, it was Monty Pyhton on *acid*.

I couldn't bring meself to watch as her aunty May, all sixteen stone of her, sang "Patricia the Stripper" and insisted on doing all the actions. I didn't have to worry about seeing it, I was sure one of her relations would have it on video.

Despite all the drink I'd had, the antics on stage kept me sober. At ten to eleven the wedding finally ended for meself and Tara. As the band played "Congratulations", we made our way out under the arch of arms the guests made. Just as we reached the door, the police were coming in.

They grabbed me, then Blue, then Brush. They grabbed about ten other blokes and frogmarched us all out. Tara was bawling her eyes out, so was her ma. But there was nothing we could do. We were all brought to different stations. Sheriff Street, Rathmines, and Pearse Street. But I knew, as I sat there, that we were all doing the exact same thing, staring at that spot on the wall. I remember the guard. I remember he slapped me across the face, full force, and before I could react I was on the floor with blood running down me cheek. I was dazed, me hands were cuffed behind me back, so retaliation was out of the question. He lashed a boot into me.

"Yeh fucking bastard, Kiely."

112

I looked up and thought to meself, you've no idea how much of a bastard I really am. But some day, some day . . .

So when he'd finished kicking the shite out of me, I rose to me feet and sat back on me chair, where I continued to stare at the wall. It was twelve hours before they released me.

* * *

I walked straight out, on to a plane and flew to Bermuda.

Bermuda was a long way off and I was stiff as a board from sitting on the plane. Tara couldn't have been comfortable either but she never let on. She was too busy bending me ear reliving every minute of the wedding and, when she realised I wasn't listening, she turned to the man sitting next to her and started telling him. I pitied the poor fucker. He was trying to get some sleep but, every time he closed his eyes, she'd nudge him in the ribs.

"Are yeh listenin teh me?"

He'd just nod his head, he was to polite to tell her to fuck off.

The only time she shut up was when the food arrived. Christ, she could eat for Ireland. She even took the stranger's cake off his plate when she saw he wasn't eating it.

When it came to ordering a drink, she was worse. Jasus, she was so common.

"'Scuse me, Miss, yeah, you with the plastered-on make-up. When yer finished showin us the exits an' sick bags, will yeh get us anudder round?"

The air hostess would glare and smile at the same time, then go and get her trolley. Tara'd order a beer for me and two vodkas for herself.

113

"Yeh better gimme two, luv, cause yer a bit slow with the aul cart."

She insisted on buying her new-found friend a whiskey, despite his insisting he only wanted a mineral.

"Ye'll have a real man's drink, all that fizzy stuff's no good for yeh. Ye'll be farting all night."

She made a sound like a whoopie cushion, a big raspberry. Then she went into convulsions of laughter, spraying vodka all over the woman sitting in front of her.

After about eight vodkas she decided it was time to liven things up. She started singing, "Una paluma blanka," at the top of her voice.

When the hostess asked her to be quiet, she sang, "Ah shut-up-a-yer-facea," in an even louder voice.

She always sang the most ridiculous songs, and always arseways.

It wrecked me fucking head.

I could see some of the other passengers laughing, it was all right for them. They were looking at the in-flight entertainment. I was looking at the rest of me life. For fuck's sake.

It was late when we arrived at the hotel. We didn't even bother unpacking, Tara's vodkas had finally taken effect and all she wanted was bed. I was delighted, she'd been talking on the coach about going on an all-night bender. Thankfully, that wasn't going to happen now. She fell on to the bed and, before I'd even undressed, she was in a coma. She hadn't even bothered taking her clothes off and I was fucked if I was going to do it.

I woke early the next morning. Tara was still in her coma. I tried to wake her but she wouldn't budge, so I went down to breakfast on me own.

Irish breakfast it wasn't, but still, it filled a gap.

The dining-room was roasting, there was a huge fan hanging from the ceiling and all the windows were open but it made no difference.

When I'd finished I headed back to the room and pulled on a pair of football shorts. Tara mumbled something about seeing me later before turning on her side and going back to sleep. I grabbed a towel and the sun cream and headed off.

The pool was like a heart-shaped lake, it was so big. It was surrounded by sunbeds, most of them full.

I stood gawking all around me, I could feel me mouth drop open at the sights. Everyone was topless, tits everywhere.

I couldn't fucking believe it. Big brown ones, small pointy ones, lopsided ones, ones with small nipples, ones with nipples the size of saucers. I couldn't stop gawking, they were everywhere. Fat ones, skinny ones, girls with none at all.

Jasus, I had to sit down. I spread me towel on the bed and sat down. I lashed on the cream and ordered meself a beer. It was crap, like lukewarm piss. I lashed on more cream and decided to have a kip.

I woke to the sound of laughter and sat up.

And there she was. Coming towards me, wearing a "Kiss Me Quick" hat and a polka-dot bikini. Jasus, what was she like? Her belly was huge and white, she looked like a pale Biafran with a spotty disease. She was shouting to me at the top of her voice.

"Oh Jasus, Johnser, I'm scarlet. Lookit them."

She was pointing at all the topless girls.

"Johnser, Johnser, quick, look! They've all got their diddys hanging out!"

I wanted the pool to open up and swallow me.

After what seemed like an eternity, she flopped down beside me and called the waiter.

"Garsun, yahoo garsun, one momento, el pleaso, if yeh don't mind. I'll have one of them that the sin-er-it-a over there is drinkin."

The waiter looked at her as if she had two heads.

"A leg-opener?"

She went into that hysterical laugh of hers.

"Scuse me, I'm a happily-married woman."

The waiter looked totally baffled.

"Sorry, madam?"

I was getting really annoyed. I went to get up but I couldn't move. I felt like shite.

"A leg-opener and a beer."

The waiter hurried away to the sound of Tara cackling. I looked at her, with her huge white belly, polka-dot bikini and that stupid fucking hat.

"For fuck's sake, where did yeh get that?"

"Wha . . . me hat . . . in Bray . . . why?"

I couldn't even answer. Me head was spinning, I felt terrible.

"Oh Jasus . . . " She thumped me in the arm and I almost fainted. "Lookit, Johnser, lookit yer woman." She was pointing at a girl with huge tits. "No fear of her drownin."

At last she looked at me.

"For fuck's sake, Johnser, the colour of yeh. Yer like a fucking lobster. What cream did yeh use?"

Before I could answer she saw the bottle.

"Ah Johnser, yeh fucking gobshite, that's me Nivea. I told yeh teh take the sun cream, that stuff's fried yeh."

I had to be helped from the sunbed up to the room.

By the time I got there, me body had swollen so much, she had to cut me shorts off. If I'd had the strength I'd have gone for her, cause she was laughing so much.

She called the doctor and he gave me tablets and a cooling cream, it looked and smelt like a carton of yogurt.

I was freezing but I couldn't bear to have as much as a sheet touching me.

Me being laid up didn't stop Tara from going out.

"I'm not the one who tried teh barbecue meself," she'd tell me as she headed out the door.

The sound of her voice travelled up from the pool, even though our room was on the second floor.

"Por-va-vor garsun."

I mean, who else could it fucking be?

At night I'd hear her coming down the corridor, knocking on doors and singing, "Oh, I'm goin teh Barbados." At the top of her voice.

Like I said before, those songs really fucked me head up. Fuck Simply Tropical for ever having released it. It's a pity Captain-whatever-his-fucking-name-was didn't crash his Coconut Airways plane, then there wouldn't have been a song. Besides, we were in Bermuda, not fucking Barbados.

Not that it would have made any difference to Tara.

She'd stumble in and fall on to the bed, on top of me. And I'd cry out in pain.

* * *

It was the second week before I was back to normal, and even then, I only ventured to the shade of an umberella.

She was there, leg-opener in hand, belly out and top off. I freaked.

"Tara! What the fuck deh yeh think yer doin?"

She jumped up off the bed, tits wobbling all over the place.

"What? I'm havin a drink, what's it look like?"

"I'm not talkin about the fucking drink. I couldn't give two shites about that. I'm talkin about . . . lookit yeh!"

She looked down at herself.

"What? Topless. Oh I see, it's all right for them, but not for yer wife, is that it? Go way, yeh fucking hypa . . . hyp . . . yeh two-faced bastard."

"It's nothin teh do with yer tits, yeh fucking eejit, yer pregnant!"

"Oh fuck me, I'm not, am I? Jasus, when did that happen?"

She was really starting to annoy me. But fuck it. If she didn't care what she looked like, why should I?

So that night, when she danced to the "Birdie Song" and looked more like a turkey about to lay an egg, I just left her to it.

Later on that night when she sang Charlie Rich's "You're Having My Baby". I just ordered a double whiskey as a chaser for the double whiskey I already had in front of me, and suddenly, Tara didn't bother me any more.

In fact, I had to admit, she was good fun.

Being heavily pregnant didn't alter the fact that Tara was a good-looker. It definately didn't stop the waiters from sniffing around. I swear to God, they'd get up on a scabby leg.

She flirted with them something terrible and, by the sheepish way Carlos acted when I was around, I was convinced that something had happened between them while I'd been laid up.

The last day of the honeymoon was spent with Tara promising to stay in touch with every cat, dog and devil she'd met.

Everyone loved her, she was the life and soul of the party. And maybe, if I hadn't been married to her, I'd have loved her too.

I could tell they were all genuinely sorry to see her go.

I was sorry to be leaving, too.

Even more sorry when the Brush phoned. Someone had squealed. He didn't know who. He warned me that as soon as I got off the plane I'd be arrested and this time I could be going down. I couldn't believe it. I thought about not going back but, fuck it, I'd better. No one was ever going to say that Johnser Kiely ran away from anything.

CHAPTER TWENTY-SEVEN

At first I tried to pan it off as wedding nerves. After all, I didn't want to marry Jeffrey, but it wasn't that. I was being sick in the mornings, every morning. I was having strange cravings. I wanted ice cream with me cornflakes. I knew, I knew even before I missed me first period. I knew from the very second that Johnser had come inside of me, that I was going to be pregnant, I wanted to be. I done a home pregnancy test but I couldn't make head nor tail of the result, I honestly couldn't. After hours of peeing into a bottle I still didn't know if I was definitely pregnant. Eventually, I went to the doctor. I didn't go to the family doctor because he knew Ma and Da too well, I went to one in Crumlin.

She was a very nice lady doctor and told me straight away. "Well, Jackie, it's positive."

I burst out crying and she put her arms around me.

"Ssh, ssh, it'll be all right. Don't worry, you'll be fine. When are you planning to get married?"

I stared at her, then, looking down, realised she was holding me left hand. I tried to smile but couldn't.

If only she knew, but she didn't and I wasn't going to tell her.

How could I? How could I tell anyone that the baby

inside me didn't belong to the man I was about to marry. What was I supposed to do? I would never be able to rear a kid on me own. I was too young, too immature. And anyway, Jeffrey wanted me and he had fucked me. He hadn't used a johnny, big fucking organised Jeffrey. Well he hadn't been so organised that night. So he could take the blame. Anyway, there was a chance that it might be his.

That night when he came over, I told him the news. He was delighted.

"You knew, didn't you? Didn't you, that's why you wanted to get married so quickly."

I told him not to be stupid but he didn't seem to believe me. He was so self-satisfied. Wasn't I a very clever woman to have planned all this on me own.

* * *

Two months later I was Mrs Adams. I was barely beginning to show when I walked up the aisle, in fact I don't think anyone even guessed that I was pregnant. I had made him swear not to tell anyone, I warned him that if me ma or da found out there wouldn't be a wedding. So, when I eventually made me announcement, Ma was delighted –

"A honeymoon baby, just like you were."

The wedding was lovely. Immediate family on both sides, a nice meal and a nice little band. Just what I wanted. We didn't make love that night. I couldn't do it, despite all the vodka inside me, I couldn't consummate the marriage.

We went to Galway on our honeymoon. Now, don't get me wrong, it's a lovely place and all that but it wasn't quite what I'd had in mind, and I wasn't with who I had in mind.

Jeffrey was like a kid with a new toy, running around,

delighted with himself. He'd got us a nice little flat and he was saving like a good thing for the deposit on a house.

I was slowly coming around to the fact that I was here for life, so I had better start making a go of it. I started to respond to him, I became a little bit nicer. I made a point of getting home first in the evening so as I could cook the dinner, and not have him getting takeaways every night. But it was still difficult, every time he kissed me I wanted to pull away, but I didn't. I was like someone trying to break a habit, only my habit was Johnser.

I decided I was really going to try and make this marriage work.

Jeffrey was great during me pregnancy. He came to all the antenatal classes and helped me with me breathing exercises. In fact, he helped me with everything, he didn't want me doing too much. He talked me into giving up me job in Caffrey's. I didn't really want to, but I knew it was for the best. I handed in me notice. There was no such thing as going out on the sick like loads of other girls did. Oh no, Jeffrey wouldn't have that. I mean to say, that would be conning the State, and us Adams didn't do things like that.

So I sat at home in our little flat, bored out of me tree. Counting the flowers on the horrible wallpaper that no doubt had been bought as a job lot. I tried to make the place look homely, but it was no good. I knew that eventually we'd be moving out. moving into our own little house. Maybe I would feel different then. The cistern in the toilet was leaking and the bowl was all stained from the people who'd been there before us and who hadn't bothered to clean it. No matter how much bleach I put down, the stains wouldn't shift. I hated the place.

The wallpaper in the bedroom was starting to curl down

at the top from all the damp it was covering. The cooker was like something that had spent twenty years in a chipper without ever having been cleaned.

The final straw came one night when I saw a cockroach. That was it, we were getting out, and there was no two ways about it.

Poor Jeffrey, he worked like a dog. Day and night, sometimes not getting home until after ten. But still he managed to be there the day me labour pains started, when me waters broke, and I was very grateful for that. He drove me to the hospital and he was there when little Johnser was born.

I didn't actually call the baby Johnser, I called him Jonathan.

But to me he was Johnser, Johnser junior. Jeffrey had never known about Johnser, neither had ma or da. So they were all delighted and thought it was a lovely name.

I loved that baby, I absolutely adored him. I couldn't spend enough time with him and I hated when Jeffrey wanted to hold him.

He's not yours, I'd think to meself, So fuck off an' leave us alone.

But I couldn't say any of that. After all, he was supposed to be the father, wasn't he? And then there was me own da, granda now, going around with a stupid smile on his face and wearing that stupid T-shirt, which Jeffrey had bought for him, with, "The World's Greatest Grandad" written on it.

I had to let him hold the baby. And there was Jeffrey's mother, and of course she had to hold him as well. They all sang stupid lullabys. I didn't want them singing to me baby, I wanted to be the only one to sing to him. I wanted to dress him, I wanted to comb his hair, bath him, change him. I just wanted to keep him all to meself. I didn't want to share him with anyone.

He was Johnser's baby all right. I could tell by his eyes, his nose, his ears, his hair. I knew that, even though he was almost bald, he was going to have lovely black curly hair. But, most of all, I could tell by the way he sucked me tits. He was a hungry little bugger, just like his father.

I came home from hospital to a new house. A new home for Jeffrey and Jackie Adams and their new baby son.

The nursery had been decorated as a surprise for me. It was a surprise all right, I hated it. All its yellows and greens, I fucking detested it. It wasn't what I wanted, but then again that didn't seem to matter. After all, it was what they wanted. Jeffrey, his mother, my mother, everyone had been consulted, everyone, that is, except me. My God, what were they trying to do, frighten the child to death? All these things hanging from the ceiling, and the wallpaper with big ugly clown's faces all over it. I mean to say, I'd be fucking frightened if I woke up in the middle of the night and saw them. But I didn't say anything. I let them have their way. Fuck it, what was the point, I'd change it in a couple of months.

Jeffrey brought his friends to see us, like we were a couple of ornaments sitting in a china cabinet waiting to be admired. They would goo and gaa over Jonathan, and I knew he hated it, I knew from the faces he made. He was like his father, he hated people who acted like gobshites. I knew that if he could, he would have told them all to fuck off and leave him alone.

When I was alone with the baby, when I fed him, while I played with his little feet, I told him about his father. I would sit for hours telling him all about Johnser, about how I'd met him, about our walks along the canal. Well, I could hardly tell him the truth about the canal. I would tell him what his da looked like, about all the nice things we used to do together. About the way he used to sing to me. Me and me baby were going to make something of our lives.

He was going to be someone who Johnser would be proud of. I remember Johnser telling me one time that he never wanted his kids to be like him. He wanted them to grow up with a good education.

"Well, don't worry, Johnser. Your son will grow up with a good education."

CHAPTER TWENTY-EIGHT

Tara was in her element as we were whisked through security.

"Jasus, Johnser, if it wasn't for the black Maria waitin outside we'd be taken for celebs."

I looked at her. How the fuck could she be mistaken for a celebrity dressed like that? With her Bermuda shorts and her belly sticking out under that stupid fucking top.

"My husband went to Bermuda and all he brought me back was this lousy T-shirt."

She thought it was hilarious, she'd bought one for all her family. Every night she'd take one out, break her shite laughing and then show it to me, expecting me to laugh too.

There was no point in telling her that she'd already shown it to me fifty times, because she'd try to convince me that it was a different one. Just because it said "Aunty" or "Uncle" or "Sister" instead of "Husband", she considered it different.

She'd bought one for me but I told her she could fuck off if she thought I was going to wear it.

I was taken to Pearse Street station where I was interviewed.

They didn't even ask me about the paintings, they went straight into the murders of the old couple. I did me usual, picked a little damp spot on the wall and stared at it. I just sat, stared and said sweet fuck all. No matter what they said, I ignored it. So fucking what if some thick-necked culchie thought I was the scum of the earth for picking on old folk, what did he know? He wasn't there, he knew fuck all. Did he really think that I was going to break down and bawl me eyes out and admit everything to him? Just because he said I'd be going away for a long time?

Then there was the aul sergeant, with his father and son routine. "Now, Johnser, be smart. Do you think that the Brush gives a damn about you? Do you know where he is now? He's at home watching television and you, Johnser, you're in here being charged with murder. Now be smart, Johnser, we all know this wasn't your job. Give us the Brush and I'll see what I can do for you. Eh?"

The stupid prick. Did he seriously think that I'd shop Brush? He just didn't know me at all.

I knew him from years back in Ballyer, when he was just a copper on the beat, he was OK back then. He might give you a clip around the ear if he caught you messing around at the shops. But sure, that was the only thing we understood back then. I thought he knew me well. And now, here he was trying to get me to rat on the Brush, what did he take me for?

I could see they were getting more and more frustrated, I knew the younger coppers wanted to lash into me.

Well go on, I thought, kick the shite outta me if it makes yeh feel better. But yeh won't get me teh budge and yeh better make a good job of it, cause I'll remember all yer faces and, some day, when yer all alone and not expecting it, I'll catch up with yeh and you'll be sorry yeh ever laid eyes on Johnser Kiely.

The aul sergeant came back at me, his eyes like a big aul sheepdog and his voice soft and sincere, "Johnser, do you realise that you're going down for this? Do you realise how long you get for murder? You'll be an old man, Johnser. And no matter what the Brush has offered you, it's not worth it."

I didn't bat an eye. The Brush would have been proud of me, proud of his adopted son.

I listened as he read out the charges, I didn't move a muscle.

CHAPTER TWENTY-NINE

The solicitor arrived. I hadn't asked for one, he just arrived.

"Gerry Davis," he introduced himself.

I knew the name. He was Brush's solicitor. I smiled to meself. "Thanks, Da."

He sat down, stoney-faced, dressed to kill in his fancy suit, wearing his little round glasses and carrying a leather briefcase. He looked like one of those telly briefs, the ones who always seemed to be losing the case, right up until the last minute. And then, suddenly, the wife breaks down and confesses everything, still leaving him time to sweep his assistant off her feet, and all this before the credits.

He was taking so long to get organised that I decided to say something just to break the ice.

"So you're here teh get me off."

He looked at me.

"It won't be that easy, Mr Kiely."

I stared at him, giving him the look I used when I wanted to intimidate someone.

"What the fuck deyeh mean, it won't be easy? I never said anything about easy, didyeh hear me say easy? I said yeh were here teh get me out, that's all. It's yer fucking job, isn't it?"

He peered at me over his glasses, I couldn't tell whether he was afraid or disgusted. I didn't give a fuck either way, I hated suits. I didn't give a shite whether he was on my side or not, all these fucking suits were the same.

He fixed the pages in front of him back into his case.

"What the fuck are yeh at?"

He leaned closer.

"Mr Kiely, may I call you Johnser?"

He looked for a sign of acknowledgment. I gave none.

"Well listen, Johnser, I was asked to represent you, but quite frankly I haven't the time or patience to put up with your attitude. I know your type, Johnser, and I know what you think about us . . . suits . . . so why don't I stop wasting both our time and leave you to rot in some cell for a few years."

He was at the door before I even realised he was finished speaking.

"I'll give you a few hours to think about it, Johnser. If you change your mind and decide you want the best defence in the country, give the Brush a call, he has my number."

I rang the Brush. He was livid.

"What the fuck dehyeh think yer playing at?"

"He pissed me off."

"He pissed you off! Do you have any idea how good this guy is? Do you have any idea how much he costs, eh? Because let me tell you, Johnser, if you want one of those legal aid fellas, you can fucking have one."

"It's not that, I just want teh get outta here."

"Don't you think I know that? But it's not that easy."

"What deyeh mean?"

"You know the story, I'm not going into it on the phone,

let's just say there's certain merchandise I need to sell, and because of all of the fuss that's going on, I'm finding it a bit difficult. I need someone to take the heat off me, and I'm asking you to be that someone."

"Bollocks! I don't give a fuck 'bout yer merchandise, I couldn't care less about the heat being on yeh. I don't give a fuck, deyeh hear me, Brush?"

I was shouting now, and I could see the copper down the hall looking at me. I turned away, trying to compose meself.

"They're talkin murder, Brush. Yeh know me, I don't mind doin me time but I'm not goin down for a murder I didn't do."

"Johnser, be very careful what you say. There are a lot of nasty people involved in this. It's not only about me. If it was, it would be different, I'd do the time myself. Besides, it's not my fault; after all, you did choose the men yourself."

"So?

"Well, my men don't rat on each other."

"Who the fuck stitched me up?"

"Now's not the time."

"Who?"

The line went silent.

I lost it again.

"Brush . . . who the fuck ratted me up?"

"Stan the Man."

"I'll fucking kill the bastard."

"This is doing neither of us any good, Johnser, calm down and listen."

"No. You fucking listen . . . I don't care who's involved, I

131

don't care what the fuck yeh have teh do, just get me outta here."

"I hear you, Johnser. But you just remember that we all appreciate what you're doing. Now all I want you to do is sit tight, say nothing and, when Davis comes to see you, listen to what he has to say. He's the best."

CHAPTER THIRTY

Davis must have been with Brush when I'd rang because he was back with me within the hour.

"The Brush holds you in very high esteem, Johnser. He only wants what's best for you."

"What's best for me is teh get outta here, but nobody seems teh be hearin that."

"We hear you, honestly we do. But you're in here on very serious charges. There's no point in me filling you full of false hope, this is going to be a hard case to win."

"Don't give me any of yer crap. Say what yeh fucking mean, that I haven't a fucking hope in hell of gettin outta here! For all yer fucking fancy suits an' yer stupid fucking glasses, yeh haven't a fucking clue."

He smiled.

"Johnser, I've been defending guys like you for as long as I can remember. I'm the best, and as the best I'm advising you to shut up and listen to what I have to say."

I sat back and sighed.

"So tell me, what's me best bet."

He looked me straight in the eye, never flinching. I liked that, I liked the fact that he wasn't afraid to tell me what I knew couldn't be good news.

"We're looking at a plea-bargain of manslaughter. They have too much evidence, they have their snitch, they're putting pressure on Blue."

"Blue'll say fuck all."

"Blue will say exactly what Brush wants him to say."

I was numb. I knew what he was saying. He was threatening me in the nicest possible way. They had me by the balls.

"What's manslaughter? How many years?"

"It's impossible to say."

I glared at him.

"At least ten, but with good behaviour you could be out in seven."

"Me, good behaviour?" I laughed.

"Well, you're the one telling me you want out, if you want it that bad you'll keep your nose out of trouble. In the meantime, the Brush will look after your wife and child. They'll want for nothing . . . "

I switched off, there was no point in arguing. I was going down.

We called in the police and I gave my statement, making sure that the Brush's name was never mentioned. I admitted that I had killed the old folks but explained that it was an accident. I'd panicked when they came in on me. I told them that I'd burnt the paintings.

I don't know how long it took to make the statement, it all became a blur.

Davis only spoke when necessary. By the time it was all over, the guards seemed happy with what they'd been told.

Davis assured me that I'd made the right decision and, that it would work in me favour in court.

I wasn't convinced.

CHAPTER THIRTY-ONE

Tara had the baby while I was on remand.

The minute I heard that she was in labour I wanted to get out and be with her. Now, I hadn't gone all soppy or anything, it was nothing like that. I just wanted to be there when me son came out.

Tara had said that she wanted me there, too. I was supposed to keep guard in case they tried to take her make-up off. She said that she didn't want to look like one of them aul ones she'd seen on the videos at the antenatal classes.

No, not Tara. She wanted to look like one of them actresses on Dallas, who had just gone through a sixteen-hour labour without getting a hair out of place or smudging their mascara.

She always insisted on going to bed with her make-up on, and then had a big fit next morning when it was all over the pillowcase.

"That never happens teh Linda fucking Evans."

It was pointless trying to tell her that Linda Evans hadn't actually slept in the bed.

She made me promise not to deck the doctor when he slapped the baby.

"Now, Johnser, he's not hittin the babby just cause it's yers, he has teh slap them all on the arse . . . teh make sure they're alive."

She needn't have worried, because they wouldn't let me out for the birth.

I could tell by the tone of his voice that the screw enjoyed relaying the refusal.

"Bastard."

I bet he didn't enjoy the broken nose that resulted from me head-butting him so much.

I spent that night in hospital meself. "A bad fall," that's what they said I'd had. Well, fuck them, fuck them all.

No one was going to keep me from seeing me son.

Eventually I got the news. A girl. Tara, the stupid bitch, couldn't even get that right. I'd gone through all that aggro for nothing. It freaked me out, I ripped me cell to bits, had another "bad fall," but I didn't care.

A girl, what the fuck was I going to do with a girl?

Don't get me wrong, girls are OK. I don't have a problem with them, for fuck's sake, I like them as much as the next fella. There's nothing I like better than to see a girl with big tits and a skirt up to her arse walking down the road.

But that was the problem!

That girl with the short skirt, with the big jugs, with the face caked in make-up, was someone's daughter.

My daughter!

I couldn't handle the idea of fellas eyeing up me daughter, asking her out, their tongues rammed down her throat, their dirty little paws all over her tits, on her . . .

I couldn't even bring meself to say the word.

Jasus, no. What was Tara thinking of, having a girl? I'd

have to kill every fucker from Ballyer to Timbucktoo . . . and back.

And, worse still, she might even be a teenager by the time I got out. It could be too late. Some scruffy bastard might even have took her cherry by then. Some gang on a corner could already have shouted –

"Get up, yeh ride."

I'll kill them, I'll fucking kill them.

CHAPTER THIRTY-TWO

It was in all the papers.

I remember reading it at the time but I didn't really pay it much attention. I knew it had been a big robbery and thought it was terrible the way those two people had been killed. Not until I seen his name in the paper, and they said they had charged him with *the crime of the century*, did I even suspect he'd been involved. "A Major Criminal," they were calling him. They must have got the name wrong, they couldn't be talking about my Johnser.

I know he was no saint, he'd rob the eye out of your head, but he wouldn't kill anyone.

He might hurt someone, hurt them a lot, he might even break a few bones, but he wouldn't kill them.

I started collecting all the cuttings from the different papers, *The Star*, the *Times*, the *Independent*, anything I could get me hands on. I cut every article out, I kept every single word that they printed about him. I still couldn't believe he would do something like this. What amazed me even more was that, on the first day of the trial, he pleaded guilty to manslaughter.

I had to go and see him. I had to go to the court and hear for meself what he had done. Hear him admit with me own ears that he'd killed two people. Two old people.

I couldn't even begin to imagine Johnser hurting someone old, he liked old people. I remember even in his hard man days in Ballyfermot he always helped old folks across the road. They were probably afraid of their shite he was going to rob them, but still and all he always helped.

Johnser respected old people. He loved his granda, he was the only member of his family he ever talked about with any affection. He'd been dead for ages, but he never forgot him. So he wasn't going to murder a defenceless old man, no, not my Johnser.

I just had to go and find out for meself.

* * *

It was only the second time I'd ever seen Johnser in a suit, but he didn't look as well as he had the first time. His hair had been cut too short and it made him look pale and drawn. He looked like he hadn't slept in days.

The court was packed with reporters busily scribbling down the facts. They were treating him like a common criminal and I hated them for it. I leaned forward, not wanting to miss one word, not wanting to miss one breath he might take. It was stupid, I know, but I felt as if I would be able to tell whether or not he was lying by the way he was breathing when he answered. Johnser stood proud and tall, he gave the guards on both sides of him a dirty look as he rose. I could see by his eyes that he wanted to spit at them and tell them to fuck off. He seemed strangely detached from it all.

I looked around the courtroom, scanning it for a friendly face, a face from the old days, for Fat Larry, Slash, Baldy, Tiny or Froggy but none of them were there.

It was then that I spotted Tara. She still looked the same, big Bambi eyes and blonde hair, though it looked more bleached than I remembered. People around her smiled as she bounced her baby on her knee. Typical Tara, she always had to be the centre of attention.

Johnser was going down, possibly for life, and here she was playing happy fucking families in the courtroom.

I had a sudden urge to fuck poor Johnser junior on to the lap of the woman sitting next to me, jump the four rows of seats that separated me from the bitch, and reef the skinny cunt around the place.

That would look great, wouldn't it? The papers would have a field day. I could just imagine the headline – *Killer's Wife KO'd in Court.*

And underneath a picture of me and Tara reefing each other.

Even then, Tara would probably still look better than me. I'd have pulled out half her hair and she'd still manage to look stunning. Needless to say, I decided against this course of action.

I couldn't help smiling to meself. Imagine the look on Jeffrey's face if he saw it. I mean to say, two skinheads walking down the road was the beginning of a riot as far as he was concerned.

I ruffled Jonathan's hair and he looked at me the way Johnser used to, I thought me heart was going to break.

There were a lot of men who looked out of place in their expensive suits sitting at the back of the court. With their broken noses and cauliflower ears, they couldn't be anything other than associates of Johnser's. Associates, me arse. They were common thugs and nothing more. It worried me to think that he was involved with these people.

They seemed to be ill at ease in their surroundings, like schoolkids standing at the back of the church, thinking they would never get out for a fag but afraid to leave in case the priest seen them. These were obviously the men Johnser was going down for.

I wanted to jump up and scream, "Johnser, don't do it, don't waste your life for these shites.

Another headline flashed through me mind – "Ex-Girlfriend Goes Berserk In Court."

Jasus, I'd probably have been locked up meself. So I quickly scrapped that idea.

I sat listening as the charges were read out.

The theft of twenty-eight paintings, the theft of three cars, but most importantly, the one I couldn't believe, the manslaughter of two innocent people. Two defenceless pensioners. How could he do something like that? Maybe I didn't really know him at all. And in the light of the murders, who really gave a fuck about paintings?

I mean to say, who cared if the *Mona Lisa* was taking pride of place in some high-falutin gallery or on the jacks wall of a tenement house in North King Street?

When the charges had been read out, the judge turned to Johnser and asked him how he pleaded. He didn't say a word, he just looked at the judge the way he would have looked at someone who dared to stand up to him outside the chipper in Ballyer all those years ago. I thought for a minute he was going to do something stupid, like jump over the judge's bench and loaf him in the head, or maybe give him a classic knee in the balls. It would have been just like the old days when we were going together and I'd heard all the stories of Johnser's exploits.

The judge asked, more sternly this time, "How do you plead?"

"Oh, Jasus," I thought. "Please don't get thick with him. Don't make Johnser react."

Johnser mumbled something, I couldn't quite make it out but I think it had something to do with bollocks. Once again the judge asked him how he pleaded. His lawyer intervened. Obviously he'd heard what Johnser had said.

"My client pleaded guilty, Your Honour."

The judge looked at him over the top of his glasses.

"I believe your client is capable of speaking for himself."

He turned towards Johnser, as if he was moving in slow motion.

Johnser squared his shoulders, took a deep breath and said, "Guilty."

It was over in minutes.

He was given twelve years with a recommendation that he serve at least ten.

I knew by the look on his face that he hadn't expected this.

He glared at his solicitor, but he was too busy packing up his briefcase to notice. The expensive suits in the back row quickly made their exit.

Johnser scanned the room, obviously looking for Tara, but he spotted me. He looked at me, the same way he'd looked at me the day I'd shown up at his mother's funeral.

He looked lost. I knew he wanted me to go to him but I couldn't.

I looked back at him desperately, me eyes pleading with him to understand.

He smiled, that special smile, then walked away. I knew he understood.

CHAPTER THIRTY-THREE

Tara came to visit me in prison. She was all full of how her da was so proud of me. And why wouldn't he be? Proud of me for being the fucking gilly, for taking the rap, for not being a snitch. It was like listening to Blue himself. I could imagine him sitting here giving me the same shite. About how I wouldn't notice the time going by, how I'd still be young enough to start again when I got out. How'd he'd look after Tara and the kid for me.

"BOLLOCKS."

Of course he'd look after Tara. Why shouldn't he? She was his fucking daughter.

Had they not listened to a word the judge said? Had they not heard him say "ten years" . . . minimum.

Had I missed something? Had he changed his mind when I'd left the court? Had Jeremy fucking Beadle jumped out and told them all it was a set-up? Cause he was right, it was a set-up but I seemed to be the only one not laughing.

I listened to her crap and watched as she flashed her legs at the screw, who was supposed to be keeping an eye on me, not fucking her. I realised there and then that the whole thing was a farce. I was sitting across from a woman who I didn't even like, never mind love. A woman I'd married

143

because she was pregnant and shouldn't be left to rear a kid alone. Well, what the fuck was she going to do now, other than rear the kid on her own? Why had I bothered? Jasus, if only I'd known, if only I'd been able to see into the future. I'd never have married the bitch, fuck her anyway. She could do what she liked, I didn't give a shite, they could all go and fuck themselves.

Time would pass quickly, isn't that what they'd said? What the fuck would they know? They weren't the ones spending ten years in an eight-by-ten cell with Victor and his smelly feet. Jasus, he was rotten, he couldn't help it but it was unbearable. He tried everything, he even left his boots outside the cell, but some fucker robbed them.

What ever happened to honour among thieves?

He used to bathe his feet in Dettol for hours but all this achieved was the loss of layers of skin. Ten minutes later the smell would be back, worse than ever.

The Professor (so-called because of his John Lennon glasses and the fact that he was never seen without a book in his hand) said that he had read that if you urinated on your feet it would solve the odour problem. So, after pissing on them for two weeks, all poor Victor got was warts.

There was a smell of pissy grannies in the cell for a month after.

People give out about the lack of space in prisons. It's no wonder there's no fucking room, the place is overrun by do-gooders. Everywhere you looked you saw them, and they all ask the same questions. Questions about your background, about your childhood, about your family.

They were obsessed with sex, wanting to know if you had been abused as a child. As if that was the only reason in the world why people turn to crime.

I mean to say, if that was the case me whole family must've been abused. In fact, there must've been some pervert interfering with every kid on our road.

One day I told one of them that I'd started robbing when I was five.

I couldn't believe it when he asked. "Was that when your father started to abuse you?"

I just laughed. They hadn't a clue.

They honestly thought that these little pep talks would change us, that we'd never rob again. How fucking stupid can you get?

Robbing was me occupation. It was like trying to tell a carpenter to stop working with wood. I'd served me apprenticeship, I'd gone through the years of doing all the shitty jobs, the ones that didn't pay. I wasn't going to give it up now. Not for some toffee-nosed do-gooder who probably broke out in a rash every time he saw Ballyfermot on a map.

I told Davis I wanted to see Brush. He told me that wasn't a good idea. I went berserk. I grabbed him by the lapels of his fancy suit, me knee was in his balls before I could stop meself. The screws moved in, but before they got to me I told him that I would rat on them all if he didn't give the Brush me message.

Two days later the Brush arrived. He walked in, laden down with cigarettes, and threw his arms around me.

"Brush, get me outta here."

"Don't worry, son, I'll look after you . . . and your family. I won't let you down."

He pulled away, looked me straight in the eye and continued, "Just like I know you won't let me down."

We sat down and he talked in a whisper, careful not to be overheard.

"I've got people in here who'll look after you, you'll be all right."

"Brush, you're not listenin. It's Stan the Man who should be in here, not me."

"Don't you worry about him, he'll be dealt with . . . in good time. Stan or Blue couldn't be trusted to keep their mouths shut, that's why it had to be you. There'll be a place waiting for you when you get out."

He reached across and touched me arm.

"You're like a son to me. I don't expect you to do anything for me that I wouldn't do for you."

I felt like screaming – "I'm not yer fucking son, don't fucking patronise me."

But what was the point in getting emotional? They had me by the balls. I was as guilty as sin. I'd stood up in court and admitted it, every newspaper in the country had printed it, so it didn't really matter what the truth was, it was too late now. I was going to do the time, like it or not.

CHAPTER THIRTY-FOUR

I decided that, if I was going to spend the next ten years in prison, I was going to be number one. No one was going to fuck with Johnser Kiely. If I couldn't be outside, then prison was going to be me kingdom.

Every night when the lights went out I replayed the court scene in me head. How had I been so stupid? How had I let them set me up like this? I couldn't believe how badly Davis had defended me. I thought he would be like Perry Mason, that at the eleventh hour he would produce some gem of evidence and the whole thing would be quashed. Needless to say it didn't happen like that. He started going on about me poverty-stricken background, about me life of petty crime, about the huge unemployment in Ballyer. He might as well have said, "Me client is as guilty as fuck."

Because it would have been the same result.

I couldn't believe the sentence, the minimum ten years, where was the seven he'd talked about? Up his fucking arse, like everything else he talked about. All he kept telling me was, "Don't worry, Johnser, we'll appeal."

"Well, I am fucking worried, very fucking worried. Deyeh realise how old I am?"

147

"You'll still be a young man when you get out. You'll still have a lot to look forward to."

"Well, let me tell yeh, Mr Young Man, there's fuck all for me teh look forward teh. Ten fucking years in the clink, ten years without a woman, ten years lookin at the same four walls, what the fuck is that teh look forward teh?"

He gathered up his papers and threw them into his case.

"There's no point in trying to talk to you," he said as he left the room.

Every night I went over and over the same things.

At first they all visited. Tara, the Blue, the Brush, all of them. It was nice to see people from the outside, it made me feel less restricted. For some reason, just talking to them made me feel as though part of me was still free. Hearing them talking about places we used to go made me feel as if I was still out there. I could almost smell the sweaty atmosphere of the Brush's snooker hall.

He would be telling me about some new kid, whizzes he called them. Some kid who was going to take the snooker world by storm, or at least make Brush some money on side bets when he sent him out hustling.

We used to sit there for hours watching these kids play, we'd watch through the haze of smoke as it mingled with the smell of sweat. Now, as I listened to the Brush talking, I was there, watching his latest whizz taking the last few bob from some poor fucker who wasn't as good as he thought.

They always brought smokes and chocolate and, though these were worth their weight in gold, I kept mine, savouring the taste of freedom they brought with them.

I used to bring them back to me room, put on me

headphones and, closing me eyes, I'd smoke and eat until I felt sick.

With me eyes closed and me music blaring in me ears, I wasn't inside, I was wherever I wanted to be. I could put on some Meatloaf and suddenly I'd be back at the Naller, and Jackie was there, her knickers around her ankles and her hand on me knob. I often thought about touching meself and pretending. But with me eyes closed and me headphones on I wouldn't know if someone came in, and with me eyes open, I was back in me little cell.

At other times I played me sixties tapes, ate me chocolate and remembered the good old days when I'd been parked beside the checkout in the Elephant.

I began to long for me visits. I forgot about me resentment towards Tara and started looking forward to seeing her in her skirts that grew shorter by the day. I had even started looking forward to Blue, because he always had a story to tell about some job that had gone down and, like the snooker hall, I could smell the atmosphere, and I was there.

After a few months the visits became less frequent. There were lots of excuses.

The baby wasn't well, there was a big job on, there was always some business that had to be taken care of. The list was endless. So it came as no real surprise when Blue arrived looking sheepish.

The conversation started with the usual excuses as to why the Brush and Tara hadn't been able to make it. Then he went straight into a story about a shopkeeper who'd refused to pay his protection money.

"You'd have loved it, the stupid fucker wasn't so brave by the time we left."

149

He laughed. Normally, I'd have laughed too, but something wasn't quite right.

"Where did yeh say Tara was?"

He looked down at the table.

"Before I forget, the Brush sent yeh smokes. Jasus, he'd kill me if I forgot teh give yeh them."

He was rushing too much, it wasn't like him.

"Tara! Blue, where is she?"

He pulled out his cigarettes. I knew he was building up to something, I said nothing. I took the cigarette he offered and let him stew.

"Yeh know how it is, Johnser, Tara's a young girl." His eyes dropped back to the table. "She's got . . . needs."

He looked up as though that explained everything.

"What the fuck are yeh shitin about?"

He paled.

"She's pregnant."

I couldn't believe it. I don't know why I thought she wouldn't be riding. For fuck's sake, it wasn't as though I'd been her first. And I hadn't expected her to stay faithful for ten years. But, Jasus . . . it had only been six months.

I looked back at Blue. He really didn't give a fuck about me or Tara. All he was worried about was whether or not I was going to rat them all up. Give me some credit. I stood up.

"Tell Tara I want teh see her."

He didn't take his eyes off me.

"Johnser, yeh won't . . . yeh know?"

I bent down and whispered, "Just cause yer tart of a daughter can't keep her legs closed doesn't mean I can't keep me mouth shut." He looked relieved.

"But tell the slut she better come an' see me."

I walked away.

"Johnser, don't forget yer smokes."

Prison life isn't easy, but it has its good points. Once you accept the fact that you're not getting out, that you're guilty, it gets that little bit easier. There were a few faces I recgonised from Ballyer, people who'd let it be known that I wasn't to be messed with. And, regardless of what the authorities say, you could get anything you want in prison.

I knew cokeheads who were stoned more in prison than they ever were on the streets. It was a farce, the gear was getting in every way. It was coming in in kids' nappies, on the tongues of lovers. One fella had it coming in in cards. The padded ones, they were full of tabs. This fella had more birthdays, anniversaries and special occasions than the whole of Ballyer put together.

If they'd built a cocaine highway through Dublin, there wouldn't have been as many drugs on it.

We all had visits from kids, we all held the babies in our arms and pulled gear from their nappies. Even if, like me, you never touched the stuff, you still had it brought in.

In prison it was important to let it be known that you weren't to be fucked with.

The first time I went down to the toilet I was followed by three heads. On me way out, one of them bumped into me. I knew the story. Before he could do anything I'd grabbed him into a headlock and ran full force into the tiled wall.

I heard the bones in his face crush and blood splattered everywhere. The other two just stood looking on, in shock.

Before they could move, I kicked them both in the balls and flushed their heads down the toilet.

I walked straight back to me landing, and into every cell

and told them all I was Johnser Kiely, and that nothing would happen unless I said so.

Only two chose to ignore me. But a couple of broken noses later, they decided to toe the line.

I was back. It was Ballyer all over again, I was head gaucho. For the next ten years, I was going to make every minute of every day hell for the screws . . . and anyone else who got in me fucking way.

CHAPTER THIRTY-FIVE

I stopped telling Jonathan stories about his father. I felt that they were all lies.

The Johnser Kiely who'd stood up in court and pleaded guilty to the manslaughter of two innocent people was only a sad shadow of the man I loved.

I'd always thought of Johnser as an unsung hero. The kind of man who inspired others to write ballads. A Jesse James, Robin Hood type of person. The ones who robbed from the rich to give to the poor.

I believed that Johnser only robbed from people who could afford it, from the banks and places that were well covered by insurance. I never considered robbing a bank to be real robbing, after all, they had thousands and thousands of pounds and even after being robbed they still opened the next day, with thousands and thousands of pounds.

He never robbed from the people of Ballyer, he never believed in doing the dirt on your own. And now, here he was, beating the fuck out of old people. I couldn't take it in, I just couldn't comprehend what he'd done.

I stopped talking to the baby about him. And started calling him Jonathan even when we were alone.

Jeffrey was becoming more and more attractive by the day.

Jeffrey hadn't terrorised old people, Jeffrey didn't hurt anybody, Jeffrey was kind and considerate, Jeffrey cared about people and at the end of the day that was important.

There was a time when I would have sneered at his "kindness", but not any more. Now I seen him for what he was, a man, a real man.

I'll never forget the night Johnser was convicted. It was the night I conceived my second child. Another boy. I called him Edward, his father's second name. I couldn't very well have called him Jeffrey, I mean what would it have been like?

Johnser, Johnser junior. Jeffrey, Jeffrey junior. Not very imaginative, is it?

Jeffrey was delighted, he preferred the name Edward. At least that's what he told me.

Jasus, when I think about it, there'd only been two men in me life and I'd had a baby for both of them. Thank God there hadn't been ten.

Jeffrey was working later and later in order to make ends meet, but he never complained. He talked about building an extension or maybe moving to a bigger house. He was always thinking of me, always making sure that I wanted for nothing. I loved him for that.

I was finally beginning to get over Johnser, and learning to love Jeffrey, when it happened.

I came down one morning, me eyes in the back of me head from lack of sleep. Edward was teething and his crying had kept me up all night. They were both asleep now, thank God. At least I could have a cup of tea in peace and get the house sorted before they woke. Jeffrey had offered to get up with Edward during the night but I'd said no. After all, he had work in the morning and it wouldn't be fair.

I filled the sink to wash up the dishes from the night before and stood with tea in hand looking out the back window. Next door's dog started barking. I knew what that meant. The postman was on his way. With that, I heard the post dropping into the hall. I smiled to meself, where would I be without that dog? I walked out and picked up the post. Bills, bills and more bills. I never opened them, Jeffrey had told me not to, he would look after them, I wasn't to worry meself about things like that.

As I flicked through them I noticed that one was a letter, addressed to me. I didn't recognise the handwriting, it was like a child's. I opened it and started to read.

Dear Jackie,

Howya? I bet I'm the last person yeh spected teh hear from. I bet yeh taught I wasn't capable of writing. I know yeh don't owe me nothin but I just can't get that night outta me head. I keep on thinking about yeh. Thinking about how much I love yeh. I can't stop thinking about the days we had together. I know yer married, me too, but things ain't working out. Don't worry, I'm not asking yeh teh marry me, I just want yeh teh come and visit me in the Joy. Visiting is next Tuesday. I hope you'll come because I want teh tell yeh what really happened.

It was signed Johnser, just that. No love or best wishes, just Johnser.

I had to sit down and take a deep breath. I couldn't believe it, Johnser had written to me. Me first thoughts were, what a cheek, expecting me to drop everything to go and see him.

What did he take me for? Did he honestly think I was going to risk what I had with Jeffrey, just to see him?

I suppose I should've torn the letter up and thrown it in the bin, but I didn't.

During the course of the day I found meself drawn back to it. I kept picking it up and reading it over and over again.

For the next few days I was like a bitch, Jeffrey could do nothing right. I criticised everything he done, I was like the old Jackie again. I wouldn't let him touch me. I couldn't bear him near me. I pretended it was that time of the month but I don't think he believed me. However, Jeffrey being Jeffrey, he accepted it and left me alone. This made me feel even guiltier. That was it. I would tear up the letter and forget all about him. I wasn't prepared to risk everything on a whim.

CHAPTER THIRTY-SIX

By Tuesday morning I knew that I would go. I had to. I had to hear him tell me that he hadn't murdered those people. I knew he'd tell me the truth, he wouldn't lie to me.

I organised me mother to mind the kids. It wasn't a problem, she loved having them. She was always going on about how she didn't see enough of them. So, after dropping them off, I went and had me hair done. I had to, that had been me excuse for leaving the kids with Ma. By half past eleven I found meself standing in line with the rest of the visitors, they all seemed to know each other. I used to think that I was afraid of no one, but by Jasus, I was afraid of some of these.

Out of nowhere appeared the fattest woman I'd ever seen. She was wearing a fur coat that smelt of mothballs and big loopy earrings that would have fit around me waist. She nudged me in the arm. Nudged! She nearly knocked me across the fucking road.

"Howya, luv, this must be yer first visit, I haven't seen yeh before."

I smiled, nodding me head.

"Don't be shy, luv, we're all in the same boat." She looked along the line. "Isn't that right, girls? We're all one

157

big happy fambily here. So what diddy do, luv? Yer fella, what diddy do?"

I was scarlet. Jasus, what was I doing here? Why had I ever come to this place?

"He's not me fella."

She folded her arms like a matron on a hospital ward.

"Well, yer brother then." She was getting impatient.

"He's not me brother, he's me friend."

"Well, yer fucking friend then. What's he in for?"

They were all laughing. I felt like a right fucking eejit standing there. I wished the ground would open up and swallow me. Suddenly the old Jackie made a guest appearance.

"I don't fucking know, I haven't fucking seen him yet, have I?"

"Oh, well, 'scuse me for fucking breathin. I was only askin, showin support is what we call it. But yeh can fuck off now."

With that she turned on her heel and made her way over to a little group huddled in a corner. No doubt to talk about me. But fuck her, who gave a shite what the likes of them thought?

Eventually the gates opened and we were allowed in. There were security guards on each side of them.

It reminded me of that time out at the airport when we were going on our school trip to France.

As "furry" passed the youngest-looking guard, she opened her coat and asked if he'd like to body-search her. Everyone laughed, even me.

I walked in and showed me pass to the guard at the desk.

"Wait over there," he told me.

Minutes later Johnser appeared.

He seemed really pleased to see me –

"Howya, Jackie? I'm glad yeh came, I knew yeh wouldn't let me down." He went to kiss me but I pulled away.

"Johnser, what's this all about?"

"I just wanted teh see yeh, Jackie, what's wrong with that?"

We sat down. He looked at me.

"Yeh didn't happen teh bring any fags, didyeh?"

I took a deep breath, I knew I was losing the head.

"Johnser, yer lucky *I'm* here, never mind yer fucking cigarettes."

He smiled nervously.

"Sorry, Jackie, maybe next time?"

"Johnser, if yeh don't start talkin, there won't be a this time, right?"

He was silent for a minute. Maybe he'd expected something more from me, I don't know. But what I did know was that if he was expecting me to be all over him, he was in for a shock. I had a family now. I wasn't going to forget about them just because he'd written one scabby letter.

"So yeh got married?"

"Yeh know I'm fucking married. So cut the crap, Johnser, why did yeh kill them people?"

He leaned forward.

"Jackie, Jackie, listen teh me. I didn't kill anybody."

"Well, what the fuck are yeh doin in here, if yeh did nothin wrong? Well, Johnser, answer me that?"

"I had no choice."

"Ah, please. Please, Johnser, I know yeh better than that. Yer not sitten here for the good of yer health. Com'on, give me some credit, I'm not fucking stupid."

He stared at me. He looked like he wanted to hit me for having the cheek to question him.

"I told yeh I didn't fucking do it."

"An' I told yeh I don't fucking believe yeh."

He sat back, throwing his hands in the air.

"Maybe it was a big mistake askin yeh teh come here."

I stood up.

"Yeah, I think you're right, maybe it was. You and me are no longer an item, Johnser, it's over. I've two kids now, I'm happy."

"Two kids?"

"Yeah, Johnser, that's what I said, two kids."

"What are they?"

"Boys."

"I always wanted a boy."

"Yeh still have plenty of time, you'll be out in a few years and Tara'll be still young enough teh have babies."

He looked up at the ceiling.

"That was the biggest mistake of me life, I should've never left yeh."

I looked at him and I knew he was being sincere. But I couldn't give in.

"That's all history now, Johnser. And, like all history, it's better left in the past."

He seemed stunned.

"I've been a right eejit. Forgive me?"

I looked at him and smiled.

"Johnser, there's nothin teh forgive. I wanted teh see yeh too."

"Jackie, I never lied teh yeh, believe me. I swear teh God I never did it. I can't explain, not here, the reason why I'd teh

160

take the blame, but yeh have teh believe me when I tell yeh that I didn't do it."

I looked at him. Looked deep into his eyes and I knew he was telling the truth.

"I believe yeh."

He stood up.

"Lookit, Jackie, I have teh go, thanks for comin. Will yeh come again?"

"Johnser, I'm sorry. I can't." I kissed him. "I won't be comin back here again."

"I know that now. I'm sorry for wastin yer time, Jackie. I'll see yeh."

He turned and walked back towards the door where the guard was waiting to let him back in. I felt so sorry for him, I felt like screaming, "Johnser, don't go, come back."

But what was the point? He was locked up and I had Jeffrey and the boys at home. That was the way things were. It wasn't how I'd planned it, it wasn't how I'd wanted it. But what could I do? It was the way things were.

CHAPTER THIRTY-SEVEN

I can't say what made me write to Jackie, but I did.

Tara had only come up once since I'd heard she was pregnant, she was huge. She'd started giving me all the crap about how I'd been away for so long and she was lonely. How she was still a young woman who needed somebody in her life. About how awful it was spending all her time with a baby. How she needed adult company.

"Adult company me arse, more like fucking male company."

I knew that at the end of the day she was just a fucking slut. A slut who'd taken me for a ride. And look at me now, I was the scapegoat for them all.

"Who's the father?" I asked.

She told me.

"Stan."

And you know, I suppose that if I'd thought about it for long enough, I wouldn't have had to ask, I'd have guessed.

"Stan the fucking Man."

Stan the man who'd stitched me up. Stan the Man who had me in prison while he was out shagging me missus. Well, that was it, we were finished, it was over. I didn't want anything more to do with them, they could all fuck off.

I was getting a reputation as a hard man, someone who wasn't to be fucked with. Even so called RAH heads were starting to respect me. There was no sectarianism on my landing. The only ones I wouldn't allow were Jockeys.

That's what we called them. They were the ones who'd interfered with kids, or beat up their wives, or messed around with old people.

I remember one inmate saying that I was a bit of a hyprocrite, after all, hadn't I gone down for killing two old people. He only said it once. I let it be known why I'd gone down and who I was protecting. Eventually, they started to believe me.

The word was out that I was a fucking Jockey hater.

You always knew the Jockeys, they tried to hide what they'd done. They were never up-front about their crimes, they'd never say why they were in, so this made them easy to cop.

I'm sure when they were all together, they'd no problem talking about what they'd done. All bragging about their exploits.

Scumbags, the lot of them. Fucking shirtlifters. They wanted to be put in solitary, but there was always a time when they'd have to come out, and we got them then, all you needed was patience.

And I was going nowhere for the next ten years, so I had all the time in the world.

Word always came through when one of them was out, I reckon it was the screws who put it about. They hated Jockeys too.

When you seen the way those bastards were treated. They were the ones being educated, getting free access to the library, going on computer courses. And why? Because they'd molested kids, and raped women. For fuck's sake. Where's the justice in that?

I fucking hated them.

Sammy Bennett came in. I knew Sammy from Ballyer, I'd heard the rumours about him, about how he was always shirtlifting the young lads.

He helped out in the church, collecting the money and the likes. Afterwards he'd be hanging around the altar boys, up to no fucking good.

I'd never had any run-ins with him of course, not ever having had the pleasure of being an altar boy, but I knew him. I knew Sammy, Sammy the shirtlifter.

He used to give the fucking knacker kids fifty pence if they'd do things for him, and we all knew that it wasn't odd jobs he wanted done.

I went through all the old newspapers that were kept in the library and found what I was looking for. There'd been a man from Ballyfermot who'd gone down for messing with kids. By right he should've been in Arbour Hill, but we all knew that Arbour Hill was full to the fucking gills with pervs, so in the meantime he was given a nice cosy little cell in the Joy.

He recognised me the minute he set eyes on me. I knew by the way the colour drained from his face and the fact that he dropped the cup he was holding, he knew who I was.

The word on the landing was that Sammy was in for tax evasion, that Sammy was in because he hadn't paid his television licence, he was in for this, he was in for that.

Bollocks. Bollocks to all that.

He was a fucking shirtlifter and I was going to sort him out once and for all.

Sammy was a sneaky little bastard, a clever cunt. He never

went to the jacks without an escort, never ate with the rest of us, never ate meat. (He knew fucking well that the cons in the kitchen made sure it was laced with shite.) You could never get him on his own long enough to do any real damage.

But I could wait, I was in no hurry.

I worked in the laundry, and when I got the opportunity I sewed blades into his sheets and hoped they would cut the fucking back off him. Then I heard that he always checked his bed at night, he knew the story. He knew what happened to people like him.

Eventually I got me chance. He was getting lax.

I walked into the dinner hall one day, and there he was sitting at a table. I decided I'd go over and talk to him. I sat down and we started chatting, like old mates who hadn't seen each other in years. I talked about me father, me uncle and how he must know them, about this person and that person and what they were doing now, about Ballyer in the old days and how it had changed. We had a great chat.

I kept this up for about a week and he became convinced that I knew nothing about his past. He thought we were best friends.

Sammy was fond of his cigarettes, he paid top whack for them.

One day I told him that I knew where there was cigarettes coming in. All he had to do was go down to the farm, (some fucking farm, more like a 4 x 4 vegetable plot) where they would be thrown in over the wall. I couldn't be seen down there because I'd be sussed.

Sammy agreed. Sammy was happy to have a friend, especially one like me, someone he thought would protect him.

I told him that everyone would be at a football match so he could sneak down without been seen. I had promised him fifty cigarettes for himself, he was delighted.

There was a football match going on that day, I wasn't lying. I knew that Sammy was no fucking eejit, that he'd check it out first to make sure he wasn't being set up.

So while the match was going on he snuck away, got the cigarettes and was on his way back through the veggie patch, that was surrounded by a wall with a little gate where you could get in and out, when he seen me. He knew instantly that he'd been conned.

I smiled.

He dropped the cigarettes and started screaming. Screams that on a normal day would've been heard by half of Dublin. But not today, not when there was a match on. And amazingly enough, at that precise minute a fight broke out on the pitch. That was sure to keep the screws busy for a while.

He made a run and ended up in a corner where he crouched down on the ground. He started crying, crying like a little baby, but I had no pity.

I laid into him, kicked the fucking shit out of him. I could hear his bones cracking under the force of me boot but I didn't stop. I smashed him in the face until there was blood everywhere, he was in bits. Even his own mother wouldn't recognise him.

He stopped crying. He was unconscious. I left. I left him there to die.

I was working in the laundry that day so I had no problem getting clean clothes.

Sammy did die. But there was nothing they could do about it. I'm sure they suspected that I was involved, but they had no proof, they couldn't touch me.

I knew the day Frankie Fitz, the main man, sent for me, that I'd entered the major league, no mistake.

CHAPTER THIRTY-EIGHT

It took me a while, but I got back into the rhythm of me life. Me life with Jeffrey and the kids. I knew I could make it work. Johnser hadn't contacted me since the day I'd gone to see him, and I was glad about that. He still meant a lot to me, but so did this life I had built, this little nest that I'd built for meself and me family.

It was by no means perfect, there were still a few things wrong, things like Jeffrey's ideas on women.

Jeffrey believed that a woman's place was in the home, he didn't agree with working mothers. He didn't agree with me having a lot of money either, he figured I didn't need it.

He paid all the bills, he came to the supermarket with me on a Friday night and paid for the groceries. He was the one who paid the bill if we went out for a meal, he was the one who paid for the drinks if we went to the pub, so what did I need money for? He didn't seem to understand that every woman likes to have her own few bob in her purse. I mean to say, why should I have to ask him for the money to have me hair done? Or, even worse, the money to buy him a birthday present? It was ridiculous.

He'd say stuff like, "You don't need your hair done, love, I think it looks lovely the way it is."

Or, "There's no need to waste money on presents for me. I have you and the kids, that's all the presents I need."

That really bugged me, it really fucking annoyed me.

Still, I suppose, none of us are perfect, least of all me.

Besides, Jeffrey's good points outweighed his bad ones, so I learned to live with his little imperfections.

Jeffrey was very well educated, he was always going on some course or another, he knew all about computers and business organisation and things like that. He had more education than he was ever going to use in Cadbury's. So, when they offered him redundancy, he jumped at it.

He was going to set up his own business, something he'd always wanted to do. He got a nice little lump sum but, to be honest, to this day I don't know how much it was. I think it was over thirty thousand, but how much over thirty thousand, I don't know.

So he started his own business and worked more hours than ever. He'd come home all excited telling me about the new people he was meeting, the contracts he was getting, the new systems he was installing. But sure I hadn't a clue.

I knew where he was going, what he was doing, the names of some of the people he dealt with, but that was it. I hadn't a notion about computers but I'd pretend to be interested.

No matter how many hours he worked he was still the same old Jeffrey, he was great with the kids, he was great with me, he was a great man. So there was no reason for me to suspect that there was anything wrong.

I did notice that we were getting a lot of letters from the bank lately but thought nothing of it. It was obviously to do with the new business.

That was until the day that knock came on the door.

I opened it and a man I'd never seen before stood on the step.

"Yes?" I said, wondering who he was.

"Are you Mrs Jeffrey Adams?" he asked politely.

"Yes, I am, why?"

"Could you tell me what time you're expecting your husband home at, Mrs Adams?"

"No, I don't know the exact time, but he'll probably ring me later on. Can I give him a message?" Suddenly, for no reason at all, I began to feel anxious.

"You might give him this? Ask him to ring me?" he said, handing me a card.

As I closed the door I looked at the card, plain white, no name, just a number that meant nothing to me.

When Jeffrey rang, I told him about the mystery caller and gave him the number. He didn't seem concerned so I decided it was nothing to worry about.

Six weeks later I opened the door to the same man.

This time he handed me an envelope. I opened it. I couldn't believe what I was reading.

It was a final notice from the bank, telling me we had fourteen days to vacate the property listed as . . . blah blah blah.

I stared at the man standing in front of me.

"No, I'm sorry, there must be some mistake, you've obviously got the wrong Mrs Adams." I was starting to feel uneasy.

"No, I'm afraid there's no mistake."

"And I'm afraid there is. My husband runs his own business, he got loads of money from his redundancy, how could he not afford to pay the mortgage?" I knew I sounded hysterical but so would you.

"I'm sorry, Mrs Adams, maybe you should talk to your husband. I'm only doing my job."

He looked at me and I could see the pity in his eyes.

"Goodbye, Mrs Adams."

I thought the day would never end.

Waiting for Jeffrey to come home was like a kid waiting for Christmas, it seemed to take forever. At last, I heard his key in the door. I ran into the hall.

"Jeffrey what the fuck is this?" I hadn't even said hello.

He took the envelope from me.

"Well, I don't know, love, I haven't seen it yet, have I?"

He laughed nervously.

I watched him as he opened it. I knew by the expression on his face that this was no mistake. I stood rooted to the spot, unable to speak. Eventually, I found me voice.

"Jeffrey what's goin on? What is it?"

He just stood there, staring at me. Then he burst into tears.

"Jeffrey, Jeffrey, please, don't do this, talk teh me, please. Why hasn't the mortgage been paid? Where's all the money gone? Jeffrey, please tell me what's wrong!"

Suddenly he lashed out, taking me totally by surprise. He caught me on the side of the head, sending me flying backwards into the sitting-room.

The kids started screaming, they didn't know what was happening. Neither did I for that matter. Before I could get meself together he was beside me. He didn't try to help me up as I thought he would, instead he started kicking me, kicking me in the stomach and screaming, "Bitch. fucking bitch, this is all your fault, your fucking fault."

It was like being in the middle of some terrible nightmare, only I was awake and I was feeling the pain, the horrible, horrible pain.

I obviously passed out because, when I opened me eyes, he was gone. I dragged meself up off the floor and went to the kids. They were sitting hunched up in a corner, their arms wrapped around each other for comfort. They didn't make a sound, I think they were in shock.

"Come on, come on, sweethearts," I said, holding them tight.

"It's all right, Mammy's here now. It's OK, it's OK."

They clung to me, still not making a sound. I thought me heart would break for them. I tried not to cry, I really did but I couldn't stop the tears. Once they seen me crying, they started.

Thank God, I thought. Thank God, at least crying was normal.

I took them into the kitchen and tried to act normal. I told them we were going to have a special tea, biscuits, cake, lemonade, anything they wanted. I was desperate, desperate to make them happy again.

And it seemed to work. Before long they were laughing and making a mess. Edward was doing his party piece, blowing bubbles into his lemonade. He knew this always sent Jonathan into fits of giggles.

I didn't know what time it was when he came home.

I was lying on the bed in the dark when I heard him come into the room.

I didn't know how long I'd been lying there replaying the whole scene over and over in me head. Why? How? Where?

That was the one that puzzled me the most. Where had all the money gone? How could you possibly go through so much money in eight months? I didn't know, I just didn't know. And then there was the violence. Where had that come from? I obviously didn't know Jeffrey as well as I thought I did. I mean, who would have suspected him of being a wife-beater? Certainly not me.

I couldn't even begin to make sense of what had happened.

And, not for the first time that night, I wished it was all just a horrible dream.

He sat on the end of the bed, quiet now.

"What's wrong? What's wrong, Jeffrey?"

He just sat there. He still seemed angry. But then, so was I, so he'd better fucking answer.

"I lost it all," he said. "I've lost everything, every penny that we ever had, I've lost it all. I'm in debt, we're in debt up to our eyes."

"What do yeh mean? I don't understand!"

"I know you don't. That's the fucking problem, you never understand. It's always the same with you, you don't give a fuck about anyone but yourself. I've had to carry this burden on me own for months. Yeah, months, because I couldn't go upsetting little Jackie. Now could I? When the business wasn't doing well, who had I got to talk to? Not fucking you. When there were risks to be taken, where were you? Sitting at home moaning because you hadn't the money to get your poxy hair done. That's where you were. That's what you were doing while I was breaking me bollocks trying to earn a living. So don't tell me you don't understand, I know you don't understand, because you don't fucking want to understand."

He must have thought I'd gone into a coma or something. I just sat there staring at him. But I have to say, I had no idea what he was talking about. None whatsoever.

Despite what he might think, he wasn't making any sense. I sat up.

"Jeffrey, am I missin somethin here? Cause if I am, I wish you'd explain exactly what it is. The last I heard about our financial situation was that yeh gotta lotta money off Cadbury's and were startin yer own business. Now, I don't know what happened after that. The main reason being, I wasn't fucking told. Now maybe yeh think I'm fucking psychic or somethin but the bad news is, I'm not. So don't think yeh can sit there an' abuse me for not fucking understandin what's goin on. As far as I'm concerned, you're the only one who knows that an' yeh don't seem prepared to enlighten anyone else."

"For fuck's sake, Jackie. What's the point in trying to explain? You're not fucking listening. It's gone, gone, gone, gone, all of it. I spent it, yes, spent it, and you should know about spending money, Jackie, God knows you've done it often enough."

I couldn't believe him. Couldn't believe that he was trying to compare the money I spent on clothes for the kids and the upkeep of the house with the thirty something, maybe even forty something, thousand pounds he'd spent. He was fucking mental.

"What did yeh spend it on?"

"You don't need to know."

"I don't need teh know! What are yeh fucking talkin about? I don't need teh know. I've a letter here tellin me that our house is being taken off us cause we haven't paid the mortgage in fucking months, an' yeh sit there tellin me that I don't need teh know where the money's gone. What deyeh think I am, fucking stupid?"

He started crying again. But I was ready for him, his whinging act wouldn't work this time. I slapped him, slapped him hard across the face.

"Tell me, yeh bastard, tell me what yeh did with all the money?"

He was sobbing now, sobbing his heart out, but I didn't care. He mumbled something.

"What? What are yeh sayin? For fuck's sake stop snivellin an' answer me!"

"Gambling."

"What!"

"Gambling."

"What kind of gambling?"

"Does it matter?"

"Yeah, it fucking does matter."

"Poker machines."

"Poker machines?" I was stunned. How could you lose so much money on a poker machine? I thought they only took ten pence at a time, not hundreds of pounds.

Over the next few days he told me everything.

How he'd always had a weakness for poker machines. Who'd have believed it? Good old reliable Jeffrey was a gambler.

I certainly couldn't believe it.

He told me it had started with a few pounds here and there, nothing much. But when he got his redundancy, he started spending more and more. Sometimes twenty, thirty even forty pounds a time. Soon he was losing hundreds, and he had to try and get it back. Needless to say, he hadn't. So now, eight months later, he'd lost it all.

There was no business, there never had been. He'd spent all day every day playing the poker machines. And, when he'd nothing left, he went to the bank and got an overdraft. An overdraft of three and a half thousand pounds. And where was that? In some scummy poker machine.

* * *

I cried me eyes out the day we had to leave the house. I couldn't believe we were going back to living in some dirty, poky little flat. I mean, here we were, five years and two kids later, going backwards instead of forward. Where was it all going to end?

Jeffrey started going to GA Meetings, he said he found them a great help.

He got a job in a shop, it was no great shakes, nothing like he'd had before, but still, it was bringing in a week's wages.

It was steady money. It paid the rent, the ESB, put food on the table, and at the end of the day that's all that mattered.

We hadn't got much but at least what we had was our own, there was nobody knocking on the door looking for money, and for that I was grateful.

But it wasn't long before that little bubble burst.

Jeffrey started drinking. He'd never been much of a drinker so this came as a bit of a surprise. Another insight into his character. I think he started drinking because he'd become disillusioned with life.

But with the drinking came more violence.

He blamed me.

He blamed me and the kids for holding him back. Blamed me for not making any contribution towards the bills.

"Jeffrey," I'd say, trying to reason with him.

"Jeffrey, you're the one who doesn't want me teh work."

And then he'd hit me.

He was always sorry afterwards, but that didn't take away from the fact that he'd done it.

175

"Jackie, Jackie, I'm sorry. Please believe me, it's not you. You know I love you, it's the frustration of working in that shop all day, that's what makes me angry. You know I'm capable of better than that, don't you? You know how bright I am? Jackie, please don't leave me, you're all I've got. You and the kids, you're all I have in the world."

Me heart went out to him. Because, deep down inside, I knew he was a good man. And I did love him. I hated to see him suffer like this, but what could I do? He still wouldn't hear of me going out to work, so how was I supposed to help?

I knew he worked hard. By the time he got home at night it was time for bed, then he was up again a few hours later and back at the job he hated. On and on it went.

One day I came home and met him on the stairs with the video recorder under his arm.

"Where are yeh goin with that?"

"I'm going to have it repaired."

"Why? What's wrong with it?"

"It's broke, didn't I tell you? I noticed the other day that it was stuck on 'record'."

"No, yeh didn't."

"Oh, I must've forgot."

I hadn't noticed it was broke. In fact, I knew it wasn't, I'd had a video on for the kids that morning. But I let him go, he was happy, he was cheerful. He was late home that evening. He brought me flowers, things seemed good.

Before the video came back, the television broke down. And Jeffrey brought that away to be repaired. I started to notice other little things going missing.

A lamp someone had bought us as a wedding present, the toaster that we never used, so couldn't possibly be broke, the lawnmower. Although we'd no garden now, we still had our old lawnmower. All sorts of little ornaments, none of them worth very much, but still they were gone.

I knew the day Jonathan's bike disappeared that Jeffrey wasn't working any more. He was gambling again. Was once not enough to lose everything? Why now? We were starting to get back on our feet, why was he doing this? I couldn't make him out. I didn't know him any more.

I decided there and then that I wasn't taking any more. I wasn't able for it. What with the beatings, the drinking and now this. It was one thing what he did to me, but to start taking the kids' toys, I wasn't having that.

I packed a few things and left.

I went back to Ma and Da and told them everything that had happened. I knew by them that they didn't want to know, they idolised Jeffrey. He was the greatest thing since sliced bread as far as they were concerned. And they didn't want to think of him as being anything less than perfect. Also, there would be the shame of a broken marriage. How were they supposed to deal with that? This was the kind of thing that happened to other people, not them.

I wondered what fucking century they were living in? Anyway, the main thing is, they let us stay.

Later on that night Jeffrey came over.

He sat there acting as though there was nothing wrong. Chatting and laughing, the way he had when we'd been going out together.

I couldn't believe him.

He told them things weren't as bad as I was making them out to be. That I was overreacting, I was bored at home, I was resentful of the fact that he was out meeting people all day while I only had the kids for company. But what could he do? He had to earn a living, somebody had to put the food on the table.

And they believed him. They understood. Who knew better than them what a selfish, demanding young woman I could be? They knew how argumentive I could be.

They were talking about me as if I wasn't there. I wanted to fucking kill them.

I got up and walked out, I went upstairs to the kids. I couldn't take any more of them.

Ma followed me upstairs.

"What are you playing at? Why are you being so bloody selfish? Why don't you, for once in your life, put someone else first?"

Why was I treating Jeffrey so badly? How could I treat someone who was so good to me like this? And what about the kids? Had I thought about them in all of this? Kids needed a good father, and I couldn't accuse him of not being that. On and on she went, until I could take no more.

"Listen Ma, listen!" I said, struggling to keep me hands from her throat.

Once again I told her what had happened. The gambling, the beatings, the drinking, the house being repossessed, everything. I told her the reason I didn't come over to see them very often was because of the black eyes and bruises I was always trying to hide. She just sat there looking at me. And I knew I was wasting me time.

I knew that she believed me, but that didn't mean she wanted to be involved. She never got involved in anything unpleasant.

Ma got up off the bed and went downstairs. She hadn't said a word.

I was halfway down the stairs when I heard her voice. I stopped.

"You, out of my house. Now!"

I'd never heard her sound so angry.

"Yes, you, out now! And if you ever dare to show your face around here again, I won't be responsible for what I do. Do you understand me? If you ever as much as look at my daughter again, never mind lay a hand on her, I will fucking kill you. K-I-L-L Y-O-U. Yes, that's what I said. Now get out of my house while you still can."

I couldn't believe what I was hearing, you could've knocked me down with a feather. Who'd have believed it? Ma, of all people. I ran down the stairs.

"Ma?"

"Oh, Jackie, Jackie. Why didn't you tell me before?" She hugged me so tight I thought me ribs would break.

"I thought it would stop. I thought I could handle it on me own."

I started to cry. Me, the greatest crier the world had ever known, hadn't cried since that first night he'd hit me. But I was certainly making up for it now.

I sobbed and sobbed into me mother's chest like I was a little girl again. Eventually, I ran out of tears.

We sat in the kitchen drinking tea.

"Jackie, why didn't you tell me about the house being repossessed? I thought the flat was only a stopgap while you were waiting for the new house to be finished. Maybe we could've helped."

"Oh, Ma, how could I? You were so proud of me. Your daughter building her own house, I just couldn't. It was easier to carry on with the lie."

"Well, there'll be no more lies. From now on you and I

are going to be honest with each other. I know we haven't been very close but it's never too late to start. Now you get yourself off to bed and have a good night's sleep. I want to have a chat with your father."

I threw me arms around her.

"Thanks, Ma. I don't know what I'd have done without yeh."

And I really meant it.

For the first time in me life, I'd had a real conversation with me mother. And, despite the subject matter, I'd really enjoyed it.

CHAPTER THIRTY-NINE

There were some really heavy people in prison.

People whose names you'd only heard but still respected.
There were also the ones who you didn't respect, the ones
who lived off other people's reputations.

Frankie Fitz had a reputation as an IRA hit-man,
although, as far as I could see, he was more a gangland thug
with connections. But, no matter what I thought, in prison he
was considered a major league player. He loved his IRA
reputation. He flew the tricolour in his cell, wore a beret and
always talked military lingo.

Other inmates always wanted to know where you stood
on the North, but I didn't really hold any opinion on it.

In Ballyer, I'd been like every other young fella who got
his hands on a tin of paint. When I got fed up writing
"Johnser Kiely Rules OK," I'd write "Up The IRA" or "RA
Land," until I got a pain in me arse and fucked the whole can
against some wall. I don't know where those American
graffiti artists got their patience from. They painted whole
blocks, whole fucking cities, they'd depict the whole history
of the American civil war, or the Mexican revolution, things
that took years to paint.

Not me, I couldn't do it. I got a pain in me bollocks after ten minutes.

Anyway, the walls in Ballyer were scruffy from all the shite the factories pumped out, and the lorries that spewed out huge clouds of smoke from their dilapidated exhausts. So, when you put your brush on the wall, you ended up with more dirt than paint. I wondered how the Americans dealt with this problem. Did the gangs come out with buckets of water and wash them down first? I could just imagine that happening in Ballyer, us sending Froggy off to get a bucket of water from some aul one, and her asking him what he wanted it for.

"We have teh clean the wall cause Johnser wants teh write, 'Up The IRA'."

All I can say is, Hispanic aul ones must be very tolerant.

There was another thing about America. All the gangs had names. I remember seeing *The Wanderers,* it was brilliant.

Hundreds of gangs all dressed in their own colours, and wearing jackets with the gang name on them. After the film, I wanted us to do the same. To have a leather or denim jacket with a dead man's skull on the back.

We were all on for it, all except Fat Larry. He said his ma'd kill him if he ruined his good jacket. Good jacket, me arse, it had been worn by at least three other members of his family before he'd finally got it.

Slash wanted us to shave our heads and call ourselves "The Ballyer Baldies". Froggy wanted us to be "The Free Spirits." When Fat Larry volunteered "The Ballyfermot Bollixes", I knew it was time to scrap the whole idea.

I was glad now, all these years later, that we hadn't named our gang. It was childish. I remember the girls called themselves "The Pink Ladies" after the girls in the film *Grease*.

Fucking eejits. Olivia Newton John, they weren't.

Back then it was the in-thing to be associated with the IRA. Bobby Sands had died on hunger strike, died for the cause.

I remember me da saying that anything worth dying for had to be right, and Ma agreed. It was unusual for her, cause me ma always felt sorry for the mothers of anyone who died. She'd no time for all the bombs and shootings. She likened Bobby Sands to Jesus.

"Christ died on the cross for the sake of Christianity and Bobby Sands for Ireland. He's a martyr."

Two days later the IRA struck again, she gave out shite about them. She blessed herself, saying, "God help the mothers of them poor soldiers."

Still, she'd never hear a bad word against Bobby.

I'd always bought *An Phoblacht* (though I never read it) and I never refused a collection box. However, I didn't agree with their attitudes towards our jobs.

If we done a big bank job, they always wanted a percentage for "The Cause." Bollocks. I often wondered if the money ever reached "The Cause." After all, I knew most of the RA heads in Ballyer and I wouldn't trust them as far as I'd throw them. As far as I was concerned, if I did a job, I was the one taking all the risks, I was the one who worked out all the plans and I was the one who'd do the time if it all went wrong. So I was never in favour of giving them any of me hard-earned cash.

The Brush used to give them money, just to keep the peace. He used to say it was one thing having the police on your case, but quite another having the IRA.

People were always talking of the Troubles ending, and I

often wondered what would happen when, if ever, that day came.

What would the likes of Frankie Fitz do for a living? At the moment he had a certain importance. He wasn't just a common criminal, he robbed for "The Cause". He didn't kick the crap out of people, he issued punishment beatings. But take away the banner of the IRA, and what then? What credentials did he have? In my view, Fitz and his like were just thugs and robbers, they were no different from me, Stan or the Brush.

As far as I was concerned, he could go and fuck himself.

So I went to see him. I was escorted down the landing to a cell at the end.

The cell door opened and there in front of me, behind a table, sat three men. The cell was in semi-darkness but I sensed that there was more than us four in there. I was ordered to take a seat. I turned the chair around, straddled it and folded me arms across its back. It felt uncomfortable but I'd seen it done in films and thought it was cool.

It looked tough, it said, "Don't fuck with me." It depicted a rebel, it screamed disrespect, at least I hoped it did. After all, James Dean, Steve McQueen and Paul Newman always sat like this. It better say fucking something, cause me jeans were stretched so tight I thought me balls would end up in me stomach.

The small man sitting between the two heavies started to read from a notepad in front of him. He never once looked up. Meanwhile, Pinky and Perky didn't take their eyes off me.

"You have been invited here today in the hope that you will be able to assist us in our struggle for 'The Cause'. You are being asked to assist by eliminating a member of this community, who has persistently carried out activities against the codes of our organisation . . . "

"What the fuck's all this shite about?" I shouted, rising to me feet. Pinky and Perky rose too, but the small man continued. "We will give you every support in your quest to carry out this task assigned to you."

"What are yeh sayin? Yeh want me teh kill for yeh? No way. I'm here teh see Frankie Fitz, not teh join yer fucking Boy Scout troop. Now, where the fuck's Fitz?"

The door closed behind me. I swung round, careful not to turn me back on the two stooges.

I'd never seen him before, but I knew that the man who came out of the shadows was none other than Frankie.

It's always disappointing meeting legends. Frankie looked like any other aul lad you might see in your local. His grey hair was slightly receding and he had a beer belly. If Hollywood got hold of his life story, they'd get Daniel Day Lewis or Liam Neeson to play the part. Yet the man standing in front of me looked more like Tom out of *The Riordans*.

"Hello, Johnser, it's nice to meet you at last," he said opening a packet of cigarettes and offering me one. I accepted, after all a smoke's a smoke. I was keeping me eye on the stooges.

It was an old trick to offer someone a smoke and, as you lit it, someone else would smack you in the jaw.

"What's all this committee shite 'bout?"

He laughed. "You really have no respect, Johnser, have you?"

I answered without removing me cigarette.

"Fuck the respect, why can't yer own gorillas do the hit?"

"I have my reasons."

185

"Well, unless yeh share them with me, yeh can go an' fuck yerself."

Fitz stubbed out his cigarette.

"Peter Brady is one of our own, we can't be seen to kill a Republican."

"So why deyeh want him dead?"

"He's dealing drugs. You know that's against our rules."

It was my turn to laugh.

"What the fuck are yeh on about? Gimme some credit. Yeh don't want him dead cause he's dealin, yer upset cause he's moved in on yer patch."

"Whatever. But we need him out of the way."

"Frankie, yer on yer own, I've no argument with Brady. So, if yeh want him dead, kill him yerself."

"You realise you're ignoring a direct order, Johnser? The result could be tragic for you."

I moved close to him, grabbing his lapels.

"Is that a threat, Frankie? I don't like threats."

Pinky approached, I swung Fitz around and threw him into his arms.

"I'll be seein yeh, Frankie."

He didn't answer.

I walked down the landing, expecting some kind of retaliation.

There was none.

CHAPTER FORTY

I hadn't slept so well for months.

I didn't know where I was when Ma woke me up with a cup of tea.

"Morning, love, did you sleep well?"

"Like a log. What time's it?"

"It's only just gone half past eight."

"Half eight, how come I didn't hear the kids?"

"Your daddy has them in the back garden playing football."

"Oh, great."

This was going to take a lot of getting used to. We were starting to sound a bit like *The Waltons*. Grandma in the kitchen baking scones while Grandpa played outside with the kids. I don't mean to sound ungrateful, but I wasn't quite ready for all this doting grandparent stuff just yet.

Ma and Da were great but I really needed to get me own place.

I was used to doing me own bits and bobs at home and, because Ma wouldn't let me help around the house, I found the days endless. I wasn't used to sitting around all day doing nothing. I just had to get back into some sort of routine and so had the kids. I decided I'd have to go down to the social and see what they had to offer. After all, I must be entitled to something, I'd paid tax and PRSI for long enough. And besides, whether I liked it or not, I was a deserted wife now so that had to count for something.

As I entered the office, I remember thinking to meself, God, I wish the aul one, "Furry", the one I'd met at the Joy, was with me now. She'd know all about deserted wives' allowance and anything else I might be entitled to.

I'll never forget that morning. I felt like a beggar asking for money on a street corner.

Some snotty fucking bitch sitting behind her desk asked all sorts of personal questions. Interrogated me like I was a fucking criminal, and for what? So she could offer me a scabby twenty pounds a week? Well, fuck her, I wasn't going to take any of her crap.

"Now listen here, you. Me husband left me, I'm livin with me ma an' da in a two-bedroom house, I've two kids an' no money. Now, what are yez gonna do about it?"

"Well, Mrs, em, Ms Adams, it's not up to me. All I can do is process your application for benefit. After that, it's out of my hands."

"An' whose hands does it go inteh?"

"Well, I suppose you could have a word with Mr Johnson, he's the supervisor."

"Well, Mr Johnson it is then."

"Just a minute, please."

She got up from her desk and almost ran to the door at the far side of the room. Where Mr Johnson held court.

Eventually she came back.

"Mr Johnson will see you now," she said, lifting the hatch like she was Saint Peter allowing me into heaven.

"Well, now, and what can I do for you?"

Was he for real? I mean, did he really expect me to believe that "Snotty" hadn't filled him in?

"Now, look here, Mr Johnson, you might have time teh waste but I haven't. Yeh know why I'm here. I need a house an' I need money so as I can get on with rearin me kids. So don't try teh convince me that dilly-dream out there hasn't already filled yeh in, cause I know she has."

"Well, Ms Adams, it's not as simple as that," he said, ignoring me outburst.

"Well, what'll make it simple?" I was really getting annoyed.

"If you'd just tell me what you told Ms Kelly outside, I might be able to help."

So, for the second time that morning, I told the story of me miserable life.

He said he'd do his best to get me sorted. He was going to put me on the priority list for housing.

Meanwhile, if I went back outside to hatch four and signed on, they would be able to sort out me benefit.

I left the office feeling exhausted.

I felt like I'd just gone three rounds with Mohammed Ali.

Although, thinking about it, that might have been easier.

A week later I had a letter from Mr Johnson, telling me how sorry he was that there were no houses available at the moment. However, if I was by any chance able to fix meself up in private accommodation, i.e. a flat, I'd be entitled to a rent allowance. All I'd have to do was get a letter and a rent book from me landlord, bring them into the office and they'd do the rest. I sat looking at the letter for a few minutes, then I thought: Well, I suppose it's better than nothing. I mean, it wasn't his fault if the corporation had no houses.

I felt no joy the day I moved into me flat.

189

I couldn't believe I was going back down this road again. The flat itself wasn't bad, nothing a good cleaning wouldn't cure. It was depressing but it was better than living with Ma and Da for the rest of me life.

Ma had been great, she really had. I couldn't believe she was the same woman I'd known all these years. She seemed to have lost about fifteen years, she was like a friend, there was nothing we didn't talk about. We'd sit in the kitchen yakking for hours.

I always remember one day when we were sitting chatting and, out of the blue, she said, "Jackie, don't ever take him back."

For a minute I didn't know who she was talking about. Then the penny dropped.

"Please, love, I know what I'm talking about. There's no such thing as a second chance. Once he's hit you the first time, it gets easier and easier. Then it turns to the kids. Hitting you in front of them, them in front of you and, before you know it, it becomes a way of life. You begin to see it as normal, you start to think everyone's the same, until suddenly, it's too late. You're an old woman and all you have to show for your time on earth is a bruised and battered body."

I looked at her and wondered how she knew so much. I mean, how could she know anything about battered wives, having spent so many years with Da? Good old easy-going Da. Then a thought struck me, surely not, not Da . . . it was as if she read me mind, "No, Jackie, don't even think about it. Your father's a good man, he always was. It was your granda. Granda Cranny, he was the bad one."

I couldn't believe what I was hearing. I couldn't imagine the kind little man who used to come to visit us on Sundays hurting anyone. He wouldn't hit Granny, she was too nice. She was so small and skinny, how could he have been so cruel to her?

I was stunned.

"So now you know, Jackie. I know what I'm talking about."

I became very determined. It was as if I'd gone on an assertiveness course. I became so confident, so sure I was going to get on in life.

I had two kids, I was a single mother, but so what, so were fucking hundreds of others. Thousands in this day and age. There were women walking down streets with five and six kids, all with different fathers, I was going to be as strong as them. I was going to get up off me arse and get a job, I didn't care what I did as long as it brought money in at the end of the week.

Ma would mind the kids, she'd said she would. Anyway, they were both at school now so there was no real minding on them.

I got a job as a cleaner. I hated it but it was better than nothing.

The mornings were a nightmare.

I got up at half past six, got the kids ready and left them over to me ma, she brought them to school. I barely had time to kiss them goodbye before I had to run. Run all the way from her house, down the road, around the corner and up to the roundabout. If I didn't run like an Olympic sprinter, I'd miss the bus.

I remember one morning the heel on me shoe broke but I had to keep running. I grabbed the shoe and ran in me bare foot all the way to the bus stop. I'd blisters on me foot for a week after that. But that didn't matter as long as I got me bus, and arrived at work on time.

Work! Now that was a fucking joke. Cleaning in a high-rise office block.

Going around all day cleaning the educated people's shite.

Sounds brilliant, doesn't it?

They were the dirtiest ignorant shower of fuckers I'd ever come across.

All the cleaning women started at the same time, we all had our own floors. We had to have everything finished by twelve and then another shift of cleaners took over. That's how dirty they were, even kids didn't need round-the-clock cleaning.

The job I hated most was cleaning the men's toilets. If you seen the way I had to clean the urinals, polish them as if they were the family china. And, despite the fact that I always left a bucket outside to let them know that I was inside, there was always some dirty bastard who ignored it.

He'd come in dressed to kill in his suit with his mickey hanging out. And he always made sure that I seen it, while he fumbled away. He'd never apologise, wouldn't dream of it.

After all, I was only a common cleaner.

One day a fella came in and told me not to mind him, just carry on, he said. Did he think I was fucking mad? I was to carry on cleaning while he pissed into the basin beside me.

I walked out mumbling under me breath about perverts.

No matter how much I hated the job, I couldn't give it up.

I really hated it when the supervisor came around. She'd point out all the places you'd missed. She'd say, "Are we asleep today? Or do we not think this window ledge needs polishing?"

She was a bitch. Showing off in front of all those snots. Trying to pretend that she was better than us, like she was one of them.

I'm not saying I was gorgeous but I wasn't bad-looking. And I think they used to make a laugh of me. I think they were of the opinion that all cleaners were middle-aged women with gansy-loads of kids. So if you were young, they immediately assumed that you were either a scrubber or an unmarried mother.

I used to see the girls laughing at me when the supervisor was giving out.

I'd see these little secretaries, jumped-up fucking nobodies, laughing. Ugly-looking, buck-teethed, fucking ponytailed, scraggy-haired bitches. I fucking hated them.

I also hated not having any money at the end of the week, not being able to get Jonathan or Edward some little present. So I put up with it, and worked till twelve every day.

Then I went home and tried to catch up on the washing and ironing and everything else that had to be done. I always tried to spend a bit of time with the kids because, despite the fact that I needed the money, I still felt guilty about leaving them. By the time they were in bed I was exhausted and I still had a night's work ahead of me.

I didn't sit down and watch telly, I still wasn't a *Coronation Street* fan. I took out me books.

I'd decided to do me Leaving Cert. I was going to educate meself at home. Books and tapes, that's how I was going to do it.

I knew it wasn't going to be easy but I was going to give it a try. And before long I started to enjoy it, I really did.

The only problem was the tiredness, I was knackered. Most nights I fell asleep on the couch, and when I'd wake up

I'd have to tidy everything away before I eventually got to bed.

Sometimes, when it all became too much, I'd call on me little friend to help me out.

I didn't call on her very often now, only the odd time. I'd stopped being dependent on vodka a long time ago. But every now and then, when I needed to relax, she'd be there.

Especially at weekends. They were the worst. The kids would be in bed by eight and the night would stretch out before me like a dark tunnel.

They were the nights when I'd think about Jeffrey, the nights when I'd think that maybe he hadn't been so bad.

The nights when I craved company so desperately that I'd have done almost anything to alleviate the loneliness, but I didn't. I called on me vodka instead.

I'd sit, vodka in hand, and think about me life, it always came back to Johnser, and that cheered me up. I'd wonder what life would have been like if things had worked out differently.

CHAPTER FORTY-ONE

I was going for me first meeting with the reform committee and had been told that I didn't stand a chance. I'd been inside four years and there was no way that someone serving a ten-year sentence for manslaughter would even be considered. They were only going through the motions.

But even so, as I sat there I couldn't help feeling a little bit hopeful. As I answered every question they threw at me, I remember thinking to meself, "Maybe one of them will take pity on me and decide I'm worthy of another chance."

But, needless to say, that didn't happen.

What annoyed me was that they, the reform committee, didn't even have the guts to tell me to me face. Reform committee, it was a fucking stupid name. It didn't sound right, what kind of a name was that? That wasn't the kind of name I'd give to people who held me freedom in their hands. I preferred the American name, the parole board. That had a certain ring to it, a certain attitude.

I'd heard through the grapevine long before I received the official letter and, even though I'd known deep down inside that I wouldn't be released, I couldn't help feeling totally pissed off at the decision.

That night, when I went back to me room (I always called

it me room because cell meant prison) I went berserk. I smashed the place to bits. I smashed up the bed, I took it apart and fucked it all over the place. And the tiny little basin that sat in the corner, I just gave that one kick and it shattered everywhere. I reefed the tap out of the wall and the water splurted up. It was like a water fountain spraying up in the air.

The screws came in, they were furious. It was the middle of the night and they wanted to take it easy, and here I was causing panic stations. One of them gave me a smack across the head, but I didn't give a fuck.

I grabbed him and pushed him against the wall, driving me knee full force into his stomach. I got him by the ear and bit, I bit as hard as I could until eventually I could taste his blood. I spat it across the room at the other two who were trying to stop the water.

I'll never forget the hiding I got that night. They kicked the fucking shite out of me, but I didn't care. I didn't care about anything any more.

Once they'd stopped the water they left.

They left me lying on the soaking mattress. I lay there all night, I couldn't move. I knew me arm was broken, I'd heard it crack, and me face felt ten times its normal size from all the punches I'd got. I was in bits.

For two weeks after that, every time they saw me they gave me a hiding. I couldn't really blame them. I mean, at the end of the day, it wasn't their fault that I hadn't got me parole.

But still, they shouldn't have fucked with me. No one fucks with Johnser Kiely and gets away with it.

Every time one of them hit me I threatened his family.

"Just yeh wait till I get out, I'll get yeh an' every member of yer fucking fambly. Just yeh fucking wait."

Eventually they stopped hitting me, and I stopped threatening them.

I'd been moved to a confinement cell while mine was being restored to its former glory. But I was back now and everything was more or less normal again.

I didn't fare any better on me second meeting with the parole board.

It was only eighteen months since I'd wrecked the place. So once again, even before I went into the office, I knew I hadn't a hope in hell of getting out.

Even so, you had to attend the hearings and explain why you thought you should be paroled. What were you supposed to say?

"Well, missus, it's like this. I haven't had a ride in five an' a half years an' I'm feelin a bit horny. So if yeh just sign the bit of paper in front of yeh, I'll be on me way."

For fuck's sake, what were they like? I mean, really, what did they expect you to say? The way I saw it was, it didn't matter what you said, you still wouldn't get out until they were ready to let you go.

Having to do without sex was one of the hardest parts of prison life.

Having been used to getting your hole on a regular basis and then getting nothing at all was enough to drive you mad. In fact, I think it did drive some fellas mad.

There was a lot of riding going on, a lot of bum-boys. Fellas who spent half their lives shagging women on the outside were now turning to other blokes for company.

I never got into it meself. I'd never be into that scene, no matter how desperate I was for a ride.

197

I remember one fella trying it on with me in the shower room and I kicked the crap out of him. I was sure I'd fucked up any last hope I might of had of early release, but what was I supposed to do? Anyway, I'd resigned meself to the fact that I wasn't going to get out one minute before me twelve years were up.

Parole visit number four.

I'd served eight of me twelve-year sentance when they finally decided that I was rehabilitated. I couldn't believe it, I was free.

Eight long hard years had come to an end and I was a free man again.

Johnser Kiely was free. Johnser Kiely was back.

CHAPTER FORTY-TWO

I stood outside the prison gates and took a deep breath. And, tucking me little bundle under me arm, I set off down the road. I never looked back.

There was a line of taxis waiting outside but I didn't want one, I wanted to walk, I wanted to savour every second of me new-found freedom.

When I got into the city I stood looking all around me like an American tourist. I kept taking long deep breaths, as if trying to prevent meself from hyperventilating. It felt great, I'd never appreciated fresh air so much in me life.

The quays were changed. It was all a one-way system now. I walked towards a bus stop looking at all the cars parked along the way and thought to meself, "Will I rob one? Will I arrive back in Ballyer in a BMW?"

But I thought better of it.

I got on a bus and headed home.

Even the buses were different, They were all one-man.

I got off the bus in Ballyer and went into a pub.

I sat down with me pint trying to get used to me freedom. It was a nice feeling and I was going to enjoy every minute of it.

I was back. I'd give it a couple of weeks to let the news circulate, let them all get used to the idea.

Johnser Kiely was back in business.

As soon as I'd finished me pint, I set off.

Some things never changed. The key was still in the front door, just like it had been when we'd all lived at home. So I let meself in. The aul fella was sitting in the kitchen with slut-head. He couldn't believe his eyes.

"Johnser!" he said, jumping up from his chair.

He looked different, he was clean-shaven, and sober. I couldn't fucking believe it.

I'd been wrong about him, I'd thought it was only a passing phase, but it wasn't, he had changed.

I knew now that if me aul fella could change, anybody could.

Even me.

I sat down and slut-head made me a dinner, it wasn't bad. I have to admit she was nice. She chatted away to me and I found meself chatting back.

Then the aul fella asked, "How's Tara? How's Tara an' the young one?"

The young one. He couldn't even remember her name.

"I don't know, Da. I haven't been up there yet."

"What? Was she not there teh meet yeh?"

"It's a long story, Da. Is there any chance of stayin here for a few days?"

Before he had a chance to answer, slut-head butted in.

"Of course yeh can, Johnser. After all, this is yer home."

I liked her for that. I liked the fact that she didn't hold it against me the way I treated her. She seemed to understand that it wasn't really her that I'd anything against. It was just that I didn't want her trying to take me ma's place.

"Thanks, Mary," I said.

She smiled.

I stayed with Da and Mary for a while. Eventually, it was time to move on. It was time to get back to work.

The first job I done, I done on me own. A little sweet shop, nothing amazing.

I bought a knife, twenty quid it cost me. A sharp little fucker, it would have cut the throat of anyone who came near me.

As I say, it was only a small shop on the northside of Dublin, so there was very little chance of me being recognised. But I wore a balaclava just the same, you never knew where they had those fucking video cameras nowadays. I wasn't taking any chances, I'd no intentions of ending up back inside.

So I ran in and held the knife to your man's throat.

"Gimme the fucking money."

He was shitting bricks in his hurry to open the till. I grabbed the money and ran.

One hundred and twenty-eight pounds. One hundred and twenty-eight scabby fucking pounds.

No way. I had to start doing bigger jobs.

I'd made a few good contacts in prison and decided it was time to check them out. I got in touch with some of them and we arranged to meet.

Before long, we became drinking buddies and met regularly. There was very little that went on that we didn't get to hear about. The other patrons of the pub kept us well-informed. Truck drivers and warehouse men were a great source of information.

We started doing big jobs.

You'd hear about them on the news. How the driver of a

forty-foot truck had been hijacked on the Naas road. How the poor fucker had been trussed up like a chicken and fucked in the back. How all the hi-fi gear had been robbed, and how he didn't know what had happened or who'd done it.

Once you were in the know and weren't greedy, you had no problem shifting the gear. There were always plenty of cash buyers willing to take cheap sound equipment.

The Brush was still running the biggest organisation in Dublin. I'd been told he wasn't too impressed when he'd heard that I was out and about again.

I decided that I was going to really get up his back, I was going to start doing the big bank jobs. His big bank jobs.

I was going to set him up.

The Brush had his own way of doing jobs, his own unmistakable style. Even the police knew when he'd set up a job. Unfortunately, they could never prove it. That is, until now.

I was going to be a copycat.

Like I say, the Brush always done the biggest jobs. So when I heard about the security van that was going to be carrying a serious amount of money, I knew he'd be making plans.

I knew his plan would be to hit the van as soon as it reached its destination.

What he didn't know was that the van was never going to arrive.

I was going to be well organised this time.

I had four men I knew I could trust. Four of the roughest pieces around, but they were level-headed. No maniacs this time.

They knew how to use a gun, they also knew how to hold one without letting it go off accidentally.

I knew what time the van would be leaving the depot, and I'd be there waiting.

The van arrived bang on time and stopped about ten feet from the shutter. They obviously felt very secure in their own surroundings because they weren't being overly cautious. They were casually loading the van when we made our move.

The security lights came on, but it was too late.

We were on them.

"Get down! Get fucking down."

I pushed the nozzle of me gun into one of the guy's stomach and he dived to the floor. Covering his head with his arms, he didn't want to see me. He knew that if he did his chances of staying alive would be very slim.

"I'm not lookin, I'm not lookin. Don't shoot, I didn't see anything."

I pointed me gun at another guy's head.

"Keep fucking loadin."

I looked over his shoulder and seen a stack of crates in the corner.

"What's that? What's in the fucking crates?"

No one answered.

I released the safety catch on me gun. I'd no intention of shooting anyone, but they didn't know that.

"Deyeh wanna die, yeh bastard? Tell me what's in the crates!"

The fella on the ground shouted, "Gold, there's gold in them."

I couldn't believe it. Gold. Jasus, this was better than anything I'd ever imagined.

"Mousy, over here, look after him."

I burst one of the crates open with the butt of me gun. A

small packet fell to the floor, no bigger than a ten-pack cigarette box. I picked it up and, sure enough, it was gold.

There was a fork-lift in the corner and I jumped into it. I lifted the crates and dropped them into the back of the van.

We were out of there.

We had to take the van because of the gold. But we'd a lock-up organised about five miles away.

The lock-up belonged to one of the lads and he'd assured me that no one knew of his association with it.

"Jasus, Johnser. Can yeh fucking believe it? What a bonus, three crates of gold on top of all the fucking money."

"Listen lads, I know yer not gonna like this but the thing is, we're not keepin the gold."

"What!"

The chorus was deafening. The van screeched to a halt.

"What deh fuck deyah mean, we're not keepin the gold?"

"Hold on, calm down. Just listen, listen for fuck's sake."

I knew this was going to be difficult but they had to be told.

"This is the way it is. I know the Brush was gonna be waitin for the van teh arrive at the bank. Now, what deh yeh think he's gonna do when it doesn't arrive? Go home an' put his feet up in front of the telly? I don't think so. So that leaves us with two options. One, we give him the gold an' we still have the money, split four ways as planned. Or two, we give him nothin an' he comes after us an' takes everything. The choice is yours."

There was silence. It lasted for what seemed like hours.

Eventually Mousy spoke.

"Right, OK. But he gets nothin fucking else. We keep all the money, an' we keep it in me lock-up."

"For fuck's sake, what deh yeh take me for? Yeh don't think I'd give him the fucking money as well? Now, do yeh?"

"Just makin sure."

"Well, what do yeh say?"

"How'll we get the gold teh Brush?"

"Leave that teh me."

"No fucking way, tell me how yer gonna do it or else the gold goes nowhere."

"OK, OK. For fuck's sake, talk about doubtin Thomas. We go teh the lock-up, unload the money, leave the gold on board, clean the van an' then I drive it teh one of Brush's lock-ups. Easy."

"How deh we know yeh won't do a runner with the gold?"

"Ah, Jasus Christ, what do yeh take me for? What deh fuck would I want with a load of gold bars I have no hope of shiftin when I've a ton of cash here waitin for me?"

"Yeah, well, OK then. We agree."

Things were going according to plan.

I was glad Brush's lock-up was only a few miles away. I mean, it wasn't as though I wanted to be driving halfway around the world in a security van. I found the lock-up easy enough. Opened it up (it's amazing what you can do with a hairclip), drove the van in, locked up and went about me business.

I know I hadn't been exactly honest with the lads, but fuck it, what difference did it make? It's not as though I'd double-crossed them, I hadn't, I'd just stretched the truth a bit. I'd wanted to set Brush up, they'd wanted the money, so now everyone was happy. They'd got their money and I'd got Brush.

The morning papers were full of the robbery.

The evening papers were full of Brush's arrest.

Who said that revenge wasn't sweet?

CHAPTER FORTY-THREE

There was nothing much happening in me life.

Yet there never seemed to be enough hours in the day to get through all the things I had to do. I didn't have time to be depressed any more. Besides, there was no point.

Sometimes I felt that me life was all a waste of time, it was going nowhere.

Me day consisted of . . . the kids, work, the kids, bed.

Don't get me wrong, I loved the kids to bits and wanted to spend all me time with them, but that didn't mean they didn't get on me nerves at times.

Take Jonathan, for instance. It wouldn't matter if I got him up at five in the morning, he wouldn't want to do his poo until we were walking out the door.

It was the same every morning, the minute I put his coat on he'd start.

"Ma, Ma quick, I have teh do me jobbies."

"Ah, Jonathan, not now, can't yeh wait till yeh get teh yer grannie's?"

But no, not Jonathan. Jonathan wouldn't do his jobbies anywhere other than at home.

"Well, hurry fucking up, then!"

He'd run into the toilet with his trousers down around his

ankles, holding the cheeks of his bum together as if it was about to come at any minute. He'd leave the door open, making sure he wasn't the only one to suffer the pong.

Christ, he was worse than a stink bomb. I swear that child had something dead inside him.

And as for the sound effects, "Oooh, aaah, eeeh, oooh." He sounded like he was trying to shite a football. I swear he did it on purpose.

I'd stand watching the minutes tick by, getting more and more frustrated with every tick.

"Jonathan, for Christ's sake, hurry fucking up!"

"Comin, Ma, just have teh clean me bum."

The cleaning of the bum took as long as the job itself. He'd peel layers and layers of paper off the roll, fold it neatly into little squares, at least four, then he'd begin his task.

I used to think to meself, how much fucking paper does it take teh clean an arse that size? Surely not the reams he uses.

"Jonathan, if yeh don't hurry fucking up I'll go in there an' redden yer arse for yeh."

I didn't want to seem mean, but expensive toilet tissue was one of the few luxuries I had left. I even cut back on me cigarettes so as I could afford it, and here was Jonathan wasting it.

I used to feel like screaming.

I tried hiding the good toilet rolls but that didn't work either. The trouble was, I'd always forget to bring me good paper with me when I had to go. And halfway through me business, when I remembered, I'd be caught in a dilemma.

Do I run to me room, knickers and tights around me ankles, and get the good stuff? Or do I suffer the sandpaper hanging beside me?

Even if I did remember to bring it with me, I'd forget to bring it out again. Result? Jonathan using a whole roll.

Eventually I stopped hiding it, it was pointless.

Finally he'd be ready and I'd have to run all the way to me ma's. The kids always dithered, and no matter how many times I'd checked their laces before we left the flat, I always had to stop and tie one. I swear they did it on purpose.

By the time I eventually got on me bus for work I was battered, bruised and breathless. I'd be hoarse from all me shouting at Jonathan and, of course, ridden with guilt for having done so. We had so little time together that I hated fighting with them. But what could I do? If I didn't shout in the mornings we'd never get out on time.

I felt very guilty about the kids and the life I'd forced upon them. The tiny flat they'd to live in, the lack of nice furniture, the lack of any decent toys to play with, everything. I felt guilty about taking them to Ma's every day, guilty for waking Edward up to take him home again, guilty because all I could ever afford to buy them was a tenpenny bag of sweets that I knew weren't going to do their teeth any good.

Guilty, guilty, GUILTY.

It was driving me mad.

Me friend Ann's husband reckoned I was starved of adult company.

"Don't be stupid, Tommy. Sure hasn't she got us an' her family? Aren't we all adults?"

"I don't mean us, I mean the quare thing."

Sex. That was Tommy's answer to everything. As far as he was concerned, riding was the remedy to all the world's problems.

Ask him what he thought about Maggie Thatcher and he'd tell you, "Ah, she needs a good slap of a mickey."

According to Tommy, there'd be no apartheid in South Africa if the frigid white bitches gave in to a bit of "Black Pudding".

He was always so graphic. There was no holding back with Tommy, he didn't mince words.

Slap of a mickey, riding, black pudding. He always said exactly what he thought.

"What yeh need's a good shag, do yeh the world of good. Why don't yeh come round when Ann's at the Bingo?"

"Yeh said a good shag, Tommy. So that rules you out," said Ann, not looking up from her ironing.

"Oh, very dry, Ann, very fucking dry." He was disgusted but he still didn't give up.

"Yeah, Jackie, I wouldn't mind rattlin yer bones. I'd say yeh wear them skimpy little knickers, the see-through ones, eh?"

"Fuck off, yeh dirty little pervert."

Ann said he was all talk, no action, but I don't know, I'd say he'd be game for anything given half the chance.

He was always making grabs at me. I'd be making a cup of tea and he'd sneak up behind me, and push himself up against me arse.

He always laughed, pretended it was a joke, but I knew it wasn't.

Still, when all was said and done, maybe he was right. I was missing a man, a partner, someone to share the ups and downs of me life with. And, yes, Tommy, every now and then I wouldn't have minded a good slap of a mickey.

209

CHAPTER FORTY-FOUR

The Brush went down. Twenty years, he got.

He was a broken man, he knew it was over for him now.

One day Blue arrived at me door, Tara and the young one in tow. "Yeh never told us yeh were gettin out."

"Yeh never fucking visited teh find out."

"I suppose yeh heard about Brush?"

"Yeah, I did. What deh yeh want me teh do? Cry?"

"Brush was a good man, he treated yeh well."

"Brush was a bollocks. He made a fucking eejit outta me, an' yeh know it. She even fucking knows it. So fuck off outta here, this has nothin teh do with me."

"Look, Johnser, I know all about the job an' I want a piece of it."

I laughed, I laughed straight into his ugly face. Did he honestly think I'd give him anything?

"Would yeh ever fuck off with yerself."

"Yeh owe me."

"I owe yeh fuck all, now get the fuck outta here before I break yer fucking legs."

"Brush isn't happy."

"I don't give a bollocks how happy Brush is. I couldn't care less if he cried every day of his poxy life. So, like I said before, get the fuck outta here an' take yer wagon of a daughter with yeh."

"Ah, Jasus, Johnser, don't be like that," she said, moving closer. I couldn't believe her nerve. She pushed the young one towards me.

"Say hello teh yer daddy, Tina. Ah, she's a bit shy," she said, turning to me. "Like her ma, ha ha ha."

I stood looking at her, she was mad. Mad as a fucking hatter.

Jasus, that laugh, no, it wasn't a laugh, it was more like a cackle, brought back memories.

Memories of the unforgettable honeymoon experience . . .

Like the day I went to get me paper. There was only one shop who sold English papers and that was in the hotel up the road. The fucking things were always a day late but I couldn't do without me racing pages and the soccer results. Although in Bermuda the page three lost some of its appeal. So there I was, strolling back along the beach, paddling me feet in the ocean, when I saw her. She was jumping around like a spring lamb chasing a volleyball. I stopped dead in me tracks –

"Tara!" She looked around –

"Ah, sorry, Johnser, you'll have teh wait till the next game. Yeh can see yerself that the sides are even."

As she turned to play her shot I grabbed her by the arm and walked her towards the beds.

"Ah, Johnser, it was me serve, ah, please, just one more shot?" . . .

"Jasus, Johnser, are yeh all right? You've gone a funny colour." The sound of her voice brought me back to the present.

"What exactly dey yeh want, Tara?"

211

"Well, Johnser, after all is said an' done, we're still a fambly."

"And?"

"An' I'm entitled teh some support."

"Tara, would yeh ever cop on, we've never been a family. So what the fuck is it yer really lookin for?"

"Jasus, Johnser, I never thought yeh could be so thick. I'm lookin for financial support."

"I'll give yeh financial support if yeh don't get the fuck outta here. You an' yer fucking aul fella."

I slammed the door.

"I'm entitled teh me alleymoney," she shouted through the letterbox. "I'm a deserted wife."

"Fuck off, Tara," I roared back at the letterbox.

"I'll see yeh in court, Johnser Kiely. Yeh little bollocks."

There was silence. I knew she was gone.

I leaned against the wall and laughed.

You'll be fucking lucky, I thought.

"Alimony, yeah, right, Tara." I said aloud as I made me way upstairs to the toilet.

She must have though I was loaded. If only she knew.

CHAPTER FORTY-FIVE

As I reached the safe house I knew immediately there was something wrong. A large cloud of orange dust hung in the air. I hurried forward. As I reached the gate it burst open, and out fell Mousey and the others. They were covered from head to toe in orange dye.

"Don't go in there, the fucking bags are booby-trapped."

"I can see that, yeh fucking two-faced bastard."

"What?"

"I thought we'd agreed teh wait?"

Mousey fidgeted nervously.

"We just wanted teh look at the money."

"Bollocks, yeh were cuttin me out."

I went to grab him, but just in time realised that I was the only one with no dust on me. They could all fuck off. I wasn't going to get a penny from the job but at least I was clean.

I turned and walked away.

"Johnser! What are we gonna do?"

I didn't even bother to stop.

"I don't know 'bout you, but I'm goin for a pint."

How unlucky can a man get? The papers were talking in terms of millions and here was me without a penny. I should have been the wealthiest fucker in Dublin, living it up. Instead, here I was living in Ballyer on handouts from me aul fella and his bit of skirt.

Still, at least I had me freedom, which is more than Brush had.

News of the job had spread like wildfire throughout the underworld. And it wasn't long before every scumbag I'd ever known was knocking on me door, all looking for a few bob.

They all knew about the job but none of them seemed to know how wrong it had all gone. One night while I was sitting in the pub, a complete stranger came up to me and stuck what felt like a gun into me side.

"Frankie Fitz wants teh see yeh."

I finished me pint, I wasn't going to jump for any bollocks. Regardless of whether he was holding a gun or not. We walked outside and sitting in a car across the road was Frankie.

As we walked towards the car, the stranger kept his gun pressed into me side.

"If yeh don't get that gun outta me ribs I'll fucking kill yeh."

I got into the car, and Frankie came straight to the point. The IRA wanted their cut. And, as an associate of theirs, he was here to collect. I tried explaining about how the job had gone wrong, but it was useless. Eventually I lost the head –

"Lookit, Frankie, how many times do yeh have teh be told, I've no fucking money. But yeh don't have teh take my word for it, ask anyone who was involved in the job."

"I don't care what yeh say, Johnser. Yeh done the dirt on

me inside, an' yer not gettin the chance teh do it again. I'm givin yeh twenty-one days . . . that's three weeks . . . "

"I know how long it fucking is."

"Three weeks, an' I'll be back to collect our cut. Don't disappoint me."

I didn't bother answering, there was no point. There'd be other days, days when I wouldn't have a gun stuck in me side. That's when I'd sort them all out.

CHAPTER FORTY-SIX

I decided that life was passing me by.

Ann and Tommy were right. I needed a life away from the kids.

Teaching meself at home was all very well, but at the end of the day, I had to admit that I wasn't getting any younger. I'd have to start putting meself forward more.

Of course, I wasn't going to walk into a pub on me own and, though I enjoyed Ann and Tommy's company (well, Ann's anyway), I was a firm believer that three is a crowd.

The girls, us cleaners, were all great crack. It was like a big deserted wives' club, and even the girls with husbands never disagreed with our motto, "All men are bastards". The only advantage they had over a vibrator was that they could buy a round of drinks.

Nights out with the girls were a riot. Once I'd got over the guilt of leaving the kids (it was only a few hours once a week), I really began to enjoy meself. It gave me an inner confidence, something I hadn't had since me days with Johnser.

We'd head out dressed up to the nines and take over the pub.

We took our revenge on the whole of the male population,

216

on all the fuckers who looked down on us when we were wearing our blue smocks. When we were in our blue smocks, they treated us like dirt. Shut doors in our faces as we struggled to get through with our buckets and mops. Now that we were glammed up, it was a different story.

I'm not saying that the supermodels had hit town, but we cleaned up well. And the one thing we all agreed was that, no matter what, we'd never let on that we were cleaners. You could be anything you liked, as long as you weren't a cleaner.

You could be the first sixteen-stone air hostess, the first Irish woman to work for NASA, a Bond girl. And the gobshites believed every word, just like we believed every word they said. So there we were, the sixteen-stone air hostess from Oliver Bond talking to the brain surgeon from Stonybatter. The silent partner in the Body Shop talking to the black sheep of Ireland's richest family.

It was amazing how all these would-be celebs were gathered in this kip of a pub. But it didn't matter, it didn't matter how full of crap we were, it passed the night. It was light entertainment. It wasn't as though any of us were going to fall down and the brain surgeon would be called upon to do his stuff. It was fun, stupid childish fun. And the next day, as we relived the antics of the night before, it helped to relieve the boredom of our work.

We'd be in tears at the break, literally. The tears would be rolling down our faces. You'd swear we were peeling onions.

"Jackie, what did yer man say he did for a livin?"

"He said he was the elephant trainer in the Zoo."

They all laughed.

"That's right, an' yeh asked him was there any chance of him gettin a bucket of shite for yer ma's roses."

217

We'd be nearly pissing ourselves laughing.

" . . . An' listen, shurrup for a minute, listen. He said there'd be no problem, he'd bring it with him tenigh if I promised teh meet him."

"Jasus, can yeh imagine the smell of him sittin on the bus."

We just laughed and laughed.

Even the snotty supervisor coming in and ordering us back to work didn't bother us as much as she usually did.

Every now and then, when our hormones were really acting up, we'd go on a serious manhunt. We must have frightened the life out of many a fella on those nights. We were like a pack of wolves in heat and our language was atrocious.

"Jasus, lookit the arse on yer man."

"What I'd do if I got me hands on that."

"It's not me hands I'm thinkin 'bout gettin on him."

"Yer a scruffy wagon, Catty Simpson."

"Shurrup you, Ger Byrne. When were yeh fucking canonised?"

To anyone listening I'm sure it sounded as if the girls were about to reef the hair out of each other. But we knew different, it was only harmless slagging.

"Hey you, would yeh like me teh save yeh a trip teh the sperm bank?"

"Howd yeh like teh use fifty pence worth o' rubber on me?"

And on and on it went all night. How we got away with some of the things we said to those fellas, I'll never know.

We knew all about the dangers of casual sex, but when the drink got into your bloodstream and your hormones were dragging at your knickers, wanting to get out and ravage the nearest fella, it was hard to think about safety. We were all on the pill so there was no fear of us becoming pregnant, but we all swore that, in order to protect ourselves against disease, we'd never do it without a rubber. Needless to say, there were many nights when we did.

Robert was gorgeous. He was like a model, tall, dark and handsome. Don't ask me what label his clothes were, it had been years since I'd read a fashion magazine and I didn't know the difference between Armani or Arnott's. But I knew what I liked and it was standing twenty yards away from me at the end of the bar.

We all agreed, he was a ride.

"I'd let him eat chips outta me knickers any day," Cathy informed us lustfully.

"Yeah, an' put the salt in me belly button," added Ann.

"Here, you," I said. "Yer supposed teh be happily married."

"I am, but I wouldn't climb over him teh get teh our Tommy."

We couldn't take our eyes off him. We had him stripped naked in five minutes and, every time one of us spoke, his mickey grew another inch. By the time we were finished it should have been the length of his leg.

When we were eventually thrown out of the pub we headed to a disco. It was the first Tuesday of the month and we'd got our children's allowance and had decided to treat ourselves to a late night. It was ladies' free night and everyone knew that, where the ladies went, the men would follow.

They seemed to think that free night meant free ride, and if we were randy enough they were right, if not, they could fuck off. The bouncers knew us well.

"Howyeh girls, back again?"

"Yeah, that's right." Cathy would say. "Back teh spend our mickey money."

This always got a laugh. But that's what it was known as, mickey money. Money for having babies.

Once we'd organised the drinks and found a seat, we'd make our way on to the dance floor. We'd dance around our handbags until some fella came over and asked one of us up.

I always thought it was a fucking stupid thing to ask. I mean there you were standing in the middle of the dance floor and he'd come over and say –

"Are yeh gettin up?"

Getting up where? Up on the roof, the stage? Surely he could see that you were up, standing on your own two feet. It sounded so fucking stupid.

After that it was like ten green bottles, every time you looked around there was another one gone and you prayed that you wouldn't be the last green bottle left sitting on the wall.

Nine times out of ten, Cathy was the first to fall. It was always hard to figure out who'd made the first move. The song wouldn't even be over and you'd see them in the corner wearing the face off each other, and you'd know that very soon they'd be making their way to the carpark to do in private what they couldn't very well do in public.

He appeared out of nowhere. I looked up and there he was, standing in front of me, swilling his pint in his hand. Jasus, he was gorgeous, even the way he held his pint was yummy. What was I like? That was the kind of thing the kids would say about a cream cake. But he was yummy, he was like a big cake, with lots of extra cream and cherries and . . . Jasus, Jackie, get a grip . . . for fuck's sake, he's only a man.

"Do yeh want a drink?"

"Yeah, vodka an' orange," I croaked.

So there is a God after all, I thought, as he went to get the drink.

He came back and sat down.

"What's yer name?" he asked.

After that, the time seemed to fly. We talked about everything (at least I did), but he didn't seem to mind. I told him I was a cleaner and for the first time ever I wasn't ashamed of what I done for a living. Every now and then, I'd say, "I'm sorry, I'm borin yeh."

But he'd just smile, kiss me hand and say, "No, not at all, Jackie, you're the most interesting person I've ever met."

Jasus, I thought I'd died and gone to heaven. He certaintly knew how to make a girl feel good about herself, he said all the right things at the right time. It was great, he was great.

Ger came over with her latest catch, some fella who looked old enough to be her granda.

"Jackie, you'll be all right, won't yeh? If I take a lift off me new friend." She looked at him, waiting for him to give his name but he was past remembering.

"Go on, I'll be grand," I assured her.

She looked Robert up and down, making sure he knew exactly what she was thinking.

"I want all the juicy details temorra, right?" And she was gone.

We watched as she staggered across the room towards the door.

"Mind how yeh go, Ger. Yeh don't wanna be gettin a rise in yer mickey money." The bouncer laughed as he opened the door for her.

221

Robert looked at me quizzically.

"Mickey money?"

"It's what we call our children's allowance."

All of a sudden the lights came on and the bouncers were shouting for us to leave. Where had the time gone? How come the nights you spent at home on your own or the hours you spent in work always seemed to drag by? Yet the minute you met someone nice and wanted the time to drag, it flew by.

"Com' on, Jackie, have yeh no car teh go teh?"

I laughed but Robert wasn't amused

We walked, his arm around me, to his car.

The minute we were inside he kissed me, his hands moving quickly to the buttons on me blouse. I pulled away.

"So tell me 'bout you, I've been so busy yakkin on all night and yeh haven't told me a thing about yerself."

He moved closer, his hands homing in on me tits.

Jasus, Robert, slow down, I thought. It's waiting for you but don't rush it.

Again I pulled away.

"So how come yeh aren't married?"

He was all over me, like a bad rash.

"Please don't ruin this, slow down," me mind screamed.

He mumbled something into me neck, still struggling with me buttons.

"What? What did yeh say?"

It was like wrestling with an octopus.

"I'm married."

I pushed him away.

"Yer what . . . "

"Don't start playin fucking games. Yeh must've known I was married. Anyway, what difference does it make?"

But I hadn't. I know it sounds stupid, and I'm sure everyone else in the disco knew he was married, but I swear to God I didn't. Of course he was married, did I honestly think that someone who was single and as gorgeous as him would be interested in me? Of course not, how could I have been such a gobshite?

I was numb, and while I sat there being numb he was still dragging at me blouse. He couldn't get the buttons open so he ripped it. I panicked.

"Fuck off."

His hands pulled at me bra and me tits fell out. He grabbed them and it hurt.

I tried to pull away but he was too strong for me. I started screaming.

"Shurrup, yeh slut," he hissed.

He was pulling at me skirt now, tearing me good skirt that had cost me £10.99 in a half-price sale. Jasus, was I going mad? Here I was just about to be raped and all I could think about was me skirt. Even if it was me favourite, it still wasn't worthy of me thoughts at this minute.

He was talking a mile a minute and I was only catching bits of what he was saying.

"Yeh fucking slut, yeh think yer so fucking smart, when all yeh are is a piece of shite. You're nothin, deh yeh hear me? Nothin. You're a fucking scrubber, yeh clean piss for a livin, that's all you're good for, you're a nobody."

He slapped me.

"Are yeh listenin? Lookit yeh, what are yeh like? I'm

223

doin yeh a favour by being with yeh, deh yeh understand that?"

I tried to do something, say something, shout, anything, but nothing happened. He had me seat right back and he was on top of me fumbling with his zip.

"No, please don . . . " But he wasn't listening, he was like a crazed animal. And I remember thinking to meself. This is it, Jackie, you're gettin a slap of a mickey whether yeh like it or not.

CHAPTER FORTY-SEVEN

Following the cease-fire in the North, most IRA divisions had been disbanded. Frankie could say what the hell he liked about the IRA but I knew he was out on his own now.

The IRA weren't interested in the likes of me any more. The disbanding of their army brought a whole new criminal element to the streets of Dublin. A whole bunch of hard necks, gurriers who were used to terrorising people and weren't going to stop because of a cease-fire. Deep down they had a passion for violence, this was probably the reason they'd joined the IRA in the first place.

Drugs had taken over the city. It hadn't been like this in the old days. OK, we'd had the bit of gongie and there'd been the odd coke-head, but nothing like this. Every street corner, every road, every patch of waste ground had its own dealer. You could spot them a mile away, they all dressed the same, all wore the same shell track suits and baseball caps. They looked like the gangs you seen in those rap videos on telly, giving each other high fives and talking all "Yo" and "Man". They were always ready to deal.

I hated them all, but this was where the money was. If you weren't dealing, you were nothing. Everything was dictated by drugs, and you had to know all the slang names.

People who I'd always thought of as level-headed now weren't able to get out of bed in the morning without a fix.

I realised that, if I wanted to stay on top, I had no choice but to join them.

I'd no intention of doing drugs but I'd every intention of supplying them.

I needed money, I needed something that was going to give me a quick turnover. Robbing was no longer an option, every poky little shop in the country was fitted with a security camera.

Druggies are a breed unto themselves, a shower of fucking wasters, the lot of them. But there was plenty of money to be made. Buy ten thousand pounds worth of heroin from Holland and, by the time you sold it on the street, you were a little millionaire.

I had to get meself a crash course on how to speak the druggie lingo. I stopped using words like gongie and started using words like grass, dope, pot and black. It wasn't called LSD any more: it was acid, tabs, lucy, rhubarb. Ecstacy was E, burgers, Dennis the Menace, brownies and love doves. Cocaine was crack, rock, C, Charlie, coke, dust. Heroin was China White, it was dragon, H, skeg and smack.

You even had to know the names of the amphetamines. Speed, whizz, sulph and uppers.

There was a hundred different ways of taking the stuff. Cannabis could be smoked or chewed. LSD was swallowed, so was Ecstasy. Cocaine was sniffed or injected or, as crack, it was smoked. Heroin could be smoked, sniffed, injected or inhaled. And the amphetamines were swallowed or injected.

Personally, I didn't give a fuck how they took them. I didn't care about highs or lows.

All I cared about was that if they were buying drugs they

were buying them from me. I remember thinking, how the fuck can they do this to themselves? How can anybody let themselves get into such a state? Having to spend two hundred pounds a day just to feel normal?

Luckily for me, I didn't have to deal in person very often. I had others to do the dirty work. I paid the bouncers on the clubs to do the dealing. They were perfect, they met everybody on the way in. They could tell just by looking at you whether you were into gear or not, and if so, what it was.

I'd most of the inner city clubs, the good ones. I was making plenty of money but I was greedy, I always wanted more.

I had me own apartment. I'd paid cash up front, none of that mortgage crap for me.

I knew that the neighbours looked down their noses at me but I didn't give two fucks about them. I didn't talk to them and they didn't talk to me, that kept everyone happy.

The only thing I missed was a laugh. I was earning loads of money but I wasn't having any fun. I seemed to have lost me sense of humour, I couldn't remember the last time when I'd had a bit of *craic*. Everywhere I went people knew me, they knew I wasn't to be messed with, with the result they were always on their best behaviour. They seemed to think that, just because I had a hard man reputation, they weren't allowed to laugh when in me company. Maybe they were right, maybe it was my fault.

I didn't trust anyone, so I suppose that made them nervous.

And let's be honest, who's going to start cracking jokes with you if they think you''re about to beat the crap out of them? People thought that I had it all, and they were right to a certain degree, I had all the money I needed but I had no friends. And friends were the one thing I needed more than anything else.

I couldn't go to a club because I knew that, if the police heard about it, there'd be a raid, and if they found drugs on the premises, I'd be a goner.

Even the pub had lost its appeal. I knew that the minute I walked in the atmosphere would change. Fellas would be over making small talk and offering to buy me pints. I wasn't big-headed enough to think it was because they liked me, I knew it was because they were afraid of me and wanted to keep on me good side.

There were times when I really wanted to give the whole thing up, but I couldn't. I mean, what else could I do? How would I earn a living? Like I said before, who in their right mind was going to offer me a job? So, at the end of the day, I'd no option other than to continue what I was doing.

Frankie Fitz reared his ugly head again and started threatening me. He knew fucking well what had happened to the money, it was the joke of the century in the underworld, but that didn't seem to matter to the bastard. I'd warned him to stay out of me face, stay out of me way and stay out of me life, but I knew I wasn't going to get rid of him that easy. He started going on about the drugs racket that I had, and how, if I hadn't got any money from the robbery, he'd take a share of what I made dealing. I'd no intention of sharing anything with him, I owed him fucking nothing and I told him so. He just smiled.

He glanced over at the two heavies he'd brought with him. Obviously they'd been brought along to intimidate me.

"Am I supposed teh be afraid of you an' yer heavies? Don't think for one minute that you an' them two eejits will get the better of me. If I decide that I want a partner, then I'll get a partner but it certainly won't be you. So why not take yerself an' yer two gorillas an' get the fuck off me patch, OK?"

"No, it's not OK, Johnser. Yeh have two choices, yeh either play ball with us or suffer the consequences."

I pushed him against the wall.

"Fuck you an' yer consequences, do yer worst, but I'm tellin yeh this. If yeh come after me, yeh better do a good job cause if I live teh tell the tale, I'll come after you. An' yeh can be guaranteed I'll put a fucking bullet through yer head."

He laughed as he made his way to the door.

"Maybe a bullet isn't such a bad idea. Good luck, Johnser."

The police never let up. Morning, noon and night, they were there. Always looking, always searching. They'd arrive in the middle of the night with a search warrant and there was nothing I could do about it. If they seen me in the street, they'd pull me in for a "little chat" as they called it.

But I'd just sit staring at a spot on the wall the way Brush had taught me. I'd always be grateful to him for that.

They never got anything, I never kept gear in the flat or carried it on me. I had a lock-up where I done all me dealing.

There was no shortage of women either. They were another thing that came with the territory. Granted, they were only one-night stands, but that suited me, that's all I wanted.

I was never foolish enough to think that it was me expertise between the sheets they were interested in, it was the name Johnser Kiely that turned them on. When I was younger this kind of reaction would have delighted me, but not now. Now I saw it for what it was, stupid ego.

I'd no feelings for these women. I'd take them home and fuck them, end of story. That's the way it was for me, it was only a ride, nothing more, nothing less.

I often thought about Jackie, wondered how she was getting on.

Once or twice I even thought about getting in contact, I'd have had no problem finding out where she lived, but then I'd think, no, leave her alone, you've done enough damage to that girl. She was the only woman I'd ever respected, she was the one person I knew who'd made something of her life, and I wasn't going to fuck it up on her.

Let's be honest, that's the one thing I had a real talent for. Fucking up people's lives. What was it about me? Why was it that every person who came in contact with me seemed doomed to a life of failure?

I mean, look at Tara. I know she wasn't the most reliable person on the planet, but still, she deserved better than I'd given her. Then there was Fat Larry. I'd seen him lately and he was three times fatter than I'd remembered, Jasus, he was a sight. I'm not saying I was responsible for the way he was, cause I wasn't, but he was another one who'd been a part of me life for a while. Not one of the lads I'd hung around with when I was younger had turned out any good.

We'd all ended up in trouble with the law.

Take the Brush. He'd been the top criminal in Dublin for years, the police couldn't touch him. Enter Johnser, and wham. He was locked up for twenty years.

The last I'd heard of Jackie was that she'd married some posh bloke and they were doing really well for themselves.

No matter how much I wanted to see her, I knew I couldn't. I'd no intention of ruining her life a second time.

Besides, what had I to offer her? What was I supposed to say?

"Look, Jackie, look at me, aren't I great? I'm the biggest drugs baron in Dublin. Come and live the life of luxury with me on the money I earn from other people's misery."

I didn't think so. Better to leave well enough alone.

I often wished I was back in the good old days. I know that back then I was only a hard man with no money. A great goer, as they called it. I'd still had respect, but more importantly than that I'd had *craic*. No matter how bad things were, we always had a laugh, we laughed at anything in those days. But not any more, life was far more serious these days.

I mean, how could you possibly expect to exert your authority if you were seen giggling like a schoolboy at every smutty joke you heard?

Even so, I missed not being able to giggle like a schoolboy. It was as if someone had put up a big notice saying, "No laughing, you're in the big boy's league now."

It was all becoming too much for me and I can honestly say that, if there'd been a way out, I'd have took it, but there wasn't. And I knew it.

I could never be Joe Soap on a factory floor, or somebody's gofer on a building site. Could you imagine me? Imagine me trying to mix a mountain of cement for some brickie and him mouthing off because I wasn't going fast enough. I'd end up fucking throttling him and that'd be the end of me career as a builder.

There was no way out. Well, no way that I was prepared to take. Could I honestly give up the apartment, the car, the money, the status? Was I really prepared to live on the breadline like so so many families I knew? And besides, what woman would want me? All I'd have to offer would be a life of constant struggle because I'd be on the dole. Not because of the unemployment situation, but because I was unemployable. So tell me, what woman in her right mind was going to jump for joy at being given an opportunity like that? Not too many. Anyway, like I said before, I was greedy.

The drugs market was thriving, I was making money hand over fist, and deep down inside I knew, I knew that I wasn't a strong enough person to throw it all away.

Despite what some people might have you believe, it wasn't just the under-privileged who took drugs. The reason people take drugs has very little to do with how or where they live. People from all walks of life take them.

The only thing that separates the classes is that someone from Ballyer has to rob to finance his habit. Snobs don't have to, because rich daddy will pay, but to me, they were all the same. They were all scum. Fuck it, what's the difference between fiddling your company expense account and robbing a till? None, it's all robbing. In fact, fiddling your expenses is worse. As far as I was concerned, the fella who robbed a till didn't have a choice. He'd no job, no money. The fucker fiddling the company probably had a good job, a company car and lived in a big poxy house. And still he wasn't happy. Still he wanted more, the greedy little fucker.

So as far as I was concerned, it didn't matter where they came from, they were all scum. Because, sooner or later, the money would run out and the innocent people would suffer, they always did.

I had no illusions about meself. I was as bad, if not worse, than the addicts. I was the supplier. So, in a roundabout way, I was the cause of the mileage being fiddled, I was the cause of the people being beaten up, I was the cause of the video being stolen. I was the cause of a lot of things. But, just like the addicts, there was nothing I could do about it. I couldn't give it up.

This was the career I'd chosen. This was my life.

CHAPTER FORTY-EIGHT

It was just another Tuesday night and the phone hadn't stopped ringing. I'd just had a call from one of the bouncers telling me that some other dealer was trying to move in on one of me clubs, but he'd seen him off. I told him I'd see him later and hung up. I thought that maybe it wouldn't do any harm to drop him a few bob, it always paid to show that you appreciated their loyalty.

So like I say, it was just another Tuesday night.

I was restless and sat flicking through the channels on me satellite television. I found an old Hitchcock film and soon became engrossed in it. I loved Hitchcock films, everything about them was classic, especially the way he always made an appearance himself. I loved waiting for Alfred to make his cameo.

I remember as a kid I'd be scared shitless watching his films. I remember the one about the birds, fucking hell, I was petrified of pigeons for months after.

I'd seen them all at least ten times but I still thought they were great.

Before I knew it it was half past two, I'd have to hurry if I wanted to catch the bouncers before they went home. I was no more in the humour for going out, but still, I'd better make an effort, it wouldn't do to have them think I wasn't grateful.

So I grabbed me jacket and headed to the car.

The carpark was empty except for two or three stragglers. This always amazed me. After all, it was Tuesday and most people had work the next day. How they managed to get out of their beds by seven or eight in the morning was a mystery to me.

As I walked towards the back door of the nightclub, a light in the corner of the carpark caught me eye, I could see the outline of what looked like a man and he seemed to be beating something. I slowed momentarily. It's probably a domestic, I thought, and I'm not getting involved in one of them. I was just about to turn away when I heard the scream. I ran towards the car.

* * *

Robert, lovely Robert, yummy Robert, wasn't taking no for an answer. He was starting to lose it. His voice was harsh and frightening, full of hate, the voice of someone losing control. The slaps were becoming more frequent, he was hurting me, his hands tearing roughly at me body. I was crying, angry, sick, frightened, I was everything at once. I thought about the kids and panicked.

This bastard could kill me, what would happen to me kids then?

Don't struggle, calm down and stop trying to fight him, I told meself. Think of the kids. Just give him what he wants and he'll go, come on, Jackie, stay calm.

So I lay there thinking about me kids. I didn't care if he threw me out of the car half naked and left me with spunk running down me legs, I just wanted it to be over. I wanted him to stop hitting me.

How would I explain the bruises to me ma? Jasus, the things you think about in a crisis.

His fingers were pulling me open and he was pushing his thing against me, trying to enter, but in his haste he was missing the spot. He was getting really frustrated, he raised his hand and I closed me eyes, waiting for its arrival on me face, but it never came.

I heard a click and opened me eyes. His arm was suspended in midair, held there by the hand of another man.

Oh, sweet Jasus, not a gang-bang.

I must have blacked out for a few seconds because the next thing I seen was Robert being dragged from the car by some man.

Suddenly recognition dawned.

This wasn't some man. It was Johnser.

* * *

As I made me way to the car, me only thought was to get this bloke to stop beating the woman inside.

I didn't give a shite what his reasons were, but I wasn't going to stand by while he beat the crap out of some bird. I'd no grievance with this bloke. In fact, I could sympathise with him. I knew how difficult it was to hold back, women could really get you riled, and nine times out of ten I swear they done it on purpose. They'd push and push, wanting to see how far they could go before you finally snapped.

That didn't mean I condoned violence against women.

Even the smallest man was physically stronger than most women, so there was no competition.

I didn't particularly want to get involved in someone else's argument, but at the same time I felt he'd made his point by now. I was going to tell him to give it up and leave her alone.

I tried the door and it opened. Instinctively I grabbed his arm.

"Come on, mate, give it a rest, nothin personal . . . "

Then she called me name.

That made it different, now it was personal.

I dragged him out of the car, he was shouting at me, "Fuck off an' mind yer own business!"

I threw him up against the bonnet.

"Come on, let's see how yeh handle yerself against someone who hits back."

He tried to pull away, but I head-butted him and his nose exploded. After that I lost it. Every time I thought about him hitting Jackie I went berserk.

He tried to get under the car, but I pulled him back out and kicked the living daylights out of him. If the bouncers hadn't pulled me off him when they did, I swear I'd have fucking killed him.

* * *

I sat in the car and watched as Johnser beat the life out of Robert. It was like watching a film, you see everything that's going on but you have no control over it.

I started shivering and suddenly became aware of me near nakedness. While Robert had been in the car torturing me, me lack of clothing had been the least of me worries, but now it seemed like the only thing that mattered.

I pulled up me torn knickers and fixed what was left of

me torn skirt down over me legs. The buttons had been ripped from me blouse, so all I could do was wrap it across me chest.

I couldn't stop shivering, I was freezing. I seen a jumper on the back seat and pulled it on, it made no difference, nothing could make me feel warm.

Robert was slithering around on the ground. Just like the snake he was.

Johnser was kicking him and every kick sent Robert in a different direction. Still, he made no attempt to get to his feet.

Me mind went back to years ago, to the first time I'd ever seen Johnser.

It was a Friday night outside Sergeant Pepper's disco. Someone had shouted, "Millee" And suddenly there he was, Johnser Kiely. The man I was to worship for years, the man who'd cause me heartache and pain because of his rejection of me.

Life had a strange way of evening things out.

Now someone else was suffering pain. Granted, a different kind of pain, but he was suffering it because of my rejection of him.

So here we were again. Johnser beating the crap out of someone. Me falling in love.

The bouncers pulled Johnser away, but Robert didn't move, he just lay on the ground. Johnser was kicking and screaming, telling them what Robert had done, all the time trying to break free from their hold.

The bouncers were doing their best to restrain him, while trying to explain that if he killed this low life, he'd only end up back inside.

"For fuck's sake, Johnser, leave him be, we'll deal with him. You get yerself offside."

"OK, OK, get yer fucking hands off me."

Where it came from I'll never know, but as he walked over to the car he suddenly lashed out with a chain, and the only thing I heard was the sound of breaking glass.

"Jasus, Johnser! Gimme that." The bouncer was on him again.

"Yer doin yerself no favours hangin around here. Gimme the fucking chain and get lost."

Johnser pulled me gently from the car.

"Come on, Jackie, we're goin home."

He put his arm around me and led me slowly to his car.

He brought me home to me flat and quickly got rid of the baby-sitter while I pretended to be in a hurry for the toilet. We went into the kitchen and he made tea. And tea and more tea, until it was coming out me ears. In between cups of tea, I cried, sobbed me eyes out, I couldn't help it. He held me close.

"Sssh Jackie, don't cry. You're all right, I'm here now an' no one's ever gonna hurt yeh again."

I found meself telling him everything. I told him about Jeffrey, about his gambling and the beatings. But, most importantly of all, I told him what had happened that night. And for only the second time in our lives, we sat in each other's arms and watched the sun rise.

I walked him to the door of the flat.

"Can I see yeh tonigh?"

"I don't know, Johnser, I don't really want teh leave the kids two nights in a row."

"Well, temorra then?"

"I only go out once a week."

"Ah, come on, Jackie."

"I don't know . . . "

239

"I'll ring yeh."

"NO." It sounded harsher than I'd meant it.

"I'm sorry, I didn't mean it like that. I've no phone."

Everything seemed to be getting on top of me. It was obviously the lack of sleep and the thought of facing me ma. The kids mightn't notice anything wrong, but she would. On top of all that, I still had a day's work ahead of me. Christ.

"Can I ring you, Johnser?"

He handed me a card. I read it and smiled.

"Oh, la-de-da, we have come up in the world."

"Fuck off you, Jackie Clarke."

I tried to hide the bruising with make-up, but I wasn't sure whether it had worked. I needn't worry, I'd soon be standing on me ma's doorstep, and the look on her face would give me me answer.

CHAPTER FORTY-NINE

After that night I couldn't get Jackie out of me mind.

Every waking moment was filled with her. From the back of me mind would come memories of years ago. Things we'd done together, things she'd said to me, things I'd said to her . . . stupid things . . . things that made me feel good.

I'd wake up in great humour thinking, I wonder if she's awake yet. Obviously she was, cause I rarely woke before noon.

There was no point in me getting up early, me business associates (for fuck's sake, Johnser, stop fooling yourself), OK then, junkies, wouldn't be surfacing yet. And the few that had would be busy getting the price of their next fix.

With every hour that passed I'd find meself wondering, what's she doing now? Is she collecting the kids from school? etc, etc. Amazingly enough, these thoughts always made me feel good inside.

When she'd told me that her marriage hadn't worked out, I'd been genuinely sorry. If it had been anyone else I wouldn't have given a fuck, but I knew she'd have given her all, she'd have fought tooth and nail to keep it alive. I also knew that she'd blame herself, even though it wasn't her fault. She'd told me all about posh Jeffrey and how he'd gambled everything they'd had. Worst of all, she'd told me about how the bastard used to beat her.

I swear to God, if I ever got me hands on him, I'd leave him for dead. But he was a cute fucker, no one had set eyes on him since she'd fucked him out.

I'd see her face everywhere, not the face of the other night, but the one that had helped me through many a lonely night in prison.

Her straight black hair that she always wore in a fringe (the way Kiki Dee had worn hers when she'd sang that song with Elton John), her blue eyes that were always ready to smile, her perfectly white teeth. The teeth that she always felt the need to cover up because they weren't as straight as they might have been. I used to tell her that she'd lovely teeth but she always thought I was taking the piss.

"Fuck off, Kiely, lookit yer own bleedin fangs," she'd say.

And her body, the body that hadn't changed much even after two kids. I remember the time she'd come to see me in prison, thinking to meself, Jasus, she looks great, what I wouldn't give for a ride. And she did, look great, I mean.

She'd filled out in all the right places. Her tits were bigger than I remembered, so was her arse. She'd a little bit of a belly that she hadn't had before, but it was nice. She must have seen me looking at it, cause all of a sudden she'd sat up dead straight and it was gone. She'd always been paranoid about her belly. Even when she hadn't got one, she was the only woman I knew who could sit, talk, eat and drink while holding her belly in.

And her legs still looked great, there was a bit more meat on them now but that made them look all the more shapely.

To me she was still a fine thing, she was still a ride. She

was still the same girl who'd got off the eighteen bus all those years ago.

I'm not been big-headed but I could've got better looking birds. Young ones, with silicone tits that defied the laws of gravity and skin so tight you could see every bone in their face. Dressed to kill in the latest fashions and prepared to try everything they'd ever seen on Dr Love's video.

Love video me arse, it was porn with posh voices. Just because they didn't show a Swedish bird talking flur-de-flur, and walking around with her size 38D's hanging out, didn't mean it wasn't porn. Did we really need a doctor to tell us that the girl with the mickey in her mouth was giving the Brad Pitt look-alike a blowjob? No.

But anyway, like I say, I'd had them all. It was like being a celebrity, and like all celebrities, I got bored. I craved the normal things in life, like a bus journey, a big fry and Jackie.

I started having little daydreams. No, not the horny ones you'd expect me to have, but nice ones, romantic ones. Jasus, I had it bad.

I'd always thought of fellas who were romantic as puffs. I used to think that I'd rather be run over by a train than be seen holding a bird's hand in public. That romance was just a cover-up for being gay.

And now here I was, thinking about doing things like hiring a limo and driving up to Jackie's singing "Two outta three ain't bad", climbing up her fire escape and asking her to be me pretty woman.

While down below us a wino would be stumbling across the road shouting, "Welcome to Dublin, the land of equal opportunity, where all your dreams come true."

God, I never realised how much love could change a man.

Still, she had me number and she'd said she would get in touch as soon as she was ready. All I could do was wait.

* * *

It wasn't until the following evening that the true horror of what had happened the night before finally sank in.

All that day while I was in work I'd blocked it out.

I knew Cathy and the others could see the bruises but I wasn't going to tell them what had happened. I didn't want them to know. I didn't want anyone to know what a fool I'd been. How could I have been so stupid? How could I honestly have thought that he'd want the likes of me for anything other than sex?

I know what the girls would say if I told them.

"Ah, for fuck's sake, Jackie, surely yeh must've known that he only wanted teh empty his sack."

They wouldn't believe that I hadn't known he was married. And what if he was? It wasn't as though any of us wanted commitment, we were only out for a laugh. Besides, what was the difference between lying about what you did for a living, and lying about your marital status?

But there was a difference.

Lying about your job was kid's stuff, lying about your partner was underhanded and sly.

I could just imagine the same bastard who'd slapped me around going home to his perfect little wife and his perfect little kids. His kids probably went to boarding-school to learn how to piss straight, while Mrs Robert done flower arranging and lay in the missionary position once a month.

They'd kiss each other on the cheek, while she prepared a meal. Grilled meat with a tossed salad (cause we have to watch our calories), and they'd have a glass of wine, two glasses for her if it was missionary night. And, despite her knowing what a bastard he was. she'd just play along with the charade.

Well, how was he going to explain his fractured skull, his broken arm, his bloodstained clothes, his broken teeth and his smashed headlights? How was he going to explain his presence outside a disco at that hour of the morning? And how was he going to explain the rags that had once been a woman's clothes and were now strewn all over his car?

I was glad Johnser had kicked the shite out of him.

Johnser. I'd nearly died. There were a thousand ways, a million places that I wanted to meet him.

I wouldn't even have minded meeting him in the supermarket dressed in me track suit (the one Jeffrey had proposed to me in).

I wouldn't have minded meeting him when I was cleaning the offices.

But for him to come upon me in a car, half naked, Jasus.

I should have been grateful that he'd come upon me when he had, but I wasn't. I cursed Robert for doing what he'd done to me, for ruining the fun, for frightening me, for tearing me good skirt, but above all, for letting Johnser see me like that. Yes, I was glad that Johnser had kicked his all-too-perfect white teeth in.

I began thinking about Johnser, fantasising about him, but every time I did the memory of that awful night would come flooding back. I'd remember how Johnser had seen me. And even though I knew it had all been Robert's fault, I couldn't help the feeling of embarrassment. I felt dirty and, above all, . . . cheap.

I couldn't possibly ring Johnser, no way. Jasus, I'd be scarlet.

Three days later I was standing in the phone box.

I was just about to hang up when the phone was answered. I heard his voice on the other end. He sounded distracted, as though the phone had interrupted something important.

He'd said hello for the second time before I answered.

"Hello, Johnser, it's me."

If he'd said "Who's me?" I'd have hung up. But he didn't.

His voice changed, he sounded happy to hear me.

"Jasus, Jackie, I'd almost given up on yeh. Hold on a minute, will yeh?"

He held his hand over the mouthpiece but I could hear his muffled voice telling someone to leave the room.

Me mind ran riot. It was probably some little tart, another Tara. Once again I'd hesitated, and once again someone else had got him. Well, fuck her and fuck you too, Johnser. Fuck, fuck, fuck the whole bleedin lot of yez.

Before I had a chance to hang up, he was back, full of apologies.

"Sorry about that, just a bit of business, yeh know yerself . . . Jackie, are yeh still there?"

The beeps let me know that I needed to put more money in, but as I rooted in me purse for change the phone went dead.

I cursed meself.

"Yeh fucking eejit, Jackie. Yeh stupid fucking eejit."

CHAPTER FIFTY

She'd never change, she'd always be the same old Jackie, jealous Jackie. What was it with her? What did I have to do to prove to her that she was the only one? It brought me back years, it reminded me of that time down at the canal. The time she'd kicked me in the balls, and all because she'd decided to go all prudish and put her body out of bounds. Jasus, was it any wonder I'd gone off with Tara?

But she could fuck off this time. I wasn't going down that road again. I'd been given a second chance and I wasn't about to blow it because of Jackie's childish jealousy.

She was so unpredictable, it was as if she had a continual period. You know what I mean, that time of month when you never know what to expect. One minute they're telling you how great you are and the next they're eating your fucking head off. But I wasn't going to be put off this time, I was going after her.

After all, I'd gone after everything else I'd ever wanted in life and got it. And Jackie was something I wanted.

* * *

Jonathan was very giddy. He was laughing at every little

247

thing that was happening, exaggerating his laugh, and it was really beginning to grate on me nerves. Edward was encouraging him, they were supposed to be eating their tea, but Edward was chewing his fish fingers and squeezing them back out through his teeth. I'd warned them that if they didn't stop messing they'd go to bed without any tea and we'd see how funny that was. The doorbell rang.

"Youse two better give it up, I'm warnin yez."

As I went to open the door, Jonathan started blowing bubbles into his milk. This caused more hysteria. I was shouting over me shoulder as I opened the door, "Jonathan, Edward, give it fucking up or else yis'll be sorry, I mean it."

And suddenly, there he was, standing in front of me.

"Howya, Jackie?"

I could feel meself going scarlet. Me hands automatically went to me hair, then flew to me skirt in an effort to straighten it.

"Johnser! What are yeh doin here?"

He smiled.

"Oh, that's charmin, Jackie. I'm glad teh see you've lost none of yer social skills."

"Sorry, come in."

He entered the flat in his usual confident way, as if he'd lived there all his life. He didn't look around and I was glad about that. I was glad he didn't say that he liked the wallpaper, or that the flat was nice, because it wasn't and we both knew it. He went into the kitchen where he immediatly started playing with the kids. They were in kinks. He winked at me and I smiled.

"Johnser, don't encourage them. They're bad enough."

But he did. And after tea, he brought them down to the park where he played football with them. When they came back they played some more, until eventually it was time for bed.

Then the moaning started. "Ah Ma, ah Ma, please, just anudder five minutes."

"This is all your fault, Johnser Kiely," I told him laughingly.

The kids ran to him. "Will yeh come an' play with us temorra?"

He looked at me and their eyes followed his.

"We'll see," I said. "But there'll be no chance if yez don't get teh bed . . . now."

* * *

I started visiting Jackie's on a regular basis. I couldn't help meself, I loved it over there. It was like being in a different world, a world that was light years away from the sordid one I lived in. And, strange as it may seem, I preferred hers.

Sometimes Jackie really annoyed me. She'd never let me help out. I remember offering to get the messages one time and she nearly took me fucking head off.

I didn't mean I would "get" them, it was more a case of I would pay. There was no way you'd find me pushing a trolley around a supermarket. You can say what you like about the New Man, but I was fucked if I was going to change. Maybe I'm wrong, but I still think there's something girlie about pushing anything that has four wheels and a handle. Next thing you know, they'd have you crying at weepie films and changing nappies.

Women have a way with these things, they're professionals. It's like on *The Generation Game* when Brucie brings on a confectioner, a real pro at icing a cake. He makes it look like child's play. But bring on the contestants, and the cake looks like it's been attacked by lugworms.

And it's the same with nappies.

A woman whips off one nappy, wipes arse, powders and lashes on the dry one, before the child even wakes up.

The man takes so long that the shite has dried into the child's arse, child goes hysterical, pisses straight up into the man's face and, by the time the whole operation is over, the little fucker is dirty again.

Fucking shopping trolleys have a mind of their own. Pushing one of those things is like dancing with your granny. You go one way, she goes the other, until eventually you're going round and round in circles. And they always seem to be in a hurry to get to the next aisle before you.

But women, they can push them around all day long without the slightest bit of hassle.

The thing I hate more than shopping trolleys is the fuckers who go around checking prices.

"Oh, look, honey, this jar of jam is 1p cheaper in the supermarket in Walkinstown."

"Oh, really, sweetie, well, maybe we'll get it over there."

For fuck's sake, they're supposed to be trying to save money, not driving miles and spending it on petrol.

In the old days, these fellas would have been known as fairies.

Anyway, like I say, all I'd done was offer to pay.

But, by the way she'd reacted, you'd swear I'd offered to rob the fucking place.

She'd got on her soapbox.

"I'm no charity case, Johnser Kiely. An' if that's how yeh see us, I'd prefer if yeh didn't come over any more."

"For fuck's sake, woman, give it a rest."

All I was trying to do was help. I mean, the fact that I was there for breakfast, dinner and tea had to be adding to her food bill.

There was no talking to her, she wouldn't listen. But where there's a will, there's a way. Eventually I found a solution. I began taking them out for meals a couple of nights a week and on the weekends I'd get takeaways.

End of problem. Hassle-free life. Bliss.

I was spending more and more time with them. She even let me stay the odd night. I had a change of clothes in the wardrobe and hopefully it wouldn't be long before I had me feet permanently under the table. Things were going well.

CHAPTER FIFTY-ONE

I was always promising to bring the kids for a pizza. They loved the stuff, but they'd never had a real one. It was always that frozen crap.

"I can tell yeh now, the day yeh taste the real thing you'll never eat that muck again."

"Well, we'll never know if yeh don't bring us."

"Jonathan, don't be so cheeky."

"No, Jackie, he has a point. I'll tell yez what, if it's all right with yer ma we'll go now, this evenin."

So, on Jackie's say-so, we headed off.

I took them to a favourite restaurant of mine. It served the best pizza in Dublin. The walls were adorned with covers from the *Rolling Stone* magazine. They were all there, some of them two or three times.

Dylan, The Stones, James Taylor, Tom Petty, the list was endless.

The boys were just starting to get interested in music and were amazed to find that some of their idols had been around in our day.

"God, that means that John Travolta is as old as you!"

"Go way, yeh cheeky git," I said, pretending to go for Jonathan.

"Well, that's it, no pizza for you." I made like I was trying to catch the waiter's attention.

"Ah, no, Johnser, I'm only messin, yer much younger than him."

"Jonathan Adams, yer the biggest lick I've ever seen." Jackie laughed.

"What's so special about the *Rollin Stone,* anyway?" asked Edward.

As Jackie tried to explain, I put on me best Texan voice and started to sing Dr Hook's old classic –

" . . . Yeh keep gettin richer, but I can't get me picture on the cover of the *Rollin Stone*."

They were falling about the place laughing.

"Yer makin a show of me," Jonathan was shouting across the table while trying to keep a straight face.

"That's right, yeh don't like modern music. Yeh prefer Bosco singin yer favourite bedtime songs, isn't that right, Jonathan?"

Jackie was doubled up laughing. The way she used to laugh when we were younger, when we'd be down at the Naller and she'd had a few drinks. The laugh that told me she loved me, loved the things I did, the way I moved, the air that I breathed, she loved it all and I was glad. Because, at this moment in time, I loved her more than I'd ever admit.

Soon we were tucking into two huge pizzas with every topping imaginable. The boys couldn't believe the size of them, they thought pizza was only the size of a small plate. They'd never seen anything like this.

I watched as they struggled to hold the large slices in their hands, and struggle they did, until there wasn't a scrap left (except the crust, of course). I don't think there's a kid on the planet who eats crust. As they scanned the dessert menu, I suddenly found meself thinking about me own childhood.

I know I'd only been slagging Jonathan about his baby music, but I remember as a kid that crap used to drive me mad.

Jasus, it used to do me head in. I mean, all that "I love you, you love me, we're a happy family". For fuck's sake, do they really think kids believe all that shite? Do they honestly think that kids look out the window and sing about the first thing they see?

I could just picture meself, snotty nose stuck up against the dirty window, singing,

"Oh Mammy, come look out the window
Cause the postman is right at our door
Let's guess who all the bills are from
Before they land on the floor.
Oh Daddy, here comes a man with a hatchet
He's screaming you owe him a score
He says if he gets his hands on you
We won't have a daddy any more."

Somehow, I don't think I was the kind of kid the composers of these songs had in mind when they wrote them. But still, whether they like it or not, there's a lot of kids like me out there.

As Jackie ordered a cappuccino me mind began to wander again. Cappuccino, no less, what was Dublin like, eh? We'd come a long way from the dirty chippers, where you'd be lucky to get your tea in a clean mug. And as for coffee, well, if they had it, it definitely wouldn't have been a fancy cappuccino, no, it would have been a cup of slightly brown water from a jar.

Nowadays ther were more types of coffee than beers. But at the end of the day, it didn't bother me how many brands there were, cause I was a tea man meself. None of your fancy Earl Grey, or mint, or lemon, or any of the other piss water they called tea. Just give me a little pot, with a couple of tea bags, a jug of milk, and I was happy.

I have to admit that I loved these fancy restaurants. It was true what they said about getting what you paid for. And it was funny, really, because even though I ate in the finest places, I always ordered the most basic food and drink. It was as if I was still a kid in Ballyer, the only difference being that me ma would have got her whole week's shopping for what I paid for one course.

It was odd, but I could never bring meself to order anything fancy. It wasn't because I was afraid I wouldn't be able to pronounce it, I couldn't give a fuck about that. It was more to do with not forgetting me roots. I'd order a dessert, a knickerbocker glory, or a banana split, no problem, cause they were the things of me childhood. The things we'd dreamed about. There used to be a restaurant on O'Connell Street and they had pictures in the window of all the different kinds of ice cream they sold. We'd stand for hours looking at them, trying to decide which one to have. I always picked either a knickerbocker or a banana split. I don't know why we bothered, because we hadn't a hope in hell of ever getting one. The best we could hope for (if we were lucky) was a cornet from Mr Whippy when he came around in his van. It just wasn't the same.

So now, whenever I got the chance, I bought meself one or the other.

The sound of Edward slurping his drink brought me back to the present.

God, this was a great day, everything was going brilliant.

I was really happy and enjoying being part of a family. All of a sudden Jackie's face changed, she'd stopped laughing and was looking towards the door. It was obvious that she wasn't happy at seeing whoever had just walked in.

Before I had a chance to turn around I heard the voice.

"Oh, this is cosy."

There was no mistaking whose voice that was. It was Tara's.

"Didn't take long for her teh come crawlin outta the bleedin woodwork, did it? Specially now that she knows yeh have money."

I swung around and pulled her down on to a chair.

"Sit down, Tara."

"No, yer all right, I wudden like teh intrude. I mean teh say, far be it from me teh break up a happy home, not like some I could mention."

She glared across at Jackie, who was busy trying to draw the boys' attention to the pictures on the wall. Of course they were having none of it, they wanted to know what was going on, they'd no intentions of missing this.

Tara's voice was raised and she was pointing at the lads.

"Jasus, Johnser, yeh amaze me. Here yeh are playin happy famblies with these two bastards; meanwhile, yer own kids are at home without a bite teh eat."

I spoke through clenched teeth.

"Tara, just shut fucking up an' go home."

"An' wudden yeh love that? For Tara teh fade away inteh the background with yer kids, while yeh swan round feedin some other floozzie's brats."

She was talking at the top of her voice, making sure that the other diners heard every word. All eyes were on our

256

table, and I knew from the look on Jackie's face that she would never darken the door of this restaurant again as long as she lived.

I grabbed Tara by the arm and dragged her outside, I felt like kicking her up and down the pathway, but instead pushed her into a doorway.

"Oh Jasus, Johnser. I luv it when yeh get all mass-cue-line."

She was a thick bitch. Even now, when she knew I was ready to burst her, she still had to be a smartarse.

"Tara! What the fuck deh yeh think yer playin at?"

"Me? What am I playin at? You've a fucking cheek. It's not me who's playin away from home, it's not me who's out with me tart."

"Yeh better watch yer fucking mouth."

"Why? What'll yeh do, Johnser, hit me?"

She didn't know how close she was to the truth.

"Look, Tara, why are yeh doin this? What's it all about?"

"It's about marriage, Johnser, about me bein yer wife. An' before yeh try teh deny it, remember I've the papers teh prove it."

"Fuck the papers, I couldn't give a fuck what papers yeh have."

"Well, me da says . . . "

That was it. It was bad enough that she'd made a show of us in the restaurant, without having to listen to what that bollox, Blue, had to say. I grabbed her by the shoulders.

"Now, you listen teh me. I told yeh an' yer fucking aul fella that I owe yez nothin. Deh yeh hear me? Nothin."

Passers-by were starting to move on to the road in order to avoid us, but that didn't stop them slowing down and trying to get a look at what was going on.

257

Tara soon sorted that out.

"Are yez havin a good gawk? Are yez? Deh yez want teh see the colour of me knickers while yez are at it?"

She lifted her skirt and the couple ran, obviously afraid of what might happen next.

"An' as for you, Johnser Kiely, yeh better fucking listen teh me. I'm yer wife an' I'm owed somethin for that. Yeh said till death us do part, an' that hasn't happened yet, has it? Cause I don't see a wreath over yer head." She pushed a gold chain with her name on it into me face. "An' I don't see RIP on this fucking necklace, so I reckon I'm still alive, too."

"Tara, for the last time, why are yeh doin this? Why are yeh actin like the hurt little wife all of a sudden? Yeh know that I never loved yeh."

"Luv? Luv, is that what yeh think this is all about? Since when did we ever talk about luv? Yeh never once told me yeh loved me, even when yeh were shaggin me or gettin me teh go down on yeh, I never heard yeh sayin it. So don't start tryin teh tell me now that the reason we're over is cause yeh don't luv me. At the end of the day, yer still me husband an' I want us teh try again."

She reached up and touched me face, she seemed sincere.

"An' there's the kids, the little darlins . . . "

I pulled away.

"They're not mine."

"They're more fucking yers than them two in there. After all, one of hers was born while yeh were in prison, so what are yeh tryin teh say? That yeh played with yerself an' sent it teh her in the post?"

I moved away from her.

"Tara, this is fucking stupid. Why don't yeh listen teh

me? We're over an' the sooner yeh realise it, the better it'll be for all of us. It's over, kaputt, finito."

"Don't get fucking smart with me, usin all yer fancy words. All I'm askin is that we give it anudder go? I mean, there musta been somethin there teh begin with?"

"There was . . . yeh were up the pole."

I knew that was below the belt, but I didn't care.

"Lookit, Tara, I'm sorry but there's no goin back. Like I said before, it's over. Now the only thing I'm willin teh do is support the young one, I'll take yer word for it that she's mine. But I'll be fucked if I'm gonna support Stan's bastard. That's the deal. Take it or leave it."

"By Jasus, Johnser Kiely, yeh won't get away with this. Ye'll pay all right, just see if yeh don't."

It was obvious she was never going to be satisfied, no matter what I said, it wouldn't be good enough. So what was the point in hanging around? Anyway, I was fed up with people staring at us. I turned and walked away.

She screamed after me, "Ye'll pay what yeh owe, deh yeh hear me, yeh slimey bastard? Just fucking wait."

As I walked back into the restaurant I knew the evening was ruined. The kids were very quiet and I could see that Jackie was doing her best to hold back the tears.

You could have cut the atmosphere in the car with a knife.

No one spoke. When we got home, the kids went straight to bed without a word of protest. I think they knew that something important was about to happen and they weren't sure they wanted to be involved.

After tucking them in, Jackie came back into the room and poured us both a large vodka. She handed me mine and sat down, not beside me as she usually did, but at the other end of the couch.

Things weren't looking good.

She took a big gulp of her drink before she began.

"Johnser, you'll have teh sort this out."

"I know, Jackie, I will, don't worry."

"I mean it, Johnser. Don't try teh fob me off. I can't live like this, I can't be doin with all this worry. I don't want teh be worryin that every time we go outside the door there's gonna be another scene like the one tonight. An' specially not in front of the kids."

"Now hold on a minute, Jackie. I didn't enjoy what happened any more than you did, but we both came in teh this relationship with baggage."

She stood up and walked to the window, the curtains were drawn, but she stood as if she was looking out.

"I know neither of us is perfect, but at least my past is behind me, it doesn't come back teh bite me every time I walk out the front door. I have a broken marriage too, but at least Jeffrey doesn't sneak round spyin on me. For fuck's sake, Johnser, it's like *Fatal Attraction*."

If it wasn't so serious, I'd have laughed. I could just imagine Tara boiling the kids' rabbit.

"Yeh need teh sort things out, Johnser . . . " Her voice was trembling but she continued.

"An' . . . I don't think we should see each other . . . till yeh do."

I tried to argue, but I knew there was no point. And, if I was to be honest with meself, I'd admit that I'd known from the minute Tara had entered the restaurant that this was going to happen. I hated Tara for doing this to us. I can honestly say that, if she'd walked through the door at that moment, I'd have strangled her. I knew Jackie was right, I did need to sort this whole thing out, for once and for all.

We finished our drinks and she walked me to the door. After a quick peck on the cheek, she watched as I made me way to the car. I noticed two men walking towards me, but I was so caught up with what was going on in me head, that I didn't pay them too much attention. As they passed, one of them turned to me and I felt a terrible pain in the back of me head.

I fell to the ground. The pain was getting worse and worse with every blow they landed. They were shouting at me, but I was losing consciousness and it was difficult to make out what they were saying. The last thing I heard before finally passing out was Jackie screaming.

When I came round, I was in the hospital.

Me head felt like I'd had a bellyful of drink the night before, it was lifting off me. I tried to raise it off the pillow but quickly realised that was a bad idea, a very bad idea. Jackie was sitting beside me and, according to her, I was lucky to be alive. I'd lost pints of blood and had to have twenty stitches in me head. I knew this was a bit of an exaggeration, but what the hell. The main thing was, she was here with me, sitting beside me, holding me hand.

I was beginning to think that maybe this bang on the head wasn't such a bad thing after all.

"What did them two fellas want, Johnser?"

"I've no idea, Jackie."

"Johnser, they said somethin about drugs, now what did they mean?"

261

CHAPTER FIFTY-TWO

Johnser was very good to me and the kids. He'd even helped me to get over the Robert incident.

For the first couple of weeks after the attack, I'd been a nervous wreck. I'd see a man in a suit walking down the street and I'd panic, I was convinced he was going to grab me. Of course he wouldn't, but I was petrified just the same.

Eventually, I calmed down and discovered a way of getting me own little bit of revenge.

I still cleaned the toilets in the offices and the mickey flashers still came in, but now I was ready for them. As they pulled out their wrinklies and told me to keep cleaning, I would. Unfortunately, for them, I always seemed to splash a little drop of bleach on to their suit. At one time I think there was a whole office full of bleached suits. Only tiny stains, but it meant that the suit was ruined. I know it was only a small victory, but it was a victory just the same.

Johnser was so good with the kids that it sometimes worried me. I worried in case he'd let them down, I was afraid they'd come to depend on him, that they'd start seeing him as their da, and that he'd up and leave and fuck their lives up, the way he had mine, all those years ago.

Then I'd tell meself that I was being ridiculous, and to

stop living in the past. To enjoy what I had while I had it, to enjoy Johnser. After all, I'd spent half me life wanting him, so now that I had him I should be happy. But no matter how hard I tried to block it out, there was always that little niggle of doubt in the back of me mind. OK, so we were back together, he was practically living with me, but at the end of the day what did I know about him? Nothing. I didn't even know what he did for a living. I could hazard a guess that whatever it was, it wasn't legal, but I still had no idea what it was. I suppose that, deep down inside, I didn't really want to know, because what you don't know can't hurt you. And as me granny used to say, "If it ain't broke, don't fix it."

So I didn't ask. I was happy he was here, I was happy he had money in his pocket, but most important of all, I knew he was here because he wanted to be with me and the kids. So I wasn't going to rock the boat, not unless it started to affect the kids. Besides, after years of suffering, of scrimping and scraping, I was enjoying all the attention, I enjoyed having someone to take care of me again. It wasn't just the money, either. Thanks to Jeffrey, I knew that could be gone as quick as you got it. No, it was more than that, it was the way he treated the kids, the time he gave them, the time he gave me.

I loved him for that.

I used to spend all day thinking about him. As I went about me cleaning, I'd have a smile on me face, thinking about the things he'd get up to with the kids. Like that time at Hallowe'en when he'd snuck out and rang the doorbell. The kids nearly wet themselves when they opened the door and he jumped out on them dressed in a gorilla suit.

Sometimes I'd laugh out loud and the other girls would want to know what was so funny. I'd never tell them and I knew they resented that, cause, after all, we were supposed to share everything, every little detail, no secrets; remember our motto, "All men are bastards".

But Johnser wasn't a bastard, and I didn't want them knowing anything about him. OK, so I knew that Tommy liked Ann to dress up as a nurse, and I knew that Cathy's latest fella was a cross-dresser. I even knew that Bernie Cash's husband had been caught in bed with the window cleaner the week after Bernie had been boasting about him shagging her.

But I didn't want to share mine and Johnser's secrets with them, our relationship was too important to me. Cathy's nose was knocked out of joint, she was always making smart remarks about me not telling her anything.

"Oh, don't tell her any of yer business, cause she doesn't tell us nuttin."

They all knew that I had a fella, after all, I'd stopped going out with them on Tuesday nights, because Tuesday nights weren't important to me any more. I was much happier sitting at home with me new-found family, I know it sounds boring but I loved it, it was all I'd ever wanted. Even as a young one hanging around street corners, I used to dream about settling down and having kids. I remember at the time I wanted to have eight, they were all going to be called John, or Johnser or Joan, anything that resembled his name.

Now I was happy to just sit at home with the three men in me life around me.

As I sat in the bosom of me happy family, I could forget the dinginess of me flat, the boredom of me humdrum job, me past. I could forget it all as I sat and watched Johnser lark about on the floor with the kids. Until suddenly, out of nowhere, came the doubts. I'd start worrying about us not being married, about how easy it would be for him to walk out on us whenever he felt like it. In me heart of hearts I knew he wouldn't, but it still didn't stop me worrying.

Every time we had a cross word, every time he was five minutes late, every time he offered to buy me something and I refused his offer, I'd panic. What if he got fed up with me always being so defensive, always wanting to be independent? But he didn't, he was always there for me. I knew he couldn't understand me need for independence and I couldn't blame him, there were times when I didn't understand it meself.

I'd come home from work and spend the whole night giving out about how bad me job was and about how much I hated it. This always annoyed him.

"Well, if it's so fucking bad, why don't yeh give it up?"

"No, I can't."

He'd throw his eyes up to heaven and I knew he was thinking, "Well, if yer not gonna give it up, stop fucking moanin 'bout it."

But I couldn't give it up, because regardless of how like a wife I acted, I wasn't one. We weren't married, so therefore, I never felt 100% sure of him. So I kept me job and earned me own money. No matter how small an amount it was, at least it was mine.

I was the world's greatest pessimist and, even though I hated me morbid thoughts, they were always right. If I so much as thought about the TV licence, I'd be guaranteed to get a letter in the post reminding me it was up for renewal, and it was always at a time when I couldn't afford it. If someone said the word "period", I got mine. If I saw a packet of aspirin, I got a headache. Honest to God, I was unbelievable. And despite what you might think, I did have pleasant thoughts sometimes, but they never came true. No matter how many times I thought about winning the Lotto, it never happened, or if I thought about getting a pay rise, well, that was nearly a sure guarantee I was going to get the sack. See, there I go again, pessimistic Jackie.

And so it was with me and Johnser.

No sooner had I thought, "this is too good to last," then it crumbled down around me. I mean, one minute we were sitting in the restaurant having the time of our lives, next, there she was as large as life, standing in front of me. Suddenly, all me old fears had come rushing back. I'd been having a great time until she appeared.

We'd been going through all the covers of the magazines and had come across a picture of Mick Jagger. I was telling them how some of the girls I'd palled with had been mad about him, but I hadn't. I thought he was crap, he was an anorexic with big juju lips, he was like something you'd see in the jungle. And as for the way he danced, he was like a rubber doll. We were laughing at Johnser doing his impression of "Satisfaction". The way he pursed his lips and waved his hands in the air was exactly like Jagger. We were having great fun. I remember thinking to meself this was the side of Johnser that I loved, I wished everyone could see him like this. Instead of Johnser the bully, or Johnser the convict, I wanted them to see Johnser the family man.

The problem was that most people feared Johnser. If he walked into a pub where he was known, people got nervous, they were afraid he was going to kick the fuck out of them for something they'd done ten years ago.

I suppose I should have felt privileged, really. Me and the

kids were the only ones he felt comfortable enough with to let his guard down.

So there I was, feeling like the happiest, luckiest girl in the world, and next thing that fucking bitch made her entrance.

Why did she have to find us? Why, of all the restaurants in this fucking city, did she have to walk into this one?

There she was, standing in the middle of this fancy restaurant shouting like a tinker. She might as well have been in the middle of Moore Street selling fish. If it wasn't for the kids I'd have given as good as I got, but they were there. So I couldn't. I wasn't going to let meself down in front of them. She really got into her stride when she noticed she had an audience, she didn't leave a stone unturned, she was going for the Oscar. And by the time Johnser finally dragged her outside, it was too late, everything had been ruined.

She was a cunt, she was ruining me life for the second time, and I wanted to kill her for it. I'd never forgive Johnser for what she'd done. Oh, I know it wasn't his fault, he hadn't told her where we were going. He hadn't said to her, "Oh, by the way, Tara, me an' Jackie are goin for a meal, deh yeh fancy joinin us?"

But she was his responsibility, not mine. So I felt that he was as much to blame as she was.

There and then, I decided that he'd have to sort out his problems before he became more involved with me. I knew I'd be heartbroken without him. But there was nothing else I could do.

I had no intention of becoming part of a love triangle.

When we got back to the flat, I poured us both a stiff drink and told him what I'd decided.

I could feel me eyes burning, but I knew I couldn't give way to tears, there'd be plenty of time for crying when he'd gone.

As I watched him walk away, I wanted to call him back, to tell him that I'd changed me mind, that I didn't care, that I loved him and wanted him back. But I said nothing, I let him go.

If I'd been on me own maybe things would have been different, but I wasn't. I had the boys, and they had to come first.

As I stood watching him, I suddenly became aware of the two men. And before I knew what was happening, they were on top of him, beating him with a bar and shouting something about someone called Frankie. I thought I heard them say something about drugs, but I couldn't be sure. I was screaming as I ran towards them, but as soon as they seen me they walked away.

They didn't run or panic, they just strolled casually down the road.

I thought he was dead. What was I going to do? I couldn't drive and I didn't have a phone.

Oh, sweet Jasus, help me, I prayed silently.

I ran to a neighbour's house and she let me use the phone. I cursed the ambulance for taking so long to arrive. It probably only took five minutes but, as I knelt on the ground begging Johnser not to leave me, I felt like I'd been waiting hours.

He didn't leave me, he didn't die. He'd lost a lot of blood and needed twenty stitches in the back of his head, but at least he was alive.

I promised God that, if he let Johnser live, I'd donate blood for the rest of me life.

When he came round I was sitting by his bed.

I asked him what had happened, what was going on, what

was it all about. I told him I didn't want any more lies, I wanted him to tell me the truth.

He took a deep breath. I knew he was going to tell me everything. I also knew I wasn't going to like what I heard.

I've often heard it said that the truth hurts and, by God, I can tell you, it does.

I couldn't believe what I was hearing. I was an eejit. I knew Johnser was no saint. Back in the days when we hung around the shops he'd always been up to something or other, but I couldn't believe I was sitting here listening to Johnser telling me he was a drug dealer. He didn't make excuses, he wasn't blaming someone else, he hadn't been forced to do it. No, he done it because he wanted to be the biggest, toughest criminal in Dublin.

I felt numb, I couldn't take it in, this was way over me head. It was as if he was telling me a story. A story about drug-smuggling and bank robberies and money-laundering and murder. Fucking hell, it was beginning to sound more and more like a film script. I knew we had a major drugs problem, it was always in the papers and on the telly. But I thought "major" meant the syringe left lying in the school playground, or the fella on the street corner flogging tablets to the kids. Not this. I couldn't believe he was talking about Ireland, this kind of thing didn't happen in Ireland, in Dublin, in Ballyer. No, this kind of thing only happened in Mafia films, films where Robert De Niro or Al Pacino played the baddies. But Johnser was telling me that it was happening and, worse of all, he was one of the baddies. Him and Tara's da and someone called Brush and someone called Frankie. Jasus, it was like a bad dream.

The thing that upset me the most was the drugs.

I could understand someone wanting to rob a bank, I could even forgive beating up a child molester. After all, I had kids meself and I knew that I'd want to kill anyone who interfered with them, but not drugs, no, I couldn't understand that. I'd never be able to forgive him for dealing drugs.

Jasus, when I think about how I was continually lecturing the kids about the dangers of drugs. I remember the time Edward had come home from school wearing a transfer on his arm, he said some man had given it to him. Fuck's sake, I nearly went mad, I thought it was Ecstasy. Gerry Ryan had been on the radio warning parents about transfers. I'll never forget that day.

I found out later that it was one of the other kid's fathers who'd given it to him. But nevertheless, I felt justified for the way I'd reacted.

And Johnser had been there that day. Had he agreed with me? I couldn't remember. I began thinking that maybe he was looking at me kids as his next generation of clients, was that it? Was that why he wanted to be with us? He wanted to introduce me kids to drugs.

"Stop it, Jackie, pull yerself together," I told meself.

But I couldn't. All I could think about was that I'd let this fiend, this monster into me house. I'd fed him, slept with him, Christ, I'd even left him alone with the kids. How could I have been so gullible?

I'd fucked Jeffrey out because he was a gambler and wife-beater, only to replace him with a drug dealer. Jasus, what kind of a mother did that make me?

I sat looking at Johnser, I didn't recognise him any more.

This wasn't the man I loved, this wasn't the man I'd dreamt of spending me life with.

He tried to hold me hand but I pulled away.

"I can't believe you've just told me yer a drug dealer."

"Jasus, Jackie, keep yer voice down. Deh yeh want the nurse teh hear?"

"Oh, that's just typical, worried in case anyone hears yer big black secret. Yeh know what I think about druggies an' dealers, for fuck's sake, yeh sat in me flat an' agreed with me."

"I do agree with yeh."

I stood up and screamed, "Don't yeh dare say that yeh agree with me. Yer a fucking dealer, yer worse than any junkie."

He reached for me hand again.

"But I luv yeh."

"Love me! Yeh bring drugs inteh me house, yeh bring yer drugs trade teh me door, an' then yeh tell me that yeh love me, deh yeh really expect me teh believe that? Jasus, Johnser, you an' that bitch must really love makin a fool outta me."

"Don't be stupid, it's not like that."

I grabbed me bag.

"Really, Johnser? Well that's how it feels teh me. An' I'll be fucked if I'm stayin around teh be made a fool of."

I ran towards the door and as I opened it I turned.

"Do me a favour, Johnser, if yeh really luv me, an' if yeh have any feelins for me kids, don't contact me again."

As I ran down the corridor with tears blurring me vision, I could hear him calling me back.

I went and picked the kids up from Ma's. She knew there was something wrong, but wouldn't ask in front of the kids.

"If you need me, you know where I am."

"Thanks, Ma."

It made me feel a bit better just knowing she was there for me, but right now I didn't feel like talking.

Later on that night Jonathan asked if I was still seeing Johnser. I put me arm around him.

"No, I won't be seein him any more."

After that night, Johnser's name wasn't mentioned again.

CHAPTER FIFTY-THREE

I thought about Jackie all the time. But I knew I had a lot to sort out before I even attempted to go around to see her.

I heard that Frankie Fitz and his men were trying to move in on me territory, and I let it be known that the next time one of them showed his ugly face, I'd deal with him meself.

I didn't have long to wait.

I got the word that one of his men was working one of me clubs, using the toilet as his base. I walked in and the deal he was about to make broke up. As the druggie made his way back to the dance floor, the dealer tried to follow. I grabbed him.

"Hey! Watch the fucking suit."

"Fuck yer suit."

"Hey, man, I think yer makin a big mistake. I don't think yeh realise who yer dealin with?"

"Really?"

"Yeah, one word from me an' Frankie Fitz'll have yeh."

"I'm fucking quakin in me boots." I grabbed him by his lapels.

"Now listen here, m-a-n, this is my patch, my club. So you tell Frankie Fitz from me, it'll take more than a few stitches teh make me give it up."

I kneed him in the balls and he crumbled to the floor.

"Just in case yer boss doesn't understand oral, I'd better make the message visual."

By the time I'd finished knocking him around, I could almost feel sorry. But it was his own fault and, if he was going to work in this business, he was going to have to learn the rules. The scars on his face would be a constant reminder to him that, no matter what, you didn't fuck with Johnser Kiely.

I was becoming sick and tired of the drugs business. I'd gotten too used to the easy life with Jackie and the kids, and I was missing it.

Beating the crap out of people just to show that you weren't to be fucked with was crazy. It was a mug's game. Always having to watch your back, always worrying about protecting your patch, always having to be on your toes, it was becoming too much like hard work.

It wasn't that I was getting soft, cause, believe me, I wasn't. It was because I'd began to enjoy another way of life, a life that didn't involve drugs.

The next day as I was getting ready to go out, there was a knock on the door. You can imagine me surprise when I opened it and seen Tara and Blue standing on the landing.

They came in and she started wandering around the room, picking things up and surveying them. You'd think she was an auctioneer from Christie's, here to value everything.

"Expensive taste, eh Johnser?"

The Blue put his arm around her and smiled.

"He always had, honey. Sure, didn't he marry me princess."

"I assume the two of yez didn't come here teh admire me taste in ornaments."

"Yeh know why I'm here."

"She only wants what's rightfully hers," Blue added.

"An' what are you? Her lawyer as well as her da?"

"Me da's here cause yeh owe him too."

"Oh, is that right?"

274

The Blue sat down and lit a cigarette.

"I wanna stake in yer drugs operation, yeh have the clubs sewn up. An' I feel it's time yeh shared it around."

I laughed.

"An' what would you like, Tara? Now that we're all bein' so honest with each other."

"I want you an' me back together, we all do."

She looked at Blue for support. He nodded his agreement.

"That's right, son. I know there's a lotta water gone under the bridge, but think about it, the two of us together, no one would be able teh touch us."

"That's not an option. Me an' her are finished, it was all a big mistake, an' now it's over."

"She's entitled teh somethin, Johnser."

I walked across the room to where a picture hung on the wall. I took it down and revealed the safe that was hidden behind it.

"Oh, very original." Blue laughed.

I reached in and took out a case, laid it on the table and opened it. Their mouths dropped at the sight of all the money inside.

"There's twenty-eight thousand pounds in here, it's every penny I have in the world, yeh can have it, Tara, it's all yers now."

I reached back into the safe and pulled out an envelope.

"In here are the deeds teh the apartment, an' me warehouse, here's the keys. Ye'll find all the gear I have in the warehouse, ye'll also find a note book with a list of me connections, it's in code but I'm sure ye'll be able teh work it out. So now, are yeh happy? Yeh have a nice apartment, fully paid for, a profitable business, an' loads of dosh."

I took the keys of me BMW and threw them on the table.

"An' needless teh say, ye'll need a car. Now yer probably wonderin why I'm givin yeh all this? Yeh want teh know what's in it for me."

275

Tara jumped to her feet.

"I knew it, I fucking knew it . . . "

"Shurrup, Tara, shut fucking up an' listen." Blue seemed to be losing his rag with Princess.

He turned to me.

"Go on?"

"There's two clauses attached to this deal. One each."

"We're listenin."

"You first, Tara. I don't want teh see or hear from yeh again. This is all ye'll ever get from me, so yeh better make it last. I don't want teh hear anythin 'bout the young one either, it's over, finished. Deh we understand each other?"

She didn't answer.

"An' the second clause?" asked Blue.

"The second is that I keep me security firm an' anywhere I have men employed is a drugs-free zone."

"That's a lotta clubs."

"It won't be that many, now I'm not dealin."

They sat looking at each other, as though they couldn't believe what was happening. Eventually, Blue rose to his feet and stuck out his hand –

"Sounds fair enough teh me."

Tara just nodded, for the first time in her life she was speechless. I turned and walked out.

As I waited for the lift I could hear Tara singing at the top of her voice. I should've known that her being struck dumb was to good to last.

"Money, money, money . . . "

I could picture her throwing handfuls of cash into the air as she sang.

I got out into the street and hailed a taxi. There was only one place I wanted to go, and that was Jackie's.

CHAPTER AFTY-FOUR

When I opened the door and seen him standing there, me heart done a flip. I couldn't believe that, after all I'd said to him, he'd still come back.

I ran back down the hall and closed the sitting-room door. I didn't want the kids seeing him, I didn't want them getting excited, thinking he'd come back.

"What the fuck deh yeh want, Johnser? I thought I told yeh not teh come round here any more. I want nothin more teh do with you or yer drugs."

"But that's just it, yer not havin anythin teh do with drugs."

"Johnser, don't try teh pull the wool over me eyes. Yeh done it too many times over the years."

"Jackie, I luv yeh."

"I know yeh do, Johnser, an' I luv you. An' I can put up with most things, in fact, yeh put me through a hell of a lot of shite over the years, but I'm not puttin up with yer drugs."

"Jackie, yeh don't have teh."

"Ah, Johnser, for fuck's sake, yer missin the point." I felt like screaming at him, but I couldn't risk the kids hearing me.

"Just cause I don't see what's goin on doesn't mean I'm

not affected by it. I know 'bout the dangers of drugs, an' I'm not prepared teh put me kids through that."

"Will yeh just listen teh me, Jackie. Yeh don't have teh put up with anythin, I've given it all up."

"Yeah, right."

"I swear it, Jackie. It means nothin teh me, I've given it all away."

I stood looking at him, I didn't know what to think any more.

"An' Tara?"

"You'll never need teh worry 'bout her again, I gave her an' her da everything. They have it all, the apartment, the car, the drugs business, I've nothin teh do with it any more."

Before I could react he grabbed me, pulled me close and kissed me. I pushed him away.

"Johnser, I can't handle this. I can't believe you'd do all this for me."

"For us."

He swung me up into his arms. I laughed.

"Johnser, stop. Put me down, yeh big eejit."

But he didn't. He pushed open the door and carried me over the threshold.

The kids jumped up as we entered the sitting-room, I knew by the expressions on their faces that they were as happy as I was.

That night was one of the happiest of me life.

I still couldn't believe what was happening. I couldn't believe that he'd given it all up, for me.

Suddenly a thought struck me.

"How are yeh gonna earn a livin now?"

It seemed like a very brutal question, especially after

what he'd just done for me. But still, I had to ask, I had to know.

He laughed.

"I should've known, yeh only ever wanted me for me money."

"It's not that, Johnser . . . "

"Calm down, Jackie, I'm only messin. Don't take everythin so serious. Don't worry, I've everythin under control. The only thing I didn't give them was the security business."

I kissed him.

"Jasus, Johnser. You're incredible."

"Yeah, I know. So now, how deh yeh intend teh repay me?"

I smiled as I pulled him on to the couch.

CHAPTER FIFTY-FIVE

It took me a long time to convince the bouncers who worked for me that I wasn't dealing any more. I was surprised how many still wanted to stay with me. Most of them said they were glad, and that the only reason they'd done it in the first place was because they wanted to keep their jobs. They were delighted at the prospect of turning the clubs where they worked into drug-free zones.

And they did. Every club where I had men employed was drug-free. And if the owner didn't like it, well, he could hire his doormen from some other firm. You'd be surprised at the amount of clubs who wouldn't hire us any more. But there was nothing I could do about it. At the end of the day it was their money, so it was up to them who they employed.

Eventually I was down to four clubs. But it was six nights a week, so I was still making a nice living from supplying the doormen. I was starting to feel really happy.

Don't get me wrong, I hadn't undergone any major changes. I was still the same. I still enjoyed me pint and the odd flutter on the horses. But now I enjoyed the *craic* too. When I walked down the street people actually said hello to me. People were beginning to realise that they didn't have to shy away into a corner when I walked into a room.

Unfortunately, the police weren't as easily convinced. In all honesty, who could blame them? How could I expect them to believe that one of Dublin's biggest criminals was now going straight? It certaintly wasn't going to happen overnight.

They knew that the security business had been a front which allowed me to deal in the clubs, but, fortunately for me, they hadn't been able to prove it.

The word was out that I wasn't dealing any more. And it wasn't long before others were moving in on me old patches. The police should have realised this would never have happened if I was still dealing.

There was still the odd problem every now and then, with people trying to deal in clubs where me men worked. It was small-time stuff, it never really amounted to much.

That was until the night Frankie Fitz arrived.

I'd got a phone call telling me he was hanging around one of the clubs. I got into me car and drove down. He was there all right, surrounded by four other pricks. I walked over to where he was sitting.

"Ah, Johnser, me aul mate, you'll have a drink with me?"

"I'll have fuck all with yeh."

"Now, now, Johnser, there's no need for that attitude. I'm only here for a quiet drink. I mean, what else would I be doin in a drug-free zone?"

Two of his cronies laughed.

"That's right, Frankie. A drug-free zone, an' that's the way it's gonna stay. No one brings drugs in here while I'm around."

"Well, now, Johnser, that's just it. You've hit the nail right on the head. The way I see it, yeh ain't gonna be around for much longer. Yeh see, Johnser, I'm gettin fucking sick an'

NEVILLE THOMPSON

tired of being told where teh deal, what teh deal, an' who teh deal to. So, as an' from temorra night, me men will be doin business in here. Now we won't interfere with yer bouncers, if they don't interfere with us."

I grabbed the front of his jacket and pushed him up against the bar.

"You're not dealin in here, Frankie. In fact, yer not dealin anywhere near this club. Do I make meself clear?"

Before he'd time to answer, I twisted his arm up his back and pushed him towards the door. I shoved him out into the alleyway and pressed his face hard against the wall.

"Now for the last time, stay the fuck outta here."

Me men had followed me outside, each had one of his cronies in a stranglehold.

As I walked back inside, Frankie mumbled something. His voice was muffled because of his bleeding nose. I turned back towards him.

"You an' that scumbag Blue have enough junkies dependin on yer drugs. So I'm tellin yeh now, for the last time, this club is off limits. Right?"

CHAPTER FIFTY-SIX

It was lovely to be living a normal life again.

Not that life with Johnser could ever be called normal, but it was close enough for me.

We'd moved into a nice new house and every day we had someone in doing bits and pieces around the place. If I was being totally honest I'd admit that it was no great shakes, Johnser's taste in decor was up his arse, but still, it was our home and I loved it. We were happy.

He wasn't earning huge amounts of money, but he was making a nice little living and we wanted for nothing. Johnser loved his few pints, he'd go down nearly every night and have a couple. He said it was more to do with the freedom than the drink. He thought it was great to be able to sit in a pub and talk about football, or horses, or a film. He loved the way people accepted him, the way the barmen laughed and joked with him, he thought that was brilliant. Most people would consider these things normal, but Johnser put it on a par with winning the Lotto. These are the things he'd missed out on for all those years. Everyday things that most of us take for granted.

Johnser had always thought that just because you lived in a deprived area, you had to go out and rob, but you didn't.

283

He'd never noticed that the majority of people in these areas struggled to make a decent living. They didn't take the easy way out. They didn't turn to crime and drugs just because they felt hard done by. They got up off their arses and went out looking for work. It didn't matter what it was, sweeping the streets, cleaning offices, or delivering coal in the middle of winter. As long as it paid the bills and put food on the table, they didn't complain.

Now, at long last, Johnser was starting to see this. He was beginning to realise that "Normal" could be very enjoyable, that the simple things in life could be just as exciting as the unattainable.

And it wasn't just because he'd given up dealing and was finding family life a novelty, it was much more than that. He seemed genuinely happy, he was enjoying every minute of his life nowadays.

I really loved having him around, he was great company. We'd great *craic* together. Now, I'm not saying that life was a bed of roses all the time, because we all know that's not possible. But it was a nice life.

We had our rows, just like everyone else. You know, the ones you have when the money gets a bit tight, or when he comes home an hour late from the pub, the stupid ones. And it's funny, really, because the biggest rows are always about the most trivial things. I have to be honest and say that, nine times out of ten, I started them. I'm a great one for making a big issue out of nothing, I'm the most opinionated person in the world about the most unimportant things. But we always made up the next morning, and most times we'd end up laughing at the stupidity of it all.

Every once in a while Johnser would arrive home with a blue movie. We'd have a great laugh watching it. I know they're supposed to turn you on, but I thought they were a scream, better than any comedy. I'd never seen one until Johnser moved in with me.

Jeffrey hadn't been into anything like that, he was more your straight sex man. You know the type, kinky means leaving the light on. But not Johnser.

The first time Johnser tried to tie me hands to the bedrail, I panicked. I thought he'd gone mental. There he was, as cool as you like, walking into the bedroom with a piece of rope in his hand. I was left with me mouth open.

"I hope teh Jasus there's a horse in here, cause yeh can fuck off if yeh think yer tying me up."

He broke his shite laughing. He wrestled me to the bed and tied me up.

When he had me hands tied he started touching me. He touched me in all the right places and it felt great.

I wanted to know where the fuck he'd learned to do all this, but he wouldn't tell me, he just laughed. I didn't really care, I knew he'd started to sow his wild oats a long time ago. Johnser was never a virgin.

He knew where to touch me, Jasus, he drove me mad. And when I couldn't take any more, he untied me hands and made me come.

After that we made love, it was like nothing I'd ever experienced before.

I'll never forget the day he tried to buy me a vibrator.

We were walking down Capel Street, and he pulled me into a doorway. I thought it was someone's house cause it had frilly curtains on the windows and the door was locked. This didn't deter Johnser.

He rang the bell and a gay-looking man answered it, he didn't even look at us. It all seemed very secretive.

285

As we went in, I noticed two other men already inside. I hadn't a clue where we were, I thought it was a barber-shop, but why the fuck Johnser would want to bring me to the barber's I couldn't imagine.

Less than thirty seconds later, I knew I wasn't in a barber-shop. You could have knocked me down with a feather.

There were pictures of naked women everywhere. And there was this big black thing on the counter, it must have been all of three feet long. I don't know what it was supposed to be, but the one thing I know it wasn't was a mickey, cause I'd never seen one that looked like that. I thought it looked more like a candle without a wick.

Johnser was showing me this thing that did look like a mickey, except it had straps on it.

"Jasus, Johnser, I'm scarlet."

He was breaking his shite laughing.

Every few seconds the gay guy would shout –

"Don't handle the merchandise . . . "

We were walking around the shop, Johnser kept telling me he was going to buy a vibrator, but I was telling him to fuck off, I only wanted to have a look.

I never seen anything like the stuff they had in that place.

They had mugs in the shape of mickeys, and some in the shape of tits. Jasus, what kind of pervert would drink his tea from them? One of the fellas who'd been there when we came in was fiddling with a box. I was having a sly peep over trying to see what was written on it. I nearly fucking withered when I seen what he took out, it was a pump-up pussy. I thought I was seeing things.

It was the funniest-looking thing I'd ever seen. It was called "Miss Pussy." It had no legs, or arse, or waist, or anything, it was just a lump of rubber with a bit of hair (that looked more like a bit of carpet) stuck on the front.

Your man was pumping away like a good thing and suddenly the insides popped out. I started laughing, surely to God that wasn't supposed to happen. But he kept on going, pumping away. It was starting to look like a balloon.

Meanwhile Droopy-drawers was still shouting, "Don't handle the merchandise . . . "

But your man didn't seem to hear him. He was still squeezing his pump. I could just imagine him in his bedroom, with Miss Pussy stuck on the top of his mickey and him pumping his heart out.

He'd have squashed his poor mickey to death.

Just as Miss Pussy was starting to look more like Miss Balloon, she popped. The gay guy jumped off his stool.

"Oh, if yeh broke it yeh have teh pay for it. I told yez not teh handle the merchandise."

I thought he was talking to me.

"Fuck off, it wasn't me, it's his pussy."

Johnser went into kinks, he was doubled up laughing.

We rolled out of that shop that day, vibrator-less I may add.

* * *

This was looking like a really good night.

Johnser was home early and we were going to have sex.

That was until this stranger burst into our home. He was holding a gun to Johnser's head, talking to Johnser but looking at me. He sounded like someone out of a film.

"Johnser Kiely, I'm your worst nightmare. I'm the last face you're ever gonna see. I've been sent teh pay yeh back for all the sins you've committed, an' I'm sure you'd like teh know me name? I'm sure that before I pull this trigger and blow yeh away, you'd like teh know the name of the man who finally nailed Johnser Kiely. Yeh always thought yeh were so smart, always changin the rules, thinkin yeh were gonna live forever. But yeh were wrong, Johnser, there's bigger people than you out there, who hire men like me to do away with scum like you. Deh yeh wanna know how much they're payin me for this? Two thousand pounds. A thousand pounds a bullet, cause that's how many I'm gonna put inteh yeh. I could use one, but there'd be no fun in that, yeh wouldn't suffer. So before I bid yeh adieu, I'm gonna tell yeh me name . . . "

"Don't fucking bother, I know who yeh are, Peter fucking Brady. I was asked a long time ago teh kill yeh when we were both in prison, by the same man who's payin yer wages."

It was like being in the middle of a bad dream.

I couldn't believe the conversation they were having.

Why wasn't Johnser panicking? Why wasn't he trying to fight? How could he just sit there chatting to someone who was about to kill him?

I tried to move, but I couldn't. Suddenly a thought struck me. Johnser didn't know about Jonathan. He didn't know that Jonathan was his son. I'd never told him. I had to get to him, I had to tell him.

"Oh, please, God, please make me legs move."

I had to go to him. I needed to see the look of pride on his face when I told him the news.

"Johnser . . . "

BANG . . . BANG . . .

I never saw his face. I was too late.

288